Praise for
and his Jacob Bu...

Strange Bedfellows

"The pace is swift; the elements fit together neatly;
the writing is assured, on-target, and often amusing,
and the characters well-drawn and likable. . . .
As well-crafted as they come."
—*The Drood Review of Mystery*

"Offers all the prime ingredients needed to keep
you hungrily turning the pages."
—*Saratoga Business Journal*

"An enjoyable cozy with well-drawn characters."
—*The Charlotte Austin Review*

"Told with warmth and wit, *Strange Bedfellows* is
a wry story that packs a wallop of an ending.
[Witten] has a skillful hand at creating likable
characters involved in believable situations."
—*Romantic Times*

"Witten is a master of characterization. . . .
Strange Bedfellows is a treat for amateur-sleuth
gourmets." —BookBrowser

continued . . .

Grand Delusion

"A success . . . **a fast, lighthearted read.** Witten presents his characters and plot twists in a straightforward and believable manner."
—*The Albany Times Union*

"**A winner.** Cozy fans are going to love this guy. The setting feels very fresh."
—Laura Lippman, author of *Sugar House* and winner of the Edgar, Anthony, and Agatha awards

"A funny, satirical novel, peopled with enjoyable characters. . . . **The self-deprecating Burns is a delight.** The mystery story does not take second place to the humor and fans of the genre will be pleased with the puzzle." —*Romantic Times*

"**A witty, fast-paced read** for mystery lovers who appreciate an engrossing puzzle. . . . I can't wait to see what [Burns] gets into next."
—Patricia Maddock, *The Chronicle* (Glens Falls, NY)

Breakfast at Madeline's

"Charming, witty, and moving . . . an irresistible read. Jacob Burns is a welcome addition to crime fiction."
  —Don Winslow, author of *California Fire and Life*

"[A] breezy, funny whodunit. The plot is fun, but it takes a backseat to the loopy, charming Jacob Burns. I hope this is going to be a series."
  —Tom Savage, author of *Valentine*

"A breezy, pleasantly clipped narrative **filled with excitement and wit.** The perfect antidote for a rainy day."
  —*Library Journal*

"Jacob Burns is a wisecracking, write-at-home dad with a nose for trouble. . . . He manages to see into the heart of his community with a great deal of humor and tenderness."
—Sujata Massey, Agatha Award–winning author of
The Salaryman's Wife

"What a great book, by a great author, in a great city." —J. Michael O'Connell, Mayor,
City of Saratoga Springs

Also by Matt Witten

Breakfast at Madeline's
Grand Delusion
Strange Bedfellows

12/2001

THE
KILLING BEE

A Jacob Burns Mystery

Matt Witten

A SIGNET BOOK

WHITING PUBLIC LIBRARY
WHITING, IN 46394

SIGNET
Published by New American Library, a division of
Penguin Putnam Inc., 375 Hudson Street,
New York, New York 10014, U.S.A.
Penguin Books Ltd, 80 Strand,
London WC2R ORL, England
Penguin Books Australia Ltd, Ringwood,
Victoria, Australia
Penguin Books Canada Ltd, 10 Alcorn Avenue,
Toronto, Ontario, Canada M4V 3B2
Penguin Books (N.Z.) Ltd, 182–190 Wairau Road,
Auckland 10, New Zealand

Penguin Books Ltd, Registered Offices:
Harmondsworth, Middlesex, England

First Published by Signet, an imprint of New American Library,
a division of Penguin Putnam Inc.

First Printing, November 2001
10   9   8   7   6   5   4   3   2   1

Copyright © Matt Witten, 2001
All rights reserved

 REGISTERED TRADEMARK—MARCA REGISTRADA

Printed in the United States of America

Without limiting the rights under copyright reserved above, no part of
this publication may be reproduced, stored in or introduced into a
retrieval system, or transmitted, in any form, or by any means
(electronic, mechanical, photocopying, recording, or otherwise),
without the prior written permission of both the copyright owner and
the above publisher of this book.

PUBLISHER'S NOTE
This is a work of fiction. Names, characters, places, and incidents either
are the product of the author's imagination or are used fictitiously,
and any resemblance to actual persons, living or dead, business
establishments, events, or locales is entirely coincidental.

BOOKS ARE AVAILABLE AT QUANTITY DISCOUNTS WHEN USED TO PROMOTE
PRODUCTS OR SERVICES. FOR INFORMATION PLEASE WRITE TO PREMIUM
MARKETING DIVISION, PENGUIN PUTNAM INC., 375 HUDSON STREET, NEW YORK,
NEW YORK 10014.

If you purchased this book without a cover you should be aware that
this book is stolen property. It was reported as "unsold and
destroyed" to the publisher and neither the author nor the publisher
has received any payment for this "stripped book."

For Ronne Israel, Felice Karlitz, Jeff Lantos,
and great teachers everywhere

ACKNOWLEDGMENTS

I would like to thank my literary agent, Jimmy Vines; my editor, Genny Ostertag; and the folks who helped me along the way: Carmen Bassin-Beumer, Betsy Blaustein, Nancy Butcher, Tara Clavell, Julia Fleischaker, Bill Harris, Joe Pittman, Mike Sauro, Larry Shuman, Benson Silverman, Matt Solo, Justin Wilcox, Celia Witten, and everybody at Malice Domestic, the Creative Bloc, and the late, lamented Madeline's Espresso Bar.

Also, I'd like to thank my son Zachary, who contributed the poem "Corn" to this book, and my son Jacob, who contributed the poem "Spring."

Finally, many thanks to Nancy Seid, who is not only my wife and girlfriend, but also a darn fierce editor.

WARNING: This book is fiction! The people aren't real! Nothing in it ever happened!

"I never let schooling interfere with my education."

—Mark Twain

1

My seven-year-old son never ceased to amaze me.

He could do math like a ten-year-old, play chess like a fifteen-year-old, read like a twenty-year-old . . . but he couldn't tie his own shoes.

Or rather, he *could* if he remembered. But usually his mind was busy with loftier matters. Right now he was so engrossed in the latest Harry Potter that he just sat there on the floor, shoestring held forgotten in one hand while he flipped pages with the other. He had been sitting like that for a good ten minutes.

I'd already asked him twice to hurry up and get those shoes tied. Both times he grunted assent, tied about half of a knot, and then kept on reading. It was making me nuts. I was in a rush to get out the door, and I was sorely tempted to snatch the book from his hands, fling it dramatically in the trash, and aim a few yells in his direction.

But if the truth be told, I acted just like him when *I* was a kid. "Just 'til the end of the chapter? *Please?*" was my favorite refrain. Whenever I complain to my father about the trouble we have getting our seven-year-old to stop reading, he chortles and says, "Serves you right."

Another reason not to yell at my kid was that if I did, my wife, Andrea, would yell at *me*. So I gritted my teeth and held my peace. I stooped down to his level so he would have to focus on me and said, "Honey, it's time to put down your book and tie your shoes. We have to go."

"Why? It's not even seven-thirty yet."

"Yeah, school won't start for, like, an hour," his five-year-old brother chimed in. The most well-organized member of our family, not only were his shoes already tied but his jacket was zipped.

Andrea came whizzing through on her way outside, gobbling a piece of toast as she sped by. Her long black hair was in disarray. On Tuesdays she teaches an eight a.m. class at the community college, and she was running late.

"Wish me luck today, honey," she said.

"You'll be great. Knock 'em dead," I told her. Today was a big day. Andrea was up for tenure this year, and the department head was observing her two Comp 101 classes.

"Have a nice day, guys," she said, gulping down her mouthful and kissing me. "Bye, Jacob. Bye, Latree. Bye, Charizard. I love you."

Latree? you may ask. *Charizard?*

Well, it's like this: our kids' real names are Daniel and Nathan. But two years ago, they decided to change their monikers to Babe Ruth and Wayne Gretzky. Then they morphed into Leonardo and Raphael (after the Ninja turtles, of course, not the painters), and then Derek Jeter and Bernie Williams, the New York Yankee stars. A couple of months ago, they switched *nom de plumes* yet again.

My older son picked Latree because he loves the way the basketball player Latrell Sprewell races down the court, dreadlocks flying, for another wild and crazy fast-break layup. So he wanted to call himself Latrell. But there was a hitch: Latrell Sprewell is not exactly the world's nicest guy. For instance, a few years back he allegedly choked his coach half to death. So my son decided to call himself Latree, on the theory it sounded similar to Latrell but was still different. This was intended to show he wanted to play basketball like Latrell, but he didn't want to *be* like Latrell.

If all this sounds a tad convoluted . . . what can I tell you? That's the kind of guy my son is. I think he was born with a few extra wrinkles and twists in his brain.

My younger son's reasons for choosing Charizard were much more straightforward. He just flat out *loved* Charizard—who, for the noncognoscenti, is a deceptively cute-looking fire Pokémon with the ability to spit forth flames so hot they can melt boulders. Nathan didn't care if the rest of the world was losing interest in Pokémon, he was staying loyal. He's a firm, no-nonsense kid who knows what he likes.

Right now he was standing by the kitchen door, impatient for me to justify the change in our morning schedule. Both my kids are big on routine; they're like cats that way. So with Mommy gone and the flurry of farewells dispensed with, they resumed their interrogation. "Why do we have to leave so early?" Charizard demanded.

"I have a meeting at your school this morning. It starts at seven-thirty," I explained.

Latree looked up from both his book and his shoes. "Is this another stupid gifted and talented meeting?" he asked in an aggrieved tone.

In fact, it was. Several of us parents with "academically gifted children"—to use the current jargon— had banded together. We were trying to muscle our school principal and our entire public school system into doing better by our kids.

Like most elementary schools, our school was

pretty much useless for the really smart kids—to use the older jargon. Latree hadn't learned anything new in second grade all year, and it was already May. Charizard was enjoying kindergarten, but he was no intellectual slouch either, and we worried about what lay ahead for him.

Our small cadre of intrepid parents had been meeting with the principal for months, attempting to drum into his thick skull the need to create new programs for "high-end kids"—to use yet another form of jargon. But creating new programs was not exactly principal Sam Meckel's strong suit. He was much better at droning on endlessly about how things had always been done.

Some of my annoyance at Meckel came out in my snappish reply to Latree. "Look, I'm doing this for *you*, you know. So you won't be so bored at school."

"Dad, you're dreaming. School is *supposed* to be boring."

"Great attitude." I guess I couldn't blame him, though; he was only picking up on my own pessimism about public schools.

Now by this point you may be thinking, "Hey, quit *kvetching*, just be glad you have a smart kid." I've heard this sentiment often, and I'll admit there's truth to it.

But poor little Latree was going bonkers. The math they were doing in his second-grade class, he already knew in kindergarten. Make that preschool. And he had to sit around twiddling his thumbs for hours and hours as the other students read aloud laboriously from Berenstein Bears books, when he could polish off a Harry Potter in two days. He told me one morning, "I'd rather stay home and clean every room in the house than go to school. I'd rather hang upside down from the curtains all day."

It broke my heart. Latree was a basically cheerful sort

who always used to love school. Now every morning I felt like I was sending him off to the salt mines.

On this particular morning, I tried to shake off these unsettling thoughts and focus on the positive. "At least you enjoy recess," I said.

"School isn't *that* boring," Charizard piped up, trying to make me feel better. Our five-year-old was rapidly becoming the family peacemaker.

"I'm glad to hear it."

"Just maybe two-thirds boring. Or, like, three-quarters or fifteen-seventeenths boring." Charizard was obsessed with fractions lately.

Meanwhile Latree had gone back to reading his book. *"Latree—"*

"Okay, okay." He put the book down. "I'm ready."

We were almost in the car when I happened to look down at Latree's ankles. Something was missing.

"Where are your socks?" I said, my voice rising dangerously.

Latree looked down. "Oh, I guess I forgot."

It took every last ounce of willpower to keep from screaming.

We were five minutes late for the meeting, but High Rock Elementary was still completely silent when we walked in. Nobody was in the hall. The door to Meckel's office, where we were supposed to meet, was shut.

"You sure there's a meeting, Dad?" Latree asked.

"Maybe I got the wrong day." Had all of my early-morning hurrying and haranguing been for naught?

But when we walked down the hall, turned the corner, and entered the library, I saw there was no need to fear. The gang was here.

Standing by the librarian's desk were Susie Powell, Elena Aguilera, and Barry Richardson, fellow hardcore stalwarts in the gifted and talented fight. Playing at the computers were the children we were fighting for: Susie's daughters Christine and Megan; Elena's daughter Luce; Barry's son Justin; and a boy named Adam Braithwaite, the second-grade son of my wife's best friend, Laura. I didn't see Laura anywhere, which probably meant she was outside smoking a cigarette. She'd been trying to break the habit ever since we met her.

My sons shouted out joyful hellos and ran over to Adam, all their annoyance at having to go to school early forgotten. Adam was Latree's soul brother, and a good pal to Charizard too. Meanwhile I walked up to the other grown-ups and threw them a brisk military salute. "Greetings, comrades."

They quickly got into the spirit. "Revolution!" Susie called out, fiercely shaking her bleached blond tresses.

Elena threw her fist in the air—although since she wasn't quite five feet tall, her fist didn't make it all that high. "Down with the ruling classes! *La raza unida jamás sera vencida!*"

"Solidarity forever!" Barry declared in his impeccable British accent.

Then we all began laughing at ourselves. After all, this wasn't the '60s anymore, and our days of sex, drugs, and rebellion had faded away like yesterday's pot smoke. The four of us weren't longhaired, peace-medallion-wearing Berkeley hippies, we were middle-class, slightly paunchy residents of Saratoga Springs, New York, a small town in the foothills of the Adirondacks that's known more for horse races than radical politics.

But you know what? We still *felt* like rebels. We were waging war against our country's most horrific institution, which is even scarier than the military industrial complex and more deranged than the Post

Office. I am referring, of course, to the nation's public schools.

With our kidlets safely stashed in front of the computers, the four of us marched around the corner and up the hall doing what we usually did when we were together: ragging on Sam Meckel.

It's not that Meckel was a bad man, or actively opposed to helping smart kids. It's just that he was . . . I can think of no more damning word . . . a *bureaucrat*. Don't rock the boat, cover your butt. We needed to light a fire under him until he realized that instead of covering his butt this time, he'd better move it.

All of us were acting pretty slaphappy that morning. Afterward, I would wonder if one of us had been acting a little extra goofy to cover something up.

"If Meckel gives us his standard goombah about 'limited resources,'" Susie declared, "I'm gonna kill him." Susie was a mild-mannered, stay-at-home mom, with a husband who was steadily if unspectacularly climbing the corporate ladder. But when it came to her kids' welfare, the lady was a tigress. Her third-grader, Christine, was a real whiz; I didn't know much about Megan, her quiet first-grader.

Elena added, "Yeah, Meckel always has plenty of resources for the *dumb* kids." Elena's bluntness took me aback sometimes, but her bark was much worse than her bite. Besides being a parent she also taught fourth grade at High Rock, and her students loved her.

"Now, now, let's not be politically incorrect," Barry chided. "It's not 'dumb' and 'smart,' it's 'academically challenged' and—"

"Oh, shut up," I said, more or less good-naturedly. Barry could be annoying, with his nose-in-the-air attitudes and sense of humor. He was elitist in a way that I was sometimes afraid I was becoming. But I liked having him around, so I wasn't the only man in the group. And coming from England, where bright kids get better treatment from the educational system, Barry gave us a fresh perspective.

We reached Meckel's office and I knocked on the door. No answer.

"What, he's not here yet?" Susie said, irritated.

"He's always late. He has no respect for parents," Elena said—but in a whisper, in case Meckel was inside after all and could hear her.

"I hope he didn't forget," Barry said.

"No," Susie said as I knocked again, "Laura called him yesterday to remind him. He said he'd be here."

Just for the heck of it, I tried the knob. It turned. I opened the door—

And a strange sight greeted me. Laura Braithwaite was standing next to Meckel's desk with her mouth hanging open. Her eyes stared at me, but they were unfocused, like she was in shock. She was gripping a large object in her right hand. A trophy, it looked like.

"Laura, hi," I said.

She just stood there staring.

Susie, Elena, and Barry crowded into the office behind me. "What's the matter, Laura?" Susie asked.

Laura pointed a shaky forefinger at the floor behind the desk. I stepped forward, stood on my toes—

And my morning Wheaties came lurching toward my throat.

Sam Meckel's body was lying there. His arms were splayed awkwardly, his eyes stared at nothing, and he had blood on his forehead.

"Mr. Meckel?" I said, somewhat idiotically. Obviously he wasn't about to answer.

I bent down to feel his pulse. Now I'm no doctor,

but so far as I could tell, there wasn't any. Behind me Elena screamed.

"What happened?" Barry asked. I guess he was talking to Laura, but she didn't answer.

"Call 911," I said. Barry grabbed Meckel's phone and did just that. I could hear him talking frantically to the emergency operator as Susie gasped, "Is Meckel alright?"

"Actually, he's dead," I said. Then I straightened back up and eyed Laura. She was swaying, like she was about to fall. I put out my hand to steady her and found myself holding the arm that was holding the trophy.

I recognized that trophy. It featured a large, shiny honeybee, standing tall with its wings spread open wide and a big joyful smile on its honeybee face. Laura's son Adam won this trophy for acing the second-grade spelling bee. He beat out Latree when, for some inexplicable reason, Latree spelled "impossible" with three s's.

The last time I was at Laura and Adam's house, this happy honeybee was proudly displayed on their mantelpiece. So what was it doing here, in Meckel's office?

And what was that unsightly red smear on the tip of the bee's left wing?

Oh, shit. It was blood.

Sam Meckel's blood.

Our friend Laura had just committed murder with her son's spelling bee trophy.

2

Finally Laura spoke up. "I . . . I didn't kill him," she stammered. "I came in here and he . . . he was . . ."

Laura Braithwaite was a tough broad with a deep throaty laugh and a ribald streak a mile wide. She and my wife and their friend Judy Demarest, the editor of our local newspaper, had a standing date every Thursday night to go bowling and trade dirty jokes. Laura's favorite joke, according to my wife, was:

How many Freudians does it take to change a lightbulb?

Two. One to screw in the bulb and the other to hold the penis—I mean, the ladder.

But with Meckel lying there dead, all of Laura's humor and toughness deserted her. She began hyperventilating. I put my arm around her. "Laura, sit down."

Then I turned around to everyone else in the room. Ordinarily I'm not the leader type; on the contrary, I'm more a sensitive *artiste* kind of guy. Been that way all my life. But two years ago I'd amazed everyone—including myself—by solving a murder that the police screwed up on. That gave me a reputation, and since then I had been called in on a couple of other murders. So, like Laura, I acted out of character now: I took charge. "You all better leave," I told

Susie, Elena, and Barry. "You don't wanna mess with the evidence."

The three of them didn't need any more encouragement to get the heck out of there. They murmured a few lame words to Laura—"Hang in there," "It'll be okay," and other useless stuff—and headed off.

"But stick around the school so the cops can talk to you," I called after them.

"We'll go check on the kids," Susie called back. They left, and I turned back to Laura. Her face was pasty, like she was about to pass out. Maybe I should find cold water to throw on her or something.

Or maybe the most merciful plan would be to just let her pass out. This was the last moment of peace she was likely to get for a long time—

And now that moment was gone. Police cars suddenly came racing our way, sirens blasting. Laura jumped to attention, sitting bolt upright. We both looked out the window as two cops burst out of their car and dashed into the building.

Oh phooey, I knew these guys. The cop in the lead was a lantern-jawed know-it-all in his early forties named Lieutenant Foxwell. The other one . . . well, I never actually learned his name, we weren't formally introduced. But I remembered his acne-scarred face sneering at me late one night after he spit at my own face. It happened a year and a half ago, in the deep dark recesses of the Saratoga Springs Police Station.

"Listen, Laura, don't tell the cops *anything*," I said urgently. "Like they say on TV, it can be used against you. And you'll need a lawyer. I recommend Malcolm Dove. He's the best."

"I didn't do it," Laura said. "I *swear*."

I wanted to believe her, but I'd been fooled before. So all I said was, "You want me to call Malcolm for you?"

Laura blinked, fighting back tears. Then she said, "Jacob? Could you . . . take care of Adam?"

"Of course," I said immediately. God, what an unlucky kid. Adam's dad had exited the planet two years earlier, courtesy of a heroin overdose. He was a momentum trader, and I guess the momentum went the wrong way. Needless to say, Adam was crushed. And now this . . .

I would have tried to say something reassuring to Laura, but just then Lieutenant Foxwell and Acne Scars came crashing into the room.

As soon as I made it onto their radar, they stopped in their tracks. Acne Scars curled his bottom lip like he was dying to spit at me again. Foxwell glowered in angry surprise. "You!" he exclaimed.

"Me," I agreed solemnly. "And him." I pointed at the body behind the desk.

Foxwell and Acne Scars went over and took a look. Sure enough, Sam Meckel was still dead. If there was a heaven, he was probably at the Pearly Gates already, trying to cover his butt with St. Peter.

Acne Scars straightened up and turned to Laura. His nostrils flared slightly, like a dog hot on the scent. "Who are you?"

"Laura . . . Braithwaite," she said, quavering.

"She found the body," I explained.

Foxwell raised an eyebrow. "Oh, really."

Outside more sirens blared, and various ambulances and cop cars pulled up. "Laura, remember what I said," I began—

But Foxwell shut me down. "Why don't you go in one of the classrooms, Mr. Burns. We'll talk to you later."

I stood up. "Don't say a word, Laura. Except 'I want a lawyer.' "

"Why, what does she have to be afraid of?" Acne

Scars asked, his beady eyes sparkling with a mean gleam.

I couldn't think of anything clever to say. So I took one last look at Laura's terrified face, gave her a little smile that was meant to be supportive but probably looked ghastly, and left. Acne Scars shut the door behind me.

I started up the hall. Three EMTs and four cops raced past me on their way to the principal's office. Nice to see such a quick response. Too bad Sam Meckel wasn't alive to appreciate it.

I headed for the library to check up on Adam and my sons. Sure enough, they were still there, along with the other kids and their parents. Everybody was shell-shocked, moving in slow motion. Adam eyed me fearfully. It looked like somebody had told the kids what happened. I wasn't so sure that had been a good idea, but I guess they'd have found out soon enough anyway, what with all the screaming sirens. Latree broke out of his daze and ran up to me. "Daddy, is Mr. Meckel really dead?"

"Looks like it," I said, and took him into my arms.

Charizard's face filled with horrified awe. "Did somebody kill him?" It was good to see that, despite their recent, too-frequent exposure to murder, my kids hadn't turned blasé about it.

"The police are taking care of everything," I said. I had zilch desire to go into detail about Adam's spelling bee trophy—especially with him standing right there.

But Adam was already one step ahead of me. "Did my mom kill him?" he asked fearfully.

I opened and closed my mouth like a gasping fish, not sure what to say. From the other side of the library, the other grown-ups and kids were watching. Then I heard a noise behind me and turned. I found myself face-to-face with a cop I knew named Bowles, a young guy with a military crewcut and shrewd eyes. He stood in the doorway drinking in every word like it was some kind of fancy imported beer.

"Of course your mom didn't kill him," I said, for the cop's benefit as much as for Adam's.

"But she said she was gonna go in Mr. Meckel's office and read him the riot act. She was super mad at him," Adam said.

Good grief, kid, shut up. He was so upset he was totally oblivious to the cop. "Adam, let's not talk about it right now," I said nervously.

"Where is she?"

"With the police. Don't worry. Your mom wants you to stay with us until things get sorted out. Why don't you go play Civilization on the computer?"

"I wanna go see my mom," he said, whimpering.

"Soon, honey. I promise," I lied.

Charizard cut in. "I wanna see Mr. Meckel's body."

"No. Why don't you play Civilization."

"Why can't we see it—"

"I said play Civilization. *Now.*"

They stared at me, thrown by the sharpness in my voice. Then they looked over at the cop. Something finally clicked, and without further argument they headed over to play Civilization. I doubt they got very high scores that day, though.

I walked over to where the other grown-ups stood huddled together. I wanted to ask them all kinds of Columbo-type questions, starting with: "Did you see anybody else wandering around the hall this morning?" and "When was the last time you saw Laura?" But Bowles still loomed in the doorway watching us. It kind of inhibited conversation—especially since I was scared somebody might say something that would incriminate Laura.

So we sat around uncomfortably for twenty minutes. It got so bad, Barry and I had to relieve our tension by talking about the Mets. What would guys ever do without sports?

I was almost glad when Foxwell and Acne Scars—who, I now learned, was more commonly known as Balducci—came and led me away to an empty classroom. Actually, *all the* classrooms were empty. School had been canceled for the day. The school superintendent showed up and turned all the buses away, sending the kids off to the middle school auditorium to be picked up by their parents. All of the teachers were sent away too.

The cops sat me down at one of the kids' desks and began questioning me. I instantly flashed back to fourth grade, when Mrs. Specter interrogated me mercilessly one morning after somebody hit her in the back of the head with a spitball. I didn't do it, I might add—or at least, that's my story and I'm sticking to it.

Foxwell started right in. "What exactly did you see when you opened the principal's door?"

I grimaced, remembering. "Laura was just standing there. By Mr. Meckel's desk. Looking totally out of it."

"Where was the trophy?"

I didn't want to answer. But these guys were almost as frightening as Mrs. Specter—no mean feat. She had a way of tapping her palm with a ruler that would strike terror into the heart of the most cold-blooded serial killer.

"Laura was holding it," I said.

"Holding it?" said Balducci.

Almost against my will, I nodded.

"Like she'd just finished using it on Meckel," Balducci went on.

"I never said that."

"What did *she* say?" Foxwell asked.

"That she didn't kill him."

If I was hoping that would bring them up short, I was sadly mistaken. Foxwell barreled ahead without pausing. "What about the trophy?"

"What about it?"

"Why'd she bring it with her from home?"

Damn, how did Foxwell find out that little tidbit? Laura must not have followed my advice. She'd spilled stuff to the cops.

"I don't know anything about that," I said.

Foxwell drilled holes in me with his eyes. "Laura was pretty angry at Meckel, wasn't she?"

"We all were, not just Laura."

"Why?"

"Well, because our kids aren't being challenged at school. We were trying to get Mr. Meckel to change that."

"And he wasn't changing fast enough for Laura?" Balducci said.

I put up my hands to stop them. "Look, Laura is my wife's best friend."

Foxwell nodded knowingly. "So you're going to protect her."

"Even though you think she killed Meckel," Balducci finished the thought.

I didn't say anything. Unfortunately, my silence said it all.

After the cops finally let me go, I headed back to the library. Susie, Elena, and Barry had already been questioned by other cops, and they and their children were gone. But Adam and my kids were still in evidence, along with Laura and two beefy cops who were "escorting" her.

Adam was hugging his mother and wailing, "But Mom, why can't I go with you?"

"It's okay, sweetheart," said Laura. "I just have to go . . . help the police for a while. You're gonna have a play date with Latree and Charizard. Goodbye, honey."

She hugged him even tighter. Then one of the cops said impatiently, "Ms. Braithwaite."

She forced herself to break away from Adam, then caught my eye. "Take good care of him, Jacob."

"I will."

She gave Adam a brave thumbs-up and a wave and took off. No doubt she fell apart as soon as she was out of his sight.

I turned to Adam and my sons, who stood there with eyes wide. "Okay, guys," I said, trying and failing to make my voice cheerful, "grab your backpacks and let's go."

"Where are they taking my mom?" Adam asked.

"I guess the police station."

"You mean jail, right?"

"Adam, everything's gonna be fine."

"How do you know?"

Once again I was at a loss for words.

"Maybe your mom just killed Mr. Meckel by accident," Charizard suggested.

"Yeah, that's not really murder, right, Dad?" Latree asked.

"They'll probably make Adam's mom pay some money, like maybe five and nine-tenths dollars," Charizard put in hopefully. "And then go to jail for, like, half a week."

"Sounds good to me," I said.

Now if we could just get a judge to go for it.

3

If anybody could cut a sweetheart deal for Laura it was Malcolm Dove, the three-hundred-pound chess-playing lawyer who represented me the time I was accused of murder. So after I got the kids home, fed them a snack, and sent them out to play croquet in our backyard, hoping to distract them with a normal-seeming activity, I called Malcolm and asked him to take the case. I informed him I'd pay his fee if Laura couldn't afford it.

And that seemed likely. She was still recovering financially from her husband's death, to say nothing of his stock trades. Her parents were both dead too, and her younger sister was an impoverished member of some misbegotten New Age commune in Arizona. That left Andrea and me as Laura's safety net. The restaurant where she waitressed, at the Golf and Polo Club, was where the Saratoga elite meet to eat; but I seriously doubted her lunch tips would cover a high-priced lawyer's nut.

I could cover it, though. I was rich—by my stan-dards, at least. I had three hundred grand socked away in mutual funds.

I should probably explain where all that cash came from, and why I was free to take care of the boys on a Tuesday morning instead of trudging off to some j.o.b. somewhere. What happened was, I got the loot two years ago with one stroke of a Hollywood pen.

It still amazed me sometimes, how a project that took me only five weeks to write could have such a huge impact on my life. The project in question was a screenplay called *The Gas That Ate San Francisco*, about poisonous gas seeping out of the ground after an earthquake and threatening to wipe out the entire Bay Area.

As you can probably tell from this description, it was not exactly an A movie. More like a double Z. But it sure was lucrative. The *Gas* movie put an end to my almost two decades of doing the starving artist thing, writing poignant, socially meaningful screenplays that never got produced and *avant garde* stage plays that did get produced—off off Broadway, for audiences of about four people, including myself.

You'd think that after selling a screenplay for a million bucks—which is what I got, before the agents, managers, producers, lawyers, IRS, and other bloodsuckers whittled it down to 300 K—my career would have taken off. And it almost did.

But somewhere along the way, a strange thing happened. I mysteriously misplaced my urge to write. I thought about churning out another hack screenplay, but I never quite got around to it.

The truth was this: even though the gas movie was a big hit, especially overseas, I never really *liked* it much. But on the other hand, I couldn't quite motivate myself to write any of the artsy-fartsy, hopelessly uncommercial stuff I used to write.

I guess you could call it writer's block. But that makes it sound like I was unhappy, and I wasn't. In fact, the last two years had been the best years of my life. I enjoyed being an at-home dad. I also enjoyed having lots of time to play handball at the Y and chess at Malcolm Dove's Monday night chess club, as well as pursue my latest hobby: renovating two houses that I bought as HUD foreclosures, and then renting them out.

Okay, every once in a while at three in the morning I'd wake up and wonder what was the purpose of my existence here on this earth. But everybody does that sometimes, right?

After I hung up with Malcolm, I was all set to call Andrea and let her know about the morning's excitement when Charizard ran in, crying.

"Daddy," he squalled, "Adam keeps hitting my ball in the bushes. It's not fair."

I rolled my eyes. "Look, give the kid a break. He's having a tough day."

Charizard mulled that over. "You mean 'cause his mom got arrested?"

"Yeah, that would kind of bum you out a little, don't you think?"

Charizard looked worried. "But they'd never arrest *my* mom, right? 'Cause she wouldn't kill anybody."

"True."

"Hey, maybe Adam's mom didn't do it. Maybe a robber killed Mr. Meckel. Or a mean space alien."

I tried not to smile. "It's possible."

He gazed at me earnestly. "Daddy? You'll find the real killer, right? Just like you did the other times?"

I sighed. I guess I'd known all along, ever since I first stumbled on Sam Meckel's body, that it would come to this. I'd be expected to work some magic. But the truth was, I'm really no magician; and anyway, I didn't think there was any magic to be worked here. I felt pretty sure the cops already had the real killer. I mean, I was very fond of Laura, but all the evidence certainly pointed straight at her.

"Daddy?" Charizard said again.

I sighed. "Sure," I said. "I'll take the case."

He clapped his hands. "Goodie! I'll go tell Adam you're gonna save his mom."

Charizard's confidence was touching. Too bad I didn't share it. As he ran back outside, I picked up the phone again to call Andrea. Then I hesitated.

Of all the possible days to get Andrea upset, this was the worst. She needed to do a good job today in front of her department head. If I informed her about her best friend's incarceration for homicide, she might screw up her classes—and her tenure chances.

So I held off on calling her. Instead I called the other gifted and talented parents—or to put it more accurately, the other parents of gifted and talented kids. Sometimes we tend to forget the distinction.

Susie Powell was the first parent I got through to. "I figured you'd be calling me," she said as soon as she heard my hello. "So you're gonna help Laura with this?"

"I'm gonna try."

"That's really great. 'Cause there's no way Laura could've killed Meckel, don't you think?"

I was pretty sure that was uncertainty I detected in Susie's voice. "I agree," I said, even though I felt uncertain too. Then I proceeded to ask Susie about this morning.

But she wasn't much help. Try though she might, she couldn't recall any evil strangers lurking in the school hallways when she came in that morning. Nor had she heard anything suspicious. She couldn't think of anybody who hated Meckel—"or not enough to kill him, anyway."

"When did you get to school?" I asked.

"Early, like seven-fifteen, seven-twenty. The front door was unlocked."

"What about Meckel's door?"

"It was closed. I went past there to the library. Adam was in there already, hanging out, but I didn't see Laura."

Maybe because Laura was in Meckel's office. "What about Elena and Barry. Were they there?"

"They showed up with their kids a few minutes later, I'm not sure exactly when."

"Who showed up first?"

"Barry did, with Justin. Then he went off to the bathroom for maybe half a minute, and Elena came in with Luce."

"And Elena stayed with you?"

"She dropped off Luce and went to her classroom to do something for a couple minutes. Then she came back." Susie paused. "Look, you don't think *we're* suspects, do you? It would've been, like, impossible for one of us to kill Meckel without the others knowing."

"Just dotting i's and crossing t's," I said. I didn't really take Susie, Barry, and Elena seriously as murder suspects—or should I say, I didn't *want* to take them seriously.

Next I got through to Elena. According to her, she and Luce had arrived in the library only moments before Barry returned from the bathroom; and Susie was already there. Then Elena went off to her classroom, which was next door to the library, for two or three minutes.

Elena's story was essentially the same as Susie's, except more colorful and with Spanish thrown in. Her key word was *loco*—Meckel was loco, his killer was loco, this whole loco thing was loco. Sometimes I wondered how a free spirit like Elena managed to survive in a buttoned-down institution like High Rock Elementary School.

My third call was to Barry at the Saratoga Trust

Bank, where he was some sort of factotum. "You going into your Miss Marple mode again?" he kidded me.

I prefer to think of myself as the Sam Spade type, but I let it go. "I'm wondering if you might have seen anything this morning."

"I'm afraid not. Sorry."

"You hear anything?"

"No . . ." Barry said, but I noticed a tiny split second of hesitation, so I tried again.

"You sure?"

"Well . . ."

"Just tell me. I promise I won't repeat it to anyone if it's something irrelevant."

He sighed, then finally took the plunge. "Okay, you know how the loo is just down the hall from the principal's office?"

"Yeah."

"Well, I was in there this morning doing my business, and I thought I heard somebody yelling."

Uh-oh. "Was it Laura?"

"I'm not sure. I'm pretty sure it *was* a woman, though."

Oh, Lord have mercy.

Theoretically the woman could have been Elena. Instead of going into her own classroom like she claimed, maybe she went to Meckel's office. But it seemed unlikely. There wasn't much time for her to do the dastardly deed and then slip back to the library.

I thought back to how Elena, Susie, and Barry had acted this morning, when I first came into the library and saw them. They had all been a little manic, raising their fists and talking revolution . . . but they had all acted basically normal. Not like they had just committed murder.

No, the only person who had acted suspicious was Laura. And now there was an eyewitness—or rather, an earwitness.

"It didn't sound, like, physical," Barry continued, apologetic, "or I would've gone in there. I thought it was just two people having an argument."

"Did you hear anything they were saying?"

"Not really. I mean, I was making noise too, you know, peeing and washing my hands and all that." He sighed. "I didn't want to tell the cops, because . . . you know."

"Yeah."

"Poor Laura."

"Poor Laura," I agreed. I thanked him dispiritedly and hung up.

Then I just sat there. I didn't even have the energy to call Andrea, though by now her last class was over. What could I do? Laura's goose was clearly cooked—

The phone rang. It was Malcolm. I heard choppiness on the line; he must be calling from his car. "I just talked to your pal Laura on the phone. I'm meeting her at the jail in five minutes. She wants you there, too. Can you make it?"

"I'd love to, but I'm taking care of the kids."

Malcolm snorted. "*Kids?* What kind of hard-boiled private dick *are* you?"

"Call me soft-boiled," I said, then: "I have to go, the doorbell just rang."

I answered it. Judy Demarest, the third member of Andrea and Laura's Thursday-night bowling trio, stood on the front steps. Forty years old, with an angular face and alert eyes, Judy was a lean, no-nonsense newspaperman—or at least that's what she wanted you to think.

"Is it true?" Judy asked, her forehead scrunched up with worry. "Did Laura really kill the principal?"

"Are you asking as her friend or as editor of the *Daily Saratogian*?"

"What do you think?" she said, offended.

"I think you're hereby baby-sitting three children for the next hour." I started past her toward my car.

"Hey, wait a minute," she began—

But then Adam came out the door behind us and yelled frantically, "Mr. Burns, I can't find my Game Boy. I think I left it in the library!"

"It's okay, we'll get it tomorrow."

"But I want it *now*." His eyes were watering from the injustice of it all. How could God take away both his mom *and* his Game Boy in one day?

"I promise I'll get it tomorrow. Judy, give them some lunch," I said, and took off before either of them could protest further.

The Saratoga Springs City Jail, where drunks, pick-pockets, murderers and other malcontents are held until their arraignments, is located in the basement of city hall, at the windowless end of the police station. Having once spent an endless night there myself, I can attest to its barbarism. The stench of every bodily fluid known to man permeates the place, and the din of busted toilets, hallucinating inmates, and vindictive cops is constant. The cells are four feet by six feet, and *less* than six feet high. Maybe that wasn't quite so bad a century ago, when the jail was built and people were shorter; but for a modern six-footer like myself, the claustrophobia was overwhelming. Especially with some nutcase in the next cell over chanting "Hare Krishna" all night long. I didn't even like that chant when George Harrison did it.

Fortunately my meeting with Laura and Malcolm wasn't held in the jail itself. When I got there, they had just been escorted to a small room down the hall. Bowles, the young crewcut cop, was posted outside.

Laura still looked shaky. Malcolm looked his usual dapper self. Don't ask me how a three-hundred-pounder manages to do dapper, but Malcolm pulls it off. My only fear was that the tiny plastic chair he was sitting on wouldn't make it through the meeting.

He stuck out his hand. "Hello, Jacob. I was just telling Laura to beware of bugs in this room—and I don't mean cockroaches."

"How's Adam?" Laura asked anxiously.

"He's fine," I lied. "He's playing croquet with the boys. Judy's watching them."

She dabbed at her eyes.

"Laura," Malcolm began, "if you can talk without incriminating yourself . . ."

Her lips turned downward into a bitter frown. "You think I'm guilty, don't you?"

"I'm a lawyer, I don't think anything," Malcolm joked.

Laura didn't laugh. She turned to me. "And so do you."

"No, I don't."

"You're lying. And you lied about Adam being fine."

"Look, we only have thirty minutes," said Malcolm. "This is no way to spend it."

Laura stood and began pacing up and down the airless room. It was more exercise than she'd get for the rest of the day back in her cell.

"I don't know what I can say that would help." She wrung her hands. "I knocked on Meckel's door and went in. He wasn't there. So I put down Adam's spelling bee trophy and went outside for a cigarette.

Two cigarettes," she corrected herself. "I was tense about the meeting. Then, when I came back to Meckel's office . . . there he was. Dead."

"Why'd you leave the trophy in there?" Malcolm asked.

"It was heavy. I figured I'd be coming right back. And I didn't want to be holding it while I tried to light a cigarette."

"Why'd you bring it to Meckel's office in the first place?" I said.

"For a visual aid. Adam is brilliant in English. I wanted Meckel to *see* that."

"Why?" said Malcolm.

She kept opening and shutting her fists. They don't let you smoke in the Saratoga jail, so on top of everything else she was going through nicotine withdrawal. "I called Meckel the night before, to remind him about the meeting. And he told me that to get into the gifted program, kids would have to score above ninety-five on the Terra Novas in both English and math."

"Terra Novas?" Malcolm asked, puzzled. Clearly he didn't have kids. Every parent in New York State, and a lot of other states too, knows about the week of multiple-choice tests—formerly the "CATs," now the "Terra Novas"—that their elementary-school children are forced to undergo each spring.

"They're standardized tests," Laura explained briefly, skipping over the intense aggravation these tests cause for teachers, parents, children and administrators alike. "The students took them two weeks ago. I haven't seen the scores yet, but no way Adam got a ninety-five in math. He's only above average in math, and besides, he had a bad fever during the testing."

"So you were concerned that Adam might not qualify for the gifted program?" Malcolm queried.

"I wasn't just concerned, I was outraged. Look, Adam is highly gifted. He reads at a ninth-grade level. He spells better than most grown-ups. Meckel is an idiot—I mean was."

Laura's pacing had put her with her back to us. Malcolm and I looked at each other. Neither of us was thinking happy thoughts.

"You told all this to the cops?" I asked.

She caught my disapproving tone. "I didn't tell them about the tests. But I did say I was worried about Adam getting into the gifted program. Look, I had to explain why I brought that trophy into Meckel's office," she said defensively. "For God's sake, I wasn't planning to kill him with it."

"But you have to admit, your outrage does kind of give you a motive."

Laura sat down, looking suddenly exhausted. "I realize that. And how can I expect you to be my lawyer"—that was to Malcolm—"or my investigator"—that was to me—"when you both think I'm a murderer?"

"Laura, I don't want to talk about this now, in this room," Malcolm said, "but if there was a scuffle . . . if you didn't mean to kill him . . . we have options."

Laura shut her eyes. "Why don't you both just go? Just get out."

But I didn't know when I'd get to talk to Laura again, so I ignored her request—or demand. "Did you see anyone while you were smoking?" I asked.

"No, I was out back."

"How about in the hallway?"

"It was empty."

Now what should I ask? I felt completely stuck. Was I revealing my hopeless shortcomings as a private dick, or would even Sam Spade himself be stumped by this case? I had come up with absolutely no clues whatsoever—

Wait. This absence of clues was itself a clue. How could the hallway have been totally empty?

"What about Meckel's secretary?" I asked with rising excitement. "Did you see her?"

"No," Laura replied, without returning my enthusiasm. "But it was only seven-thirty. Ms. Helquist doesn't come in till eight."

"*Usually.* But every other time we had an early-morning meeting, Ms. Helquist was already there."

I stood up. Laura and Malcolm both gazed up at me, wondering what I was getting at. I wasn't so sure myself.

But that had never stopped me before.

4

What did stop me was Bowles. He collared me as soon as I stepped out of the room. "Come with me, please," he said. His voice may have said please, but his arm resting on my shoulder said something else.

"Where are we going?" I asked as he led me down the hall.

"Chief wants you."

Ugh. Police Chief John Walsh and I were not what you would call bosom buddies. When somebody tries to lock you in jail forever for a murder you didn't commit, it kind of decreases your affection for him.

On the positive side, he did save my life once. I guess he gets points for that.

"Afternoon, Burns," Chief Walsh greeted me affably enough when I entered. "Have a seat." The chief was a good-looking man in his late fifties with distinguished gray hair and blue eyes. For some reason I always found something insidiously evil about those eyes. I thought he would have made a perfect Nazi colonel, sipping Rhine wine with his pinkie extended as he sent folks off to their doom.

"Thank you," I replied, sinking into the upholstered leather easy chair opposite his desk. The seat was extremely comfortable, probably to lure visitors into a false sense of security.

"Terrible tragedy this morning," the chief intoned, shaking his head solemnly.

"Yes, it was."

"Care for coffee? You like it black, as I recall."

"Chief, let's face it. We dislike each other too much to make small talk. Tell me what you want, and I'll tell you if I can give it."

He looked hurt. "You're not acting very grateful, considering I'm the guy that saved your life."

"I *am* grateful. You were courageous, and I wish I liked you, I really do. Now what do you want?"

"Nothing onerous. I just thought you might appreciate an update on the case." He chuckled at my surprised look. "Hey, what the heck. I know you have an interest in this sort of thing, and I realize the suspect's a personal friend of yours. So, do you want to hear it?"

What was the catch? The chief had never treated me like this before. Almost like a colleague. "Sure," I said uncertainly.

"No problem. Well, first of all, the county M.E. puts the time of death some time between seven and seven thirty-five, when the body was found. Now you already know about the trophy, I assume?" I nodded. "The M.E. checked it out. He says the trophy matches the contusions on Sam Meckel's temple."

"In other words . . ."

"Right. The trophy was the murder weapon."

"I figured as much."

"But did you figure this?" He leaned toward me. "We got Laura's prints here at the station, and we got her son's prints off a Game Boy he left at the library. We checked them against the prints from the murder weapon."

I tensed. "And?"

"Every single print on that weapon—and there

were five of them, including partials—belonged to either Laura or her son," the chief said triumphantly.

"Why are you *really* telling me this?" I said. "To stop me from investigating?"

The chief leaned back in his chair. "Jacob, you and I are both fathers. I don't have to tell you what this murder will do to the children in our community. Sam Meckel was a beloved figure." That was stretching it, but I didn't quibble. "His murder will be a traumatic experience for these kids. A lot of them will be having some pretty horrible nightmares." Here I thought the chief was probably accurate. "So let's not screw around. Let's get this investigation over with as soon as we can, and let the healing process begin."

"I agree. But one question: what if Laura didn't do it?"

"Come on, that's just your emotions talking. You want to see the fingerprint report?"

"What if the killer never left fingerprints? Maybe Laura covered them up when she picked up the trophy. Or maybe the killer's hands weren't sweaty enough. Or the killer was wearing gloves."

"In May?" the chief said, annoyed.

Ever since I got hooked into this whole P.I. biz, I'd been doing side reading on my own. Now I laid some of it on the chief. "From what I've read, there's all kinds of reasons why fingerprints don't happen. Usually all you get is smudges. Especially a situation like this, where the trophy was handled afterward—"

The chief's polished veneer started to chip a little. "Listen, Burns, I don't need you trying to turn this murder into a bad Hollywood movie script."

"I'd think you'd *want* my help, considering how I helped you before."

He snorted. "Right. You and I both know you just got lucky."

I have to confess, there was a certain amount of truth to that charge. I seemed to have an embarrassing habit of picking the wrong person as the murderer, and then getting the right one more or less by accident. But darned if I would admit that to Chief Walsh.

"Why don't you check the cigarette butts out back? See if you find a couple that Laura smoked. That would confirm her story."

"What, you think I'm gonna run DNA tests on fifty butts when it won't even confirm anything, because she could've smoked out there anytime? Dream on."

I stood up. "If that's all you have to say, I guess I'll be going."

"Just one more thing," the chief said, standing up too. Then an amazing thing happened. In the space of a nanosecond his face suddenly went ice-cold, like someone had flipped a secret switch and told the chief's inner Nazi to come out of hiding. "You should know, I have a nice cozy jail cell all picked out for you. So go ahead, interfere with my investigation. See what happens. I have half a mind to arrest you for obstructing justice right now."

"Obstructing justice? What have I done?"

"I'll think of something. Now get the hell out of my office."

Ah, this was more like it. This was the Chief Walsh I knew and loved.

I didn't know where Ms. Helquist lived, or even her full name. So I borrowed a phone directory at a gas station on Lake Avenue, and found only one person with her last name: Hilda Helquist. That had to be her. "Hilda" fit her to a tee.

Ms. Helquist was an efficient, serious woman with conservatively coiffed white hair and thick black glasses. She was the kind of secretary who could really run the school on her own, without the principal's help. Come to think of it, until we got an acting principal that's exactly what she'd be doing.

I drove up to 87 Ash, Hilda Helquist's address, and recognized the house immediately. It was only two blocks from where we lived, and I'd often stopped to admire her garden. From April to October she always had wild splashes of colors out there. The garden wasn't laid out in some careful, staid pattern, it was more like barely controlled exhilaration. In fact, it seemed totally at odds with Ms. Helquist's uptight demeanor. I began to wonder if she really lived here. Maybe I had the wrong Helquist.

But as I walked up to the front door, I spotted the right Helquist at the side of the house, near the driveway. Like a lot of homeowners in our working-class section of town, she didn't have a garage, just off-street parking. Myself, I kind of liked that setup. I mean sure, it could be a drag wiping a foot of snow off our cars on freezing February mornings, but I always think houses look much more aesthetic without a giant yawning garage door staring you in the face. Right now Ms. Helquist, dressed in jeans and a T-shirt—clothes I'd never seen on her before—was pruning back some aggressive grapevines that had attached themselves to her yew bushes.

I went up to her. "Ms. Helquist."

Engrossed in her pruning, or perhaps hard of hearing, she didn't answer. I moved closer. *"Ms. Helquist."*

"Aaaaah!" she yelled, and whipped her body around to face me. She was only a few feet away,

and when she raised her pruning shears toward me, I was afraid she'd clip my nose off. Of course, given the size of my proboscis, some people might say that would improve my looks.

"Hey, sorry," I said, putting my hands up and backing away.

"Mr. Burns," she said, flustered, and lowered her shears. "You startled me."

"Terribly sorry," I apologized again. "I didn't mean to—"

"That's okay, it's not your fault. I guess I'm a little . . . spooked, after this morning."

"You weren't there, were you?" I asked, hoping to sound innocently conversational. "I didn't see you."

"No, I stayed home. I have a cold."

Hmmm. She wasn't sniffling, her nose wasn't red, her voice wasn't hoarse, and she was outside gardening. I wished I could have colds like that.

She caught my doubtful look. "I know what you're thinking. I don't look sick."

"Well . . ."

"I guess I might as well admit it, since I already told Lieutenant Foxwell. I'm *not* really sick."

"Oh," I said noncommittally.

"I snuck a day off 'cause I had so much gardening to do." She gazed off toward her backyard, where I saw about eighteen colors of roses and a hundred eighty flowers I didn't recognize. "My first day off all year, and *this* happens." She ran her fingers through her stiff hair, looking far more vulnerable than I'd ever seen her. And talking more, too. Usually she had a New England reticence, but I guess today she had a lot of stuff to talk about. "Do you think if I was there this morning, Mr. Meckel would still be alive?"

I thought there was a good chance he would be, but naturally I couldn't say that. "I don't know."

She sighed fretfully. "I don't know what to do. I offered to go to the school, but the police said I'd only be in the way. So I'm just . . . pruning. Like I was going to do anyway."

I aimed a curveball at her. "Did you like Mr. Meckel?"

She seemed surprised by the question, but I didn't see any beads of guilty sweat forming on her brow. "He was okay. He wasn't bad. He was a . . . boss, you know what I mean?"

Actually I've been freelance for so long, I've pretty much forgotten what bosses are like. When I read *Dilbert*, I don't really get the jokes. But I nodded like I understood her perfectly, and asked, "Can you think of anybody who might have wanted to kill Mr. Meckel?"

She gave a confused frown. "The two policemen who came to my house said Laura Braithwaite did it."

"Maybe, but maybe not."

"They said they were sure. They caught her red-handed."

"I'm checking into it."

"Well, it's a free country, I guess," she said dubiously. "I know you were involved in a couple of murders before . . ."

"Did Mr. Meckel have any enemies?" I persisted.

"Are you kidding? He was a public school principal. Half the parents in the world want to kill their principals."

"Who wanted to the most?"

She threw me a sidelong glance. "Besides you and your friends?"

"Besides us."

"Well . . ." She turned away from me and began pruning again. I wasn't sure whether she was trying to calm her nerves or avoid my eyes. "The parents of the average kids . . ." *Snip.* "The parents of the low-end kids . . ." *Snip.*

"Was anything coming to a head?"

She moved on to the next yew bush. "No. Somebody was threatening to sue him, but that's nothing unusual."

"Who was it?"

She didn't answer. She was staring up at the top of the yew bush, where a grapevine was attacking, just out of her reach.

"You want me to get that for you?" I asked.

"That's alright." Standing on her tiptoes and straining her arms, she was able to slice off the offending vine.

"So who was gonna sue?" I repeated.

"Lou and Sylvia Robinson," she finally replied. "The couple that lives across the street from the school."

My ears perked up. I knew Lou and Sylvia, alright—they ran the mom-and-pop Xerox store where I used to get my screenplays copied. But I hadn't known they lived right near the school. That would make it easy for them to drop in on Meckel for a quick morning meeting. . . .

I thought about the school's layout. The library was located in a different hallway from Meckel's office.

For maybe ten minutes, Barry, Elena, Susie and their kids were in the library, and Laura was out back. It was entirely possible somebody who had a prior beef with Meckel could have come in from outside, gotten into a quick quarrel that ended in Meckel's freak murder . . . and then run off in a panic as fast as their legs could carry them, with nobody ever knowing anything about it. Except for Barry, hearing some indistinct shouting while he was in the john.

"What were the Robinsons so upset about?" I asked.

"Their kid has ADD. Or ADHD, I get them mixed up."

"But why did they want to sue Meckel?"

She eyed another vine, way up high on the other side of the bush. This time I didn't bother offering to help. "Maybe you should ask *them*," Ms. Helquist said as she strained her arms. "I feel a little funny talking to you. After all, you're not the police." *Snip*. Then she brought her arms down and eyed me challengingly.

It looked like this particular fountain of information was about to dry up. I might as well hit her with the question I'd been meaning to ask ever since I realized her cold was bogus. "What about *you*, Ms. Helquist, if you don't mind my asking."

"What *about* me?"

"Did you want to kill him?"

She stared at me, then broke into a laugh. "I'm too close to retirement to want to kill anybody."

But the way she pointed those shears, it sure looked like she wanted to kill *me*.

It was two o'clock already. Two hours since I'd asked Judy Demarest to take care of my kids for an hour. I should act responsible and go home. I got in my car, fully expecting to do just that.

But then somehow my Toyota Camry got all rebellious. She flat out refused to take the right turn that would have led me back home. Instead she turned left, toward Lou and Sylvia Robinson's Xerox store on Grand Street. Funny how cars will do that to you sometimes.

This particular car, an '85, had been with me so long she knew me as well as I knew myself. When I struck it rich two years ago, I thought about purchasing a sleek new vehicle. But I just couldn't bring myself to part with my old love. I mean, she only had 160,000 miles on her, that's all. And she still ran perfectly, as long as you fluttered her gas pedal just right when you started her and murmured a few sweet nothings to her engine. And the ride was nice and smooth, if you didn't mind her loud muffler and the wind blowing through her half-rusted-out doors like they were made of fishnet.

Lou and Sylvia's store, L & S Copies, was located in an old storefront that looked as weather-beaten as my car. It contrasted sharply with the shiny new Kinko's that had opened up six months ago on Broadway, right in the heart of downtown. Every time I drove past L & S, I half expected to see FOR RENT and GOING OUT OF BUSINESS signs on the front window. But so far, Lou and Sylvia were hanging in there.

My Camry shuddered to a halt. I grabbed a couple of oil-change receipts from the glove compartment and took them into L & S with me. I was the only customer.

At the front counter, Lou gave me a big welcoming smile when I came in. Lou was an amiable balding guy in his forties who'd given up a steady gig at Quad Graphics, a local printing company, to run his own business. I wondered how he felt about his career choice now that the two-ton chain-store gorilla had just come storming into town.

"Hey, Hollywood, where you been?" Lou greeted me. For a large man, over six feet tall and two hundred pounds, he had a surprisingly high voice. "Hanging out with Arnold and Keanu?"

"No, I've been around, Lou. Just haven't written any screenplays that needed Xeroxing."

"And here I thought you deserted me for Kinko's like all the rest of my fair-weather *fiends*." But despite the harsh words, Lou still had that smile. He could be loud and opinionated—we used to have raucous arguments about Ross Perot, back when Lou was a big supporter—but he never seemed to get too perturbed by anything. He rolled with life's punches pretty well. It was hard to picture him seriously threatening to sue Meckel—or killing him.

What about Sylvia, though? She was off to the side doing some Xeroxing. Also in her forties, with a pronounced vertical worry line creasing her forehead, she was never very communicative; she let Lou handle the customer relations. Maybe she was the strong, silent type. Or maybe not. I tried to picture her as the screaming woman that Barry had heard in Meckel's office this morning . . .

She felt me watching her and looked up. "Hey, Sylvia," I said.

"Hi, Jacob," she replied with a brief smile, then went back to work.

"So is that writer's block still kicking your butt?" Lou asked. "You could make a movie out of this place. Right, Syl?"

"Maybe a short one," she said dryly.

I handed Lou the oil-change receipts. "Got a couple of pages for you. Two copies."

"On the house," he said, going over to the funky old Xerox machine at the front of the store and setting to work. "But when you finally get around to writing your next movie, I better not catch you at that other place."

I laughed, allowed a brief pause to come in, and then said, "So that's pretty terrible about Meckel, huh?"

"No kidding. Wouldn't wish it on my worst enemy—which is pretty much what he was."

"Why's that?"

From behind her machine, Sylvia said, "Honey, don't be speaking ill of the dead."

"Yeah, yeah, I know," Lou grumbled. "I just don't appreciate the way he treated our son."

"*Lou*," Sylvia said warningly.

He threw up his hands in surrender. "Alright."

But I wasn't about to let the subject die so easily. "Was it something about your son having ADD?"

Voicing that magic acronym was all it took for Lou's dam to break. "That's a bunch of bull," he spilled out. "Mark doesn't have ADD, ADHD, or any other kind of D."

"I didn't mean to say—"

"He's got this complete joke of a teacher, Melanie Wilson, straight out of college, doesn't know diddly-squat about teaching. Only reason Meckel hired her, she's got a nice ass. You can ask Sylvia, she volunteers in the class—"

"Let it go, Lou," Sylvia said.

But it would have been easier to stop Niagara Falls than to stop Lou right now. "All the other boys are running wild too, and screaming, even worse than Mark. But this stupid broad singles out *my son*, says he's got 'attention deficit hyperactivity disorder.' Horseshit. If Ms. Wilson was a half-decent teacher, Mark would start paying attention just fine."

I clucked my tongue and said, "That's awful," to prime the pump a little more.

Sylvia tried to staunch the flow with, "I'm sure Jacob doesn't want to hear this—"

It didn't work. "Kid's in fifth grade. None of his teachers ever complained about him before," Lou said. "You'd figure Meckel would see through Ms. Wilson's crap, right?"

"Yeah."

He waved my oil-change receipts at me. "But this lazy quack psychologist they have, she and Wilson are thick as thieves. She just rubber stamps whatever Wilson says. And Meckel backs them up. Sticks a label on my kid, wants to put him on some kind of *drug*. For my money, Meckel was nothing but a pusher," Lou spit out. "May he rest in peace or rot in hell, either way is fine with me."

Obviously I'd overestimated Lou's ability to roll with life's punches. Of course, this was one heck of a punch, having somebody tell you something is seriously wrong with your kid.

That must be the biggest punch there is. God knows if someone ever said anything like that about Latree or Charizard, I'd feel like strangling him.

"I hear you were gonna sue Meckel," I said.

"I was thinking about it, that's for damn sure."

I took a flyer and tried, "Yeah, his secretary said you had a meeting with him this morning."

Lou wrinkled his forehead. "Not this morning, no."

"Oh, maybe it was Sylvia." I looked over at her.

She looked back at me. Something I couldn't define flickered across her face.

Lou, intent on putting new paper in the machine, didn't notice anything. "No, Syl was here at the store from, like, seven o'clock. We got a big order from the arts council. Thank God we still have a few loyal customers."

Sylvia stepped away from her Xerox machine. The way her bright green eyes flashed fire at me, she should have been nicknamed Charizard herself. That

look could melt boulders into cinders, easy. "Why
are you asking us about this morning?"

"No reason," I squeaked nervously.

But I didn't fool her for a second. Jabbing her finger at me, she turned toward Lou. "Do you know
what he's doing?"

Lou stared blankly at the two of us for a moment,
then he got it. He eyed me in astonishment. "Are
you *interrogating* us?"

"Look, I'm talking to *everybody*, okay? I'm just trying to get my friend out of jail—"

"And you waltz in here acting like *my* friend?" He
threw my Xeroxed pages at me. They landed on the
floor. I bent down self-consciously and picked them
up.

"I'm sorry," I said, for at least the third time that
day.

"Yeah, you're sorry, alright. Get your sorry ass out
of my store."

That sounded like good advice. So I took it. But as
I opened the door, I turned back and checked out
Sylvia one more time.

I'm lucky I didn't go up in smoke.

5

My Camry wanted to head over to the Saratoga County Arts Council on Broadway so I could check on Sylvia and Lou's alibi. However, I managed to wrestle the steering wheel into submission and drove home.

When I got there, Judy Demarest's car was gone. But my wife's minivan was in the driveway now. She must have caught wind of Meckel's murder and come home early.

That meant my child-care services weren't needed, and I was free to go hit the arts council after all. I just had to take off before Andrea and the kids spotted me and I got too busy with all my domestic duties to pursue Meckel's killer.

So I fluttered the old gas pedal again, said, "Come on, baby" to the engine in my sexiest voice, and started off. Two minutes later I was back downtown, driving past Kinko's and parking in front of the brand-spanking-new Saratoga Cultural Arts Center. This complex, complete with high-ceilinged art gallery, fancy theater, classrooms, and office space, was the million-dollar brainchild of Gretchen Lang, the executive director of the Saratoga County Arts Council. A vibrant woman in her fifties with big dreams and a big heart, she had dedicated the past ten years of her life to nurturing the local arts scene and making the center a reality.

When I walked into the elegant gallery, Gretchen herself was behind the front desk doing paperwork. "Jake!" she said warmly. "Just the man I wanted to see!"

"Nice exhibit, Gretchen," I said, pointing to the abstract nudes all around me. Some of them had one head, some two or three, and their arms numbered anywhere from zero to a dozen. The arts council used to specialize in bland watercolors of flowers and racehorses, but when Gretchen took over she really livened things up.

And she was still as exuberant as ever. "Hey, Jake, how would you like to judge the Annual Children's Poetry Contest?" she asked, her voice chirping cheerily.

Perish the thought. "I don't think I'm your man."

"Why not?"

"Well, to start with, I hate poetry."

"But you're a writer."

"I know, I know," I said, a little sheepish. "But poems always seem like just *words* to me."

"You'll love *these* poems, Jake." She held up a folder full of the darn things. "They'll warm the cockles of your heart. Maybe they'll even inspire you to write again."

Why did so many people seem to think I was so eager to write again? I was perfectly happy with my life just the way it was . . . wasn't I?

"I *need* you, Jake," Gretchen cajoled. "You know I'll just keep bugging you till you say yes."

She had me there. "Okay," I said resignedly, holding out my hand for the poems. "Warm my cockles."

"You won't regret it."

"I already do. Listen, I have a question. Did L & S do any Xeroxing for you today?"

"Yes, for our annual fund-raiser."

"You happen to know what time they finished the job?"

"Let's see, I called at ten and they weren't done yet. Then they called me right before lunch and I picked it up. Why?"

"How big a job was it?"

Gretchen shrugged. "Not all that big. Four pages, double-sided, eleven hundred copies."

Having done a lot of Xeroxing in my life, I did some mental calculations. That kind of project wouldn't take more than half an hour or forty-five minutes. And it wasn't like the Robinsons had a lot of other jobs competing for their attention.

"So it sounds like they didn't go in early this morning to finish your job." There went their alibi.

Gretchen cocked her head at me. "What's this about?"

"Uh, nothing important. Hey, thanks for the literature." I headed for the door.

"I need the three best poems from each grade level by Friday," she called after me.

"No problem. I'll just throw them all down the stairs, and whichever poems go the farthest are the winners."

I was just acting grouchy for effect. The truth was, I expected to like the kids' poems more than I like most grown-up poems.

I mean, at least the stuff would probably rhyme.

When I'm alone in my trusty Camry, I like to sing. So on my way home, I fought the creaky windows and succeeded in rolling them up. Then I let loose with the old chestnut "What do you do with a drunken sailor?" Except instead of "drunken sailor" I substituted the words "busted alibi."

I was hoping my choral efforts would loosen up

the old mental neurons and get them inspired. But it didn't work. They seemed frozen solid. I knew there was no point in going to Chief Walsh with my too vague suspicions about the Robinsons. But what else could I do?

When I got home and asked Andrea for advice, her neurons weren't working any better than mine. She was distraught about Laura's incarceration, though for the first few hours we didn't get a chance to talk about it in much detail. We were too busy keeping the three boys—especially Adam—distracted.

First we went outside to the driveway and played basketball with them, to wear them out. Then we cooked Adam's favorite dinner, plain unbuttered noodles and popcorn. After that we rented his favorite movie, the old Fred MacMurray version of *The Absent-Minded Professor*. When we put them to bed, I read aloud a few chapters of his favorite book, *Redwall*.

Despite our herculean efforts, though, Adam burst into tears four or five more times that evening. And he didn't get to sleep until after midnight.

When our baby-sitting chores were finally done— for today, anyway—Andrea and I lay in bed exhausted. We spoke quietly, so we wouldn't wake up the kids in their bedroom down the hall. "So what do you think?" Andrea asked.

"I think I should go down to Grand Avenue tomorrow, by Lou and Sylvia's store, and find out if any of their neighbors saw them there around seven-thirty—"

"I mean about Laura."

"Oh." I scratched my head. The fact was, despite my best efforts to convince myself Lou or Sylvia was the killer, in my heart of hearts I still felt it was Laura. But if I admitted to Andrea that I suspected

her bowling buddy and dirty joke guru of murder,
would she jump down my throat?

I decided to take the coward's way out. "I don't
know. What do *you* think?" I said.

Andrea bit her lip. "Adam is Laura's baby. Ever
since her husband died, Adam is all she has. She
lives for him. But . . . *killing* for him?"

"Whoever did this probably didn't mean to kill
the guy."

She poked at the pillow with her finger. "I feel
guilty even *thinking* she might've done it. But she
does have a temper. I ever tell you about the guy at
the bowling alley?"

If she had, I'd forgotten. Another symptom of
my onrushing middle age. Either that or it's a
symptom of being married for so long I only listen
to my spouse intermittently. "It doesn't ring a
bell."

"This jerk tried to kick us off our lane at eight-
thirty for a nine-o'clock league. Laura gave him such
a tongue-lashing, I bet his balls are still shriveled."

Andrea never used to use such salty expressions.
She learned them from Laura.

"I think she's still mad at her husband for
OD'ing," Andrea went on. "And that makes her kind
of mad at the whole world."

We both lay there silently for a moment. Then I
said, "So . . . what are you saying? Do you want me
to go easy on the sleuthing till we see if Laura
confesses?"

Andrea flushed. "Of course not. I'm just saying . . .
Oh God, I don't know *what* I'm saying. Laura didn't
do it. She *couldn't* have." She shivered. "What's
gonna happen to her?"

"Near term? Tomorrow she gets arraigned. The
judge will set bail."

Andrea turned onto her side and looked at me. "Laura won't have money for bail."

That was my cue. I hesitated, but only briefly, and said, "We can pay it. I doubt she'll run away."

Andrea's eyes peered into mine. "You sure you're okay with that?"

I shrugged, with more nonchalance than I truly felt. "Of course. She's your buddy."

"I love you," said Andrea. "You're the best man in the world."

Then she started making love to me. I was so wiped out, I didn't expect to respond.

But I did.

As we lay in bed afterward, I heard Andrea say, "Honey?"

Like most guys I'm not big on postcoital conversation, so I was tempted to pretend I was asleep. But I managed to say, "Mmm."

"Are you awake?"

"Mmm," I repeated.

"You know," Andrea said with feigned casualness, "you never did ask how my classroom observation went today."

Now I really did wake up. I propped myself up on my elbow. "I can't believe it—I forgot. How'd it go?"

"Not good."

Oh, no. Did this mean curtains for Andrea's tenure chances? "Are you sure?"

"I'm afraid so." Then she gave me a sly smile. "It wasn't good, it was *great*. Henry said watching me teach was *inspirational*."

"Hallelujah." Henry was the department chairman. "So you're in like Flynn?"

"Looks like it." Her words may have been low-key, but she was grinning ear to ear.

"I can't believe you kept this to yourself all day."

"We had so much craziness going on, I was looking for the right moment to spring it on you."

"So you're actually going to be one of the few people left in America with honest-to-God job security?"

"Unless I'm found guilty of moral turpitude, yes."

"Honey, I'm so proud of you." I kissed her. "You've worked so hard for this."

"There's only one thing that bothers me."

"Yeah?"

"What exactly *is* moral turpitude?"

"I doubt making love to your husband qualifies," I said, and kissed her in a different place.

She giggled. "Honey, what are you doing?"

"Trying to pretend I'm twenty years younger and can actually do it twice in a row."

But before I had a chance to pretend any further, Adam started screaming.

I threw on some pajamas and went to the kids' bedroom. Adam had woken up with a nightmare about a giant machine that crushed people. He was sitting up, still whimpering with panic, and Latree and Charizard were awake too.

I held Adam in my arms for a long while as he sobbed. I wasn't sure what to say to him, so mostly I just prayed silently. I don't do that much, because I'm not convinced there's Anyone out there listening, but that night I prayed: Please, God, let this poor kid's mom be innocent.

Eventually Adam lay back down. The three kids' breathing slowed, and they finally fell asleep again.

Then I went back to bed myself, but I was too restless to sleep. There had to be a clever way to investigate Sylvia and Lou—something slicker than just canvassing the neighbors. What would Sam Spade do? I got out of bed again and threw on some clothes. Singing in the car hadn't given me any brilliant insights. Maybe a walk in the brisk night air would do the trick.

I stepped outside. It was two a.m., and eerily silent except for the occasional buzzing street lamp. Even at the height of racing season in August, Saratoga Springs is more or less comatose at that hour. On a Tuesday two a.m. in May, the town is dead and buried.

I walked up and down the streets of my West Side neighborhood. I passed Ms. Helquist's house, with its multitude of flowers rising out of the dark earth. I went by the Gideon Putnam Burial Ground, Saratoga's oldest cemetery. Then I headed up High Rock Avenue and found myself outside Lou and Sylvia's house. I guess that's where I was planning on going all along, though I hadn't realized it. I eyed the house, a modest Colonial much like my own, and wondered what evil lurked therein.

Unfortunately I'm not psychic, so I didn't feel any vibrations emanating from the house. I walked across the street toward the elementary school and imagined what might have happened there yesterday morning. Dredging up my old screenwriting habits, I created a little movie scene in my head that went something like this:

EXT. STREET—MORNING.

Sylvia Robinson, 40s, mother and small businesswoman, steps outside to pick up her morning paper. Her face is pale and lined and she's been up all night, worrying about her beloved but troubled son . . . and about the imminent doom of her small business. She sees a car driving past. It's Sam Meckel, school principal, pulling up in front of the school.

A terrible rage grabs hold of Sylvia. Her son has been viciously maligned by this man. Declared defective. She

*hurries across the street, follows him into his office, and
confronts him, screaming. Off screen, Barry Richardson is
in the john and hears it. Laura Braithwaite is out back
smoking.*

*In the office, Meckel tells Sylvia to shut up and get the
hell out if she can't control herself. He's not listening to
her anymore, her kid is screwed up and that's that. Sylvia
can't take it. She snaps. Grabs the nearest weapon, not
wanting to kill him necessarily, just hurt him like he
hurt her. . . .*

Were there any flaws in this scenario? I gazed
thoughtfully at the darkened school—

And suddenly a light came on inside Sam Meckel's office.

It was so small and dim and stayed on so briefly
that at first I thought I'd just imagined it. But then
it came on again.

It was a flashlight.

Who was snooping around with a flashlight in Sam
Meckel's office in the dead of night?

I moved closer to the office window, hoping it was
too dark outside for the mysterious intruder to spot
me. But before I could see who was in there, an un-
seen hand pulled down the Venetian blinds. Now I
couldn't look in anymore.

Should I just stay put and wait for the intruder to
come back outside?

But what if he or she slipped out the back door
and I never even found out who it was? I'd feel like
a flaming idiot. Chief Walsh would never believe I'd
seen what I'd seen.

Should I call the cops right now? But where was
the nearest pay phone? Probably Washington Street.
How long would it take me to run over there?

Seven or eight minutes, probably. Too long.

I made up my mind. I ran swiftly across the

schoolhouse lawn. I almost tripped on a thick branch that must have just fallen from the big oak tree that shaded the front of the school. On an impulse I reached down and found the branch in the darkness. Then I snapped it in two with my feet, so I had a manageable weapon about as long as a baseball bat.

Then I hurried toward the front door again, taking my AAA card out of my wallet as I went. From experience I'd learned that certain AAA cards—the flexible ones—do a better job of opening locked doors than your average credit card.

It's funny, I'll bet I get more emotional satisfaction from my successful burglaries than I get from my hit movie or any of the stage plays I've written. In my most primal reptilian soul, being a macho-type law-breaker is a lot more fulfilling than being a sensitive *artiste*.

I looked around for security alarms and motion sensors, but didn't see any; Saratoga's not as security conscious as larger cities. I put my hand on the door handle and was about to work my AAA razzle-dazzle, but then stopped quickly. It looked like I wouldn't get a chance to showcase my amazing lock-picking skills tonight. Somebody had already unlocked the door.

How rude of them.

I opened it and walked in, then closed it gently behind me. Not a sound. No scurrying mice, no electronic hums. It was pitch-black. The Exit sign at the far end of the hall shed no light way over here.

Holding the branch in my left hand, I put out my right hand and felt my way along the wall. After a few steps, the wall turned into a window. This, I knew, was the window to the front office, Ms. Helquist's domain.

The window gave way to empty space. I'd come to

the intersection of two hallways. I turned the corner, reached out, and felt the window again. Still the front office. But then the window ended and my hand felt another wall. I kept going, slinking as softly as I could in my Nikes. At last the wall gave way to a door.

Mr. Meckel's door.

It was shut. And the intruder was inside.

Doing what—looking for something?

Maybe something that would implicate him or her in the murder . . . if the cops ever got hold of it?

Suddenly it struck me: that couldn't be Laura in there, she was in jail. Despite my fear, I was thrilled. This could mean Laura didn't kill Meckel after all.

I put my ear up to the door crack. Stone-cold silence. Damn, had the intruder heard me? Was he or she inside there lying in wait? I doubted it; I'd been awfully quiet. Probably the intruder was moving around in there, and I just couldn't hear any noise through the solid wooden door.

I stood there, mustering up my courage to burst inside. Then I decided I'd be better off staying where I was, and ambushing the intruder when he or she came out. That felt safer than barging in. So I held my branch high and waited.

And waited some more.

Seconds passed. Minutes. Actually I don't know how much time passed, but it was excruciating. My inner eye summoned up an extremely disturbing movie scene:

INT. DEAD MAN'S OFFICE—NIGHT.

Intruder tiptoes to window. He or she did *hear footsteps in the hall. Even as Jacob Burns, the world's most absurd P.I., stands out there waiting, the intruder is carefully, noiselessly lifting the Venetian blinds and the window . . .*

*then jumping out through the opening, falling onto the
soft ground outside, and running off down High Rock
Avenue, leaving nary a trace behind.*

*And Jacob Burns would waste his one and only chance
to find out who killed Sam Meckel.*

I strained my ears. To no avail.

This was insane. My reptilian brain began to rebel.
What was I so damn scared of? First of all, the intruder was probably a woman, not some big bruiser
of a guy. I was betting that the intruder was the same
woman Barry had heard screaming in Meckel's office.
Second, there was no way she had a gun. Or at least
that's what I told myself. The murder had been a
freak accident, I thought, a sudden momentary emotional spasm, not some kind of well-planned contract
hit by a well-armed gunman.

I should quit acting like a mouse. Sam Spade would
never stand out here in the hallway scratching his arm-
pits while the killer eased out of a window barely ten
feet away and headed home for a cup of hot cocoa.

So I took a deep breath. I stealthily slid my hand
down the door until I found the handle. My body
tensed, I bent my knees—

And threw the door open, brandishing my branch.
"Freeze!" I shouted immediately, without even thinking. I guess I wanted to sound like a cop. I wonder,
did I really think yelling "Freeze!" was going to stop
a murderer?

But there was nobody there. Or nobody I could
see. The flashlight was off. Was the intruder gone?
Had my nightmare scenario come true? I stepped
around the door—

Suddenly I became conscious of movement to my
left. Branch held high, I whirled quickly.

But not quickly enough. A hard object—the flashlight?—smashed into the back of my head. Then another hard object—the floor—smashed into the front of my head.

And then my brain gave an angry squawk and went on hiatus.

6

Why was I lying on my stomach on a cold hard floor?

Had I passed out in a bathroom or something? Was I back in college suffering the aftereffects of a Wild Turkey overdose? Did that explain why some evil imp was hammering at my skull?

Suddenly, in between the pounding, it all came back to me. The realization of what had just happened hurt even worse than the physical pain. Damn, had the bad guy—or bad girl—escaped for good? Leaning on Meckel's desk for support, I struggled to my feet. Then I wobbled to the school's front door. I opened the door and looked out.

Nothing.

So I wobbled to the back door and looked out that way.

Still nothing.

I teetered back down the dark corridor to the boys' bathroom. I went inside and turned on the light. It seared my eyes. My brain was on fire. I turned on the cold water and dunked my head in the sink.

My body shivered, but meanwhile my brain began to cool off. I turned my head sideways and let some of the water flow down into my mouth. I gave my head another turn with the increasingly frigid water, then took another drink, and in a couple of minutes

I felt more or less fit enough to stumble back to Meckel's office.

I had a job to do. I was going to redeem myself.

First I went over to Meckel's window and felt the blinds to make sure they were still down. They were. Thus reassured, I turned on the overhead light.

The office looked neat and untouched, aside from the branch lying on the floor. If the intruder had indeed been searching the place, it was done so circumspectly nobody would ever know. The only thing that seemed a little off was that the middle right drawer of Meckel's desk had been left partially open. The intruder must have been in the process of going through it when he or she heard me.

Now I was hoping it turned out to be a *he*. Okay, call me sexist, but I'd feel better about getting knocked cold if a guy did it.

Since the middle right drawer was where my predecessor had left off, that's where I started. I found cafeteria menus, classroom schedules, and an open bag of pretzel sticks.

Now there was a new theory of the crime: somebody was ripping off Meckel's pretzel sticks, and when Meckel caught him in the act, the thief whacked him.

I took a guess that the intruder had started with the top drawer and was working his way down. So I decided to work down, too. In the bottom drawer I found more pretzel sticks, lying on top of about a million folders containing about a gezillion memos. They came from school board members, superintendents, assistant superintendents, and others of their misbegotten ilk. Sifting through these memos, which covered every minute aspect of school life from insurance to radon testing to the price of lightbulbs, gave me a touch of sympathy with Meckel's stubborn resistance to tackling any new projects. The man had his hands full just answering memos.

But none of these memos, however aggravating, seemed worth killing over.

I opened the drawers on the other side of the desk and rifled through them. Nothing jumped out at me. Then I went over to the bookshelf, where a bunch of manila folders lay flat. I didn't want to press my luck and spend any more time in Meckel's office than I had to, so I searched especially for files with labels that might relate to Sylvia and Lou, like "ADHD" or "Psychological Reports" or, simply, "Robinson."

I drew a blank. But underneath a three-inch-thick pile of memos about officially sanctioned procedures for hiring janitorial assistants, I did find a folder marked "Terra Nova." Out of curiosity, I opened it.

The folder contained the Terra Nova test results for every child in High Rock Elementary School. I was surprised Meckel had gotten the results back from the test scoring service already. The students had taken the Terra Novas only two weeks ago.

Then I read the cover page at the top of the folder and realized these were just preliminary Terra Nova results, put together and presumably scored by Meckel himself. The cover page explained that he was using these unofficial results for administrative purposes, including giving him a head start with placing kids in the gifted program. Also he was using the scores to help him evaluate teachers.

As I flipped through the folder, I noted that in general the High Rock kids did quite well. Most had scored above the seventieth percentile for the state. Saratoga Springs schools usually scored pretty high in the statewide standardized tests; but High Rock was the poorest elementary school in town, socioeconomically speaking, and tended not to do as well as the other local schools. These scores would give High Rock parents something to crow about this year.

I turned to the page with the second-graders' scores. Since it was alphabetical, Adam Braithwaite was near the top. In English, he had scored a 98. In math, though, he only got an 89.

It was just as Laura had predicted. Her son hadn't scored high enough, according to Meckel's rigid criteria, to make it into the gifted and talented program.

No doubt Chief Walsh would view this as further evidence that Laura killed Meckel in her outrage over her son's academic placement. And I suppose I couldn't argue with that line of thinking. A few years back, a mother in Texas tried to kill somebody in order to get her daughter onto the high school cheerleading squad. So why shouldn't Laura Braithwaite kill somebody to get her child a good education?

There were plenty of worse motives for murder. In fact, if our public schools get much worse, maybe "disgruntled parents" will replace "disgruntled former employees" as the most common crazed killers. Instead of "going postal," people will "go parental."

I found Latree's test numbers right below Adam's. His name was circled. He had scored 100 in English and 96 in math, which meant he made the cut. Of course, with Meckel dead, these criteria might no longer be in effect.

Barry's kid Justin made the cut too. He had scores of 97 and 96. I noticed Justin's name was also circled—evidently Meckel had circled the names of the kids he was planning to include in the gifted program.

As I searched further in the folder, I noted that Susie and Elena's third-grade daughters, Christine and Luce, did not have their names circled. Both of them fell just shy of the magic 95—they got scores in the low 90s.

I shook my head, giving my concussion a little added thrill. This whole Terra Nova business was nuts. I'd spent time with both Christine and Luce, and there was no question they belonged in a more challenging program. Why is this whole country so hopped up on standardized multiple-choice tests? All they do is teach children to give quick answers to superficial questions.

And as for placing kids in gifted programs . . . instead of using these lame tests as the ultimate criteria, why not use grades and teacher recommendations? And what about kids who are super-gifted in one area, like English, math, art, or music, but not others? Children aren't computer statistics, and their educational program should reflect that—

Suddenly my musings were cut off by a soft noise. A small *bink*. I stood still. Where did that *bink* come from, the hallway? Was it just a random night noise—or was it, as I feared, the front door closing?

Then I heard a new sound. This one was unmistakable. *Clomp clomp clomp*—footsteps. Coming closer.

Was the killer returning? With a gun?

I had left Meckel's door open. I sprang up and shut and locked it, all in one motion.

Just in time, too. Because as soon as I turned the lock, somebody rattled the doorknob. Then pounded on the door.

"Police. Open up—now!" shouted an angry voice, which I instantly recognized as Lieutenant Foxwell's.

Well, at least it wasn't the murderer. But the cops weren't all that much better, as far as I was concerned. Chief Walsh and his minions would sneer at my explanation of how I ended up in Meckel's office, and would take great joy in nailing my derriere to the wall. I better make tracks, fast. I dashed to the window, pushed the shade out of my way, and tried to shove the window upward—

But there was nothing to grab onto, for me to shove. Then I realized it was one of those windows with handles. You're supposed to turn them round and round and gradually the window opens. So I tried to turn the handle—but it was stuck. I turned harder . . . and it came off in my hands.

And meanwhile Foxwell kept pounding on the door. "Open up or we break it down," another voice yelled—Sergeant Balducci.

Should I call out and explain there was no need to break the door down, they could simply use their AAA cards? No, maybe that wouldn't be wise. I looked down at the handle in my hands, then up at the window. Suddenly I realized I'd forgotten to un-lock the window. That's why the handle didn't work. I quickly unlocked it, then started to stick the handle back on its appropriate screw.

But I couldn't get the handle back in place. My panicked hands were too fumbly.

Behind me, either Foxwell or Balducci was throw-ing his shoulder at the door. The wood began crack-ing and splintering. If I didn't jump out that window pronto, it would be too late.

Finally the handle went onto the screw. I turned it, and the window began opening . . . but slowly. Then it got stuck. The handle was still screwed up somehow. I pushed the window hard, but that didn't help. The window wasn't open enough for me to jump through—

Crash! The dynamic duo charged the door again, and the wood split even worse. A long vertical crack ran from the top of the door down to the doorknob. One more assault and that door was history.

I jumped onto the radiator by the window. Then I squeezed my body through the narrow opening and dove down onto the ground outside. Luckily my hands hit the ground first, not my head.

Behind me there was a huge violent crash as the door burst open, then more crashes as it fell down and smacked into the desk and floor.

I did a quick roll, leapt to my feet, and ran off through the bushes to my left. My adrenaline must have been pumping big time, because I no longer felt the pain in my skull. I did feel a stabbing pain in my left shoulder, though, when I tripped on a tree root and landed hard on the shoulder as I went down.

I scrambled back up and looked behind me. Foxwell had figured out some way to get the window wide open, and now he was tumbling outside. Meanwhile Balducci was running out the front door of the school. They must have decided to split up.

I took off again. I tried to run quietly, but I snapped some twigs. Balducci shouted, "He's over there!"

I turned the corner and tore down Walworth Street, with maybe a fifteen-yard head start. Foxwell shouted, "Stop! Or we'll shoot!"

How clichéd. I kept on running. Of course they wouldn't shoot—

BANG!

Damn. I zigzagged left into Marvin Alley. There was a van right near the corner, and I hit the ground and rolled under it. My shoulder was killing me. Seconds later the cops raced up to the corner too. Then they halted. They breathed heavily as they looked around. I tried to silence my own breathing. From underneath the car, I could see the dark outlines of their legs. They were so close, if I were a gorilla I could have reached my arm out and touched them.

"You see him?" Foxwell said.

"No," said Balducci. "Could be in one of these backyards."

"You get a good look at him?"

"Not good enough."

My heart leapt. So they didn't know it was me! I had a fighting chance to make it out of this mess.

"Go back to the car, radio for backup," Foxwell said. "I'll try down the alley."

I watched Balducci's feet run off in one direction and Foxwell's feet run off in another. That backyard idea didn't sound half bad. I waited about twenty seconds, then crawled out from under the van and scuttled behind a hedge. From there I crab-walked through backyards and side streets, managing to wake up about five sleeping dogs before I made it even halfway home.

More frightening than the barking dogs were the police cars that began streaming into the West Side. There must have been ten of them. They kept their sirens off, but I could hear their tires squealing and see their headlights flashing as they rushed to the scene.

On Ash Street, I came out from behind some juniper bushes and started across the street. But then two cops on foot rounded the corner and headed up the sidewalk. They must have heard me, because they shone their flashlights in my direction. I dove back into the junipers.

"Who's that?" one of the cops called out.

I crawled around to the other side of the bushes, silently cursing every dried leaf that crackled under my knees.

"You hear someone?" the cop asked his partner.

"Yeah. I think he's behind those bushes."

I couldn't see the cops. But I could feel them approaching, and I could see the lights from their flashlights sweeping through the bushes in front of me.

I thought about running. But the cops were too close, and except for the junipers, the yard I was hiding in was way too open to give me good cover. Maybe the other cops had been shooting in the air, but maybe not, and I was in no mood to get shot at again.

Their feet crunched the sidewalk gravel as they came my way. I was doomed.

But then I got a last-ditch inspiration.

"Meow," I said. But loud, and with feeling.

The footsteps stopped.

"Meow," I said again.

"Hell, it's just a cat," the first cop said.

"Great. Let's try Hyde Street," the other one said, and they took off.

I waited the obligatory twenty seconds and took off myself. I scrambled across Ash and veered left, avoiding Hyde. Then I hit another couple of backyards, woke up another couple of dogs, climbed a fence, and plopped down into my own backyard. I ran up to my back door and let myself in.

Hallelujah. Safe at last. I felt exhilarated and incredibly macho—

"Honey, is that you?" Andrea called from the front of the house. She must have had trouble sleeping and come downstairs.

I walked toward her voice. "Yeah, it's me—"

But then I stopped.

She wasn't alone. Two men were standing with her in the front hall.

Foxwell and Balducci.

"Have a nice little walk?" Foxwell asked pleasantly.

I was dumbfounded. "How'd you find me?"

Balducci snorted. "Wasn't hard. Who else would be dumb enough to do what you just did?"

Andrea watched me, frightened. She was dying to know what it was I'd done, but she couldn't very well ask me with these servants of the law around.

"Let's go, pal," Foxwell said.

"Where?" I asked.

"Where do you think? We gonna need handcuffs?"

I went over to Andrea and gave her a kiss. "See you soon, babe. Don't worry, it's nothing serious."

"But I wouldn't hold breakfast for him if I were you," Balducci said.

7

By eight o'clock that morning, I'd spent an hour in the police station interrogation room giving my story about fifteen different times to Foxwell and Balducci. I'd used my one approved phone call to reach the trusty Malcolm Dove, and I gave him the story, too. Then I passed another two hours sitting around various waiting rooms, being thankful they hadn't thrown me in the clink—yet. Now I was sitting in Chief Walsh's office, telling my tale yet again. The more I repeated it, the more preposterous it sounded, even to me.

My adrenaline was long gone and the pounding in my skull was back. My shoulder was aching too. I'd asked for aspirin, but they hadn't brought me any. They did bring me coffee. If anything, it made the pounding worse.

"So you just *happened* to be hanging around outside the school at two-thirty in the morning," the chief said sarcastically.

"I told you, I was hoping for inspiration."

"And then you just *happened* to get knocked out without seeing who did it. How convenient."

"The guy bashed me with a heavy flashlight!" I was shouting with frustration. "How else do you think I got this big bump on my head?"

"Running from the police."

"I swear, that's not how it was." I stomped the floor for emphasis. "Don't you get it? Laura Braithwaite didn't kill Meckel, somebody else did. And that person snuck back into Meckel's office last night to cover it up."

The chief pointed an accusatory finger at me. "You went to see Laura yesterday. In jail."

"Yeah. So what?"

"What did the two of you talk about?"

"She told me she was innocent."

"Oh, did she now?" He flashed me a knowing grin.

"Look, what's your point?"

"This." The chief lifted a manila folder out of his Inbox and held it up for me to see. It was the Terra Nova folder. "You left this on Meckel's desk."

"Yeah, I was reading it."

"Why?"

I tried to recall. "I don't know, I was curious."

"Don't play your idiotic games with *me*," the chief snapped angrily, stepping into his alternate personality. I seemed to bring out the worst in the guy.

"I called Hilda Helquist this morning," the chief continued, his perfect white teeth bared. "She told me all about these tests, and how Meckel was using the preliminary scores to decide who got in the gifted program." He came around the desk and got in my face. "Laura knew about the test scores, didn't she? She knew they gave her a murder motive. So she asked you to break into Meckel's office and get rid of them."

"But—"

He leaned in even closer. I could smell the mint-flavored toothpaste on his breath. "Admit it. You broke into that office."

"No—"

"There was a coverup last night, alright. You were covering up the murder yourself."

Enough was enough. The toothpaste smell was getting on my nerves. "Don't be a damn idiot," I shot at him. His head snapped back. "Laura already told the police she was pissed off at Meckel. That's your so-called murder motive, right there. So why would she care about some stupid folder? It doesn't add anything new to your case."

"Sure, it does. It's the icing on my cake," the chief said triumphantly, waving the folder at me. "These test scores are what sent her over the edge. See, Laura admits she talked to Meckel the night before. Logical conclusion is, he told her about Adam's scores being too low for the gifted program. So the very next morning she goes berserk and kills him." He shrugged his shoulders, smiling. "Makes a nice simple story that even the most dim-witted jury members will be able to follow, don't you think?"

Unfortunately I agreed with him, but I kept that to myself. "Laura says Meckel didn't tell her Adam's test scores. And anyway, the scores still don't prove a thing. Susie and Elena's daughters scored too low, too. So why not suspect Susie and Elena?"

As soon as I said that, I realized I actually meant it. Both Susie and Elena could get pretty intense when their children's welfare was threatened. And neither of them had totally ironclad alibis.

But the chief wasn't interested in my insinuations. "I'll be glad to inform them you said that," he said sarcastically. "But luckily for them, they weren't found next to the dead body holding the murder weapon."

"Listen, Chief," I began, in a pleading tone.

But he cut me off. "Look, Burns, Laura Braithwaite is going down for this. The only question is: how far down do you want to go with her?"

I got a powerful desire to bash Chief Walsh right

in the middle of his arrogant face. Where was that spelling bee trophy when I needed it?

"Here's the deal," the chief said. "You drop your ridiculous little fairy tale about what happened last night, and you confess to the break-in. Then I'll let you cop to a misdemeanor. Otherwise it's felony B and E, to say nothing of obstruction." The chief broke into a sudden twisted smile. "So what do you say?"

I gritted my teeth. I'm far from the world's most courageous guy, but after hours of listening to all these bozo cops with bad breath giving me crap, it was time to satisfy my inner reptile. "You sure you want to play it like this, Chief?"

"You kidding? I'm enjoying every minute."

"Yeah, but throw me in jail and guess what? The entire upstate New York media rehashes our whole history. How we tend to have little disagreements from time to time, and how I tend to be right and you tend to have your head so far up your ass it's looking out through your belly button." I clicked my tongue sadly. "I'd hate to see you go through the shame, the embarrassment, the public ridicule. . . ."

"Hey, it goes with the job." The chief pushed a button on his desk. Balducci entered.

"Read this guy his rights," the chief told Balducci. "Then throw him away."

Maybe I should have kept my inner reptile locked up.

The jail was just as ugly, smelly, and all-around gross as I'd remembered. The good news was, I was only there for half an hour before all of us heavy-duty criminals were taken upstairs for arraignment. In addition to myself, there was an elderly gentleman who'd walked backward down the middle of Broadway after the bars closed, urinating on the yellow stripes as he went; a skinny kid who'd shoplifted some condoms and chocolate bars from CVS; and a Peeping Tom who'd made the strategic error of peeping a policeman's wife.

Just another fun Tuesday night.

But then another inmate joined us on our way up the steps to the courtroom. It was Laura, fresh from the women's section of the jail, which consisted of exactly one cell. Being a suspected murderess, she made our motley little crew a lot more interesting. We stood taller and walked with more pride once we had her with us.

Laura did a double take when she saw me. "What the hell happened to you?"

"Had a bit of fun last night," I said, and repeated the whole saga yet again—or at least the broad strokes, since we only had a minute before we hit the courtroom and the judge gaveled us into silence.

"God, I feel terrible. I got you in trouble," Laura said. But her face glowed with excitement, not remorse. I didn't blame her. Finally, she had at least one other person in the world who believed in her innocence: me.

Now if only I could convince Chief Walsh and his mighty minions.

Heck, if only I could convince them of my *own* innocence, I thought as we filed into court and took our seats in the jury box up front, with three cops standing guard over us.

The joint was jam-packed with spectators and media creatures from as far away as Albany. They were buzzing, whispering and wiggling their finger bones at me and Laura. I felt like an animal in a very cramped zoo.

I turned to Laura. "Shall I treat them to my stoned chimpanzee imitation?"

She didn't respond. She was rigid with fear. I put my hand on her arm. "It's okay, Laura," I said gently. "We're not alone. We have lots of support."

"Oh, is that what all these cops are doing here—supporting us?"

I pointed to the front row. "Look over there: Andrea, Susie, Elena, Barry . . . and last but not least, our fearless attorney—"

"All rise!" some courtroom factotum declaimed.

We all rose, and the judge entered. He was a short bald man who looked rather goofy in his long black robe. But he made up for it with a commanding bass voice. I'd encountered this Little Napoleon before, and I knew you messed with him at your own peril.

Little Napoleon dispensed with the preliminaries quickly and announced the first case. Since he was going alphabetically, it was Laura's.

"The People versus Laura Braithwaite," he pronounced stentoriously. After Laura and Malcolm stepped up to the bench, he continued, "Ms. Braithwaite, you are charged with murder in the first degree. How do you plead?"

She gulped, and said nervously, "Not guilty."

"Mr. Hawthorne, does the D.A.'s office have a recommendation?"

"Yes, Your Honor," said Hawthorne, the assistant D.A. He had gotten all duded up for the occasion, even going so far as to put a folded white handkerchief in his breast pocket. "Given the severity of the crime, and the terrible effect it has had on our entire community, the People request that bail be set at five hundred thousand dollars."

"Oh, knock it off," Malcolm Dove broke in scornfully. "This woman is no threat to anybody, and she's not escaping to Argentina, either. She has a seven-year-old boy to take care of. We request that she be released on her own recognizance, so she can go home to her child."

"This *is* a murder case," Little Napoleon said dubiously.

"A remarkably flimsy one. Totally circumstantial, no eyewitnesses . . . and new evidence has come to light in the last few hours which strongly indicates the real murderer is not in custody."

"What new evidence is this?" Little Napoleon asked.

"It's a complete fabrication," Hawthorne interrupted. "A friend of the defendant burglarized the scene of the crime. When he was apprehended, he tried to pretend somebody else had broken in before him—and this 'somebody else' must be the real murderer."

"The individual we're speaking of is Jacob Burns," Malcolm declared. "His reputation—"

"I know his reputation," Little Napoleon said, and then gave a sniff. I got the feeling my reputation didn't impress him all that much. In fact, he looked straight at me with narrowed eyes while he said, "The suspect is ordered remanded to the county jail. Bail is hereby set at four hundred thousand dollars."

Malcolm sputtered, "But—"

Little Napoleon brought down his gavel. "Next case. The People versus Jacob Burns."

As I stepped up to the dock, I had trouble focusing at first. Damn, four hundred grand. If I was really bankrolling Laura's defense—and it sure looked like I was—then I'd have to spring for ten percent of that, or forty grand, for a bail bondsman. Suddenly my three hundred K nest egg didn't feel quite so large.

Forty thousand dollars. That was more than I used to make in three years as a starving artist. How much more dough would I end up spending on Laura's defense? And how much would I need to shell out for my own bail?

The answer, as it turned out, was five thou, because the judge set my bail at fifty thou. He also gave me a stern warning to avoid any "shenanigans" related to Laura's case. Malcolm told me later that fifty K was way higher than the average bail for B and E's in Saratoga County. Especially for a first-time offense. Okay, they were hitting me for obstruction of justice too, but still, what was the deal here? Was Little Napoleon buddies with Chief Walsh? Or maybe he saw my *Gas That Ate San Francisco* movie and didn't like it.

Speaking of movies, the way my finances were getting zapped, I might be forced to crank out another Grade Z flick after all.

Laura and I were removed in separate police cars to the Ballston Spa County Jail. Meanwhile, Andrea feverishly set to work contacting bail bondsmen and imploring our mutual funds to wire emergency cash to our bank account.

Fortunately, she managed to untape enough of the red tape that my fellow crimie and I were released at 5:27, just before the administrative office of the jail closed up for the night. Andrea was waiting for us at the front desk, and Laura and I took turns hugging her. My concussion-induced headache, which had held me tightly in its grip all day, began to dissipate.

"God, Andrea, I don't know how to thank you," Laura said, tears streaming.

"Hey, I had to make sure you don't miss bowling tomorrow night," Andrea replied.

After we got into Andrea's car—a red Honda minivan that made me feel hopelessly suburban—I said to them, "Guess what, ladies? I have a couple of hot murder suspects for you."

Laura leaned forward eagerly from the backseat.

Andrea's hands gripped the steering wheel tight. "Like who?" she asked.

"Hold on to that wheel. You ready?"

"Come on, who?" Laura said.

"Susie and Elena."

Laura gave an explosive sigh and sat back again. "Oh, brilliant."

"Hey, why not?"

Andrea wasn't too joyful either. "Bad enough the cops are after Laura. Now you want them hounding all our other friends, too?"

"Hey, Susie and Elena may be our friends, but I always liked Laura best."

Andrea took her eye off the road and threw me a sharp look, almost running into the black Buick in front of her. "Jake, this isn't funny. Laura didn't kill Meckel, and neither did Susie or Elena. Get real."

"They do have motives. We can't let ourselves be blinded by misguided loyalty."

"Look, there's no way Susie or Elena could have done it, or Barry either for that matter," Laura said. "None of them was out of each other's sight for more than a minute."

"Their time line isn't quite that clear," I said. "Susie and her two daughters got to the library at seven-fifteen. Susie could have slipped out and done the deed."

Andrea said, "But—"

I interrupted her. "And Elena says she went to her classroom for a few minutes. But maybe it was a little longer than that, and maybe she went to Meckel's office, not her classroom.

This time it was Laura who said, "But—"

I interrupted again. "And if we can think up a motive for Barry, he's a possible too. Maybe he didn't really go to the bathroom."

"But none of them had much of a window of opportunity," Andrea said.

"More like an infinitesimal crack," said Laura.

"You gotta remember, passions were running real high," I said. "It wouldn't have taken them long to get into a knockdown, drag-out fight with Meckel. Especially if Susie or Elena had just found out their kids were getting excluded from the gifted program."

"I still think the Robinsons make much better suspects," said Andrea.

"That's because you don't care about them as much," I said.

"What Robinsons? What are you talking about?" asked Laura.

I was still filling Laura in on the Family Robinson when we arrived home and Latree, Charizard, and Adam immediately raced outside to greet us. Before we even made it out of the minivan, we were smothered in embraces.

It was a big day for this hugging stuff. I picked up both my kids at once, thereby ensuring a week's worth of back pain, while Laura held Adam. Meanwhile Judy Demarest stood and watched from the front door.

"How was jail, Daddy?" Latree asked.

"Not too bad," I replied, burying my nose in his hair. I love the way my sons smell.

"Did you catch the murderer yet?" his little brother queried.

"I'm working on it."

"I hope you catch him before Saturday, because there's a Pokémon tournament at the mall."

I laughed. Charizard looked hurt. "What's funny?"

"Nothing, honey. I'm just glad to be home."

"Did you really break into the principal's office?" Latree asked, wide eyed.

"Sort of. Actually, I just *walked* in."

"Did you find the skateboard?"

"What skateboard?"

"The one you were looking for," Charizard piped in.

Where do kids come up with this stuff? I gave them my condescending grown-up voice. "No, you don't understand. I was looking for *evidence*."

"We *know* that, Dad," Latree said impatiently. "But Mommy said something about the Robinsons, so we thought you were looking for Mark's skateboard."

"Mark?"

"Yeah, their kid. He's really big. He's in fifth grade," Charizard said. "Mr. Meckel constipated his skateboard."

"You mean *confixated*," Latree corrected him.

"Whatever. Mark was, like, yelling and stuff at lunch. About how mad he was 'cause Mr. Meckel stole it."

"He used some really bad words," Latree added sanctimoniously.

"When was this?"

"Last week. Thursday or Friday."

Curiouser and curiouser. "Why didn't you tell me before?"

"We didn't think about it till we heard Mommy talking about the Robinsons," Latree said, and added reproachfully, "If you'd tell us more about your investigating, then we could help you more."

"So did you find the skateboard or not?" Charizard demanded.

"Not."

"It wasn't there?" Latree asked, excited.

"I don't think so."

"Then maybe me and Adam are right!"

"About what?"

"We think Mark stole it back."

Charizard cut in, "Don't forget me, I think so too!"

"But then Mr. Meckel caught Mark," Latree went on. "So Mark killed him."

"Or else Mark's dad killed him," Charizard suggested.

"Or his mom," said Latree.

"Or his grandma, or his great grandma," Charizard added enthusiastically. "Or his great great grandma. Or his great great great—"

"I doubt it was his great great great grandma," I said.

But some of these other folks were definitely worth considering. My kids were turning into peewee Sherlock Holmeses.

I went up to Andrea, interrupting her chat with Judy. "Honey, I have an errand to run. I'll be back as soon as I can."

Andrea grabbed my arm. "What kind of errand?"

"I'm going to see the Robinsons. I promise, I'll be careful."

"I can't believe you broke into the school last night," she said. "You could've been killed."

"It just happened. I didn't mean to do it—"

"We should get a cell phone, so you can call me next time something like this happens. Or you can call the police."

Andrea had a point. But I've made it a personal goal to avoid having a cell phone for as long as possible. I hate the darn things. So I nodded vaguely and said to Andrea, "I'll see you, honey," and started off.

Judy called after me, "Hey, wait, I just ordered pizza."

"Save me some."

"You can't go, I was counting on you for my big page-one scoop. That's my baby-sitting fee."

"You want a scoop, just ask my kids. They know

more than I do," I told her, and jumped back in the minivan.

It was getting on toward seven as I drove to the Robinsons' house. The West Side was pretty quiet. Most folks were inside, chowing down. Every once in a while, though, I'd come across kids shooting hoops or playing hopscotch. And when I got to the Robinsons' house, there was a kid riding a skateboard on their driveway. But he couldn't be Mark Robinson, because Mark was only in fifth grade. This guy had to be a high school freshman or even older. He was tall and stocky.

"Hi," I said, giving him a false smile.

He stopped his skateboard and eyed me warily. He had thick eyebrows, his eyes were set close together, and he looked like he spent a lot of his life being unhappy.

"You a friend of Mark's?" I asked.

His sullen expression didn't change. "I *am* Mark."

Man, this kid would be ready for the NBA by the time he hit tenth grade. Come to think of it, he was already big enough to knock off Meckel with one well-aimed spelling bee trophy.

"I'm Jake Burns," I said. "You know, Latree and Charizard's dad."

Mark stood and waited, bushy eyebrows knit tight, like he was wondering why this grown-up was bothering him.

"My kids tell me you're a really good skateboarder. I used to be pretty good myself," I lied.

Mark had had enough of my blathering. He started to skateboard up the driveway away from me.

I felt sleazy interrogating an eleven-year-old, even if he did look more like sixteen, but I couldn't see any way around it. "I hear Mr. Meckel confiscated your skateboard," I called out.

Mark was so surprised, he fell off the board. It came rolling down the driveway toward me. I picked it up and held it out to him.

But Mark wasn't coming anywhere near me. "That's none of your business," he said from the top of the driveway as he dusted himself off. He looked worriedly over his shoulder, back toward his house.

"How'd you get it back?" I asked.

"He gave it to me."

"When?"

"Look, I don't want to get in any more trouble," he said, his voice turning plaintive.

"When?" I repeated.

He hesitated. "Friday afternoon."

"You're lying."

"No, I'm not, I swear. I went in his office and told him I was sorry for skateboarding on school property, and he gave it back."

"Mark!" a woman's voice shouted. It was Sylvia, coming out the side door of the house wearing an apron and carrying a wooden spatula. But she didn't look like a Happy Housewife, she looked furious. "What the hell is going on out here?"

"We're just talking," Mark said.

Sylvia came storming down the driveway straight at me. I involuntarily stepped back away from her, and my foot landed on something squishy. Hopefully it wasn't dog poop. "Why are you bothering my son?" she snapped.

"Did you know Mr. Meckel confiscated his skateboard?"

She looked from me to Mark. "So what?"

"You sure you want to talk about this in front of the kid?"

"I don't want to talk about it *ever*."

"How'd Mark get his skateboard back?"

"That's none of your business," she said, sounding remarkably like her son.

"I can't help wondering if this skateboard had something to do with Meckel's death."

My words hung in the twilight air like poison gas. I was watching both Sylvia and Mark. Finally Sylvia was able to speak. "Get off my property," she said.

"You want me to go to the cops with this?"

"Don't you dare threaten me with cops. I'll tell them you're harassing my son."

"Sylvia—"

"I hear they threw you in jail last night. You want me to give them something new to bust you on?"

I could just imagine Little Napoleon licking his chops if I gave him an excuse to revoke my bail. "For your own sake, Sylvia, don't you want to get to the bottom of this?"

She advanced on me. "I want you gone!" she screamed, and raised her spatula high like she was about to whack me with it.

For a moment I got an image of Sylvia in Sam Meckel's office, holding that trophy up and getting ready to bring it down on his head.

Then the moment was over. Sylvia bent down, picked up the skateboard, and stalked back inside her house, pulling Mark along by the side of his collar.

After they were out of sight, I got back into the minivan. Then I sniffed the air and confirmed my worst suspicions.

It was dog poop, alright.

8

I opened all of the minivan's windows to get some fresh air and looked across the street toward the school. In the darkening light I saw that hundreds of flowers had been placed along the sidewalk leading up to the front door. There were a lot of lit candles, too. It was a moving sight. There had been a memorial ceremony at the school while I was in jail. According to Andrea, several hundred children had come to the ceremony. The media had come from as far away as New York City.

As I watched, a car drove up. A little girl and her father got out. She was crying, and he held her hand. She put several flowers—dandelions, it looked like—on the sidewalk. Then the two of them stood there a while.

I drove around the corner, got out of the minivan, and scraped off my shoe. Then I plotted my next move. I was eager to have my first real meal after a day of jail food. I wanted to catch a few Z's, too; I hadn't slept at all last night. But first I drove to Ms. Helquist's house. Maybe she'd know if Mark had been skating around the truth with his skateboard story.

I walked past a bed of daffodils and knocked on her front door. Her house lights were on, but there was no answer. Maybe she was out back getting in a last bit of gardening before it got too dark. I went around the front of the house, headed up her driveway—

And saw a strange thing. Or thought I did. It hap-

pened so fast and the light was so faded that I wasn't
sure. But for a split second, it sure looked like I was
seeing a sudden flash of white hair—Ms. Helquist's—
disappearing through the bushes. When I called her
name, though, she didn't answer. And when I tiptoed
through the tulips in her backyard searching for her,
I came up empty.

Was old Ms. Helquist running from me? But why?

"I guess she figured you wanted to talk about the
murder, and she wasn't in the mood," Andrea suggested as we lay in bed together that night.

"Because she has something to hide?"

"Or because she's just plain tired of talking about
it. It was late. And didn't you say the cops woke her
up early this morning to ask questions?"

"I still think there's something fishy here. Ms. Helquist is the world's most pathologically punctilious
employee. So why does she suddenly decide to take
a day off on the one day her boss gets murdered?"

Andrea was trying to scratch her back, but not
doing a very efficient job of it. I helped her out for
a while and listened to her sigh with satisfaction. But
then the sighing stopped on a dime. "Hey, honey,"
she said, "does Elena have tenure?"

"Why the *non sequitir*?"

"I was just thinking . . . if Henry ever told me he
was opposing tenure, I'd want to strangle him."

I blinked. "Who makes the tenure decisions in elementary schools—the principal?"

"Basically, yes." She sighed deeply, but not with
satisfaction this time. "I feel like a traitor, but maybe
we should look into Elena and Susie after all. And
Barry, too. We owe it to Laura."

"Sounds good," I said. "Let's see how many friends
we can alienate."

*   *   *

The next morning, two days after Sam Meckel's fatal encounter with the spelling bee trophy, High Rock Elementary School was officially open for business once again. At the breakfast table, Charizard and Latree were totally unenthused about going back to school.

"What if the murderer comes back?" Latree said as he downed a spoonful of Rice Krispies.

"He won't," I said in my deepest, most authoritative voice, intended to portray utter certainty.

Charizard looked at me, a milk mustache on his solemn face. "Why not?"

How many "why" questions does the average child ask his parents? I'm thinking at least thirty per day, beginning at about age two and a half. By that estimate, now that Charizard was five and a half, the number of "why" questions he'd asked me had reached a total of approximately thirty-three thousand.

"He just won't," I replied. "He didn't mean to kill Mr. Meckel, anyway."

Latree pointed his finger at me like it was a gun. "What if he comes into school with a machine gun this time and shoots everybody, like at Columbine?"

Oh, Lord. Every year around the Columbine anniversary, the TV news stations while away the odd hours replaying horrific videotapes of dead children, and every year we religiously turn off the TV whenever that stuff comes on. It's way too disturbing. In general, we don't let our kids watch most news programs, because they present such a warped, inaccurate perspective of the world. But evidently some TV pollution had slipped past our defenses.

Andrea was already off at her community college, teaching her eight a.m. class, so this little piece of parenting was up to me.

"Latree," I said, "and Charizard, too. Listen to me. Nobody will hurt you today. I promise."

"What if we get run over by a car?" Charizard asked brightly. Sometimes he likes contradicting me just for the fun of it. "Or what if a big man steps on our shoes by mistake. Or the teacher yells at us, and hurts our feelings."

"Okay, somebody might hurt you," I admitted. "But nobody will kill you. On purpose, anyway."

"But they might kill you, Dad," Latree said gravely. "Right?"

"Of course not."

"If I was the killer, I'd kill you," said Latree. "Because you're such a great detective, and you're gonna find out who he is."

"Thanks for the vote of confidence. Look, I was safe and sound the other times I caught the murderers, right? And I'll be safe and sound this time."

"Yeah, because you're really fast," said Charizard. "And tricky. Like, if somebody tries to shoot at you, you can just duck, like Rapidash." Rapidash was another fire Pokémon. "And then the bullet hits the wall, and then you jump at them like Rhyhorn, using a ram attack—"

"Exactly. Now enough already. Finish your breakfast." I picked up Latree's latest find, one of the old Wizard of Oz novels, and handed it to him. "Here. Read a book."

Latree was so surprised I was asking him to read—usually I'm bugging him to *stop* reading—that he picked up the book without further comment. Meanwhile Charizard began treating me to obscure details about psychic Pokémon, and that was the end of our heavy discussion, thank God. Talking to kids about death makes me uncomfortable. I've never quite figured out how to pull it off.

Then again, I've never figured out how to talk to *myself* about death.

As the kids ate, I thought about the murder for a while. Then I headed into the other room and called Laura. "Good morning," I said. "You taking Adam into school today?"

"I don't know. Maybe later. I can't decide if it would be good for him or not."

Good question.

"I feel so guilty putting him through all this," Laura said. "Even though it's not really my fault."

As I listened, I felt a wave of guilt that I had ever doubted Laura's innocence. I'd make it up to her, though. By God, I was going to get Laura and Adam out of the purgatory they were in.

"Anyway," Laura continued, "for now we're gonna stay home and hang out and play Monopoly."

"Sounds like fun. Can I talk to him for a minute?"

I explained what I wanted, and she hesitated. "I'm not sure if I want to get Adam involved," she finally said. "It might be too hard on him."

"I'll be as gentle as I can. But I could use his help."

Laura fretted for a while, then put Adam on the phone. "Hi," he said nervously.

"Adam, I have a question for you. Remember when your mom dropped you off at the library on Tuesday?"

"Yeah."

"And then she left to go see Mr. Meckel and smoke a cigarette, right? And then Susie came, with her two girls."

Adam was silent, listening.

"My question is, after Susie came, did she leave again? Did she leave you and Christine and Megan alone for a while?"

"I was playing Civilization," Adam finally said. "On the computer. I don't know if she left."

"You sure you can't remember?"

"I'm sorry. It's a really complicated game. I wasn't thinking about anything else." He paused for a moment, then asked, "Do you think maybe Susie killed Mr. Meckel?"

I couldn't think of an evasive answer that would be good enough to fool Adam, so I said, "Maybe. But I don't think so. Listen, don't tell Christine or Megan. They might get upset."

"Yeah," said Adam. "They would."

I said good-bye and hung up. I was dying to ask Christine and Megan about their mother's activities on Tuesday. But was there any graceful way of doing that?

A few minutes later, after Latree and I had our usual tug of war getting him to put down his book and tie his shoes, I drove the boys to school. We talked Pokémon the whole way, analyzing their relative fighting ability. I guess it was the kids' way of dealing with the violence that had entered our lives.

When we got to the school, the kids looked out at the flowers and candles and got quiet all of a sudden.

After a moment, Latree said, "Daddy, did Mr. Meckel have kids?"

"I think so, yes. Two teenagers."

"Oh." Then he and Charizard got out of the car.

"I love you, Latree. And you, Charizard."

"Don't forget, Daddy. Duck like Rapidash," Charizard said, and the two of them headed up the sidewalk toward the school.

I sat there and watched them go. The street in front of the school was pretty crowded. A lot of parents had driven their children to school today instead of putting them on the bus.

Several cars up, I spotted Susie Powell dropping off her two daughters. They looked tentative this morning, just like my kids.

Eight-year-old Christine was taking her six-year-old sister Megan by the hand and leading her into the school. Susie was watching them from her car.

I got out of my own car and walked up to Susie, leaning in her window. "Hi."

"Aauh!" she yelped, almost jumping out of her seat belt. Then she settled down with a nervous laugh. "You scared me." .

"Sorry, didn't mean to. How are your girls doing?"

"Okay, I guess. Megan's a little freaked out."

"She's lucky to have such a sweet big sister." I watched Christine holding open the door for Megan. Both of them had long coltlike legs and light brown ponytails. I knew Christine reasonably well; she was in the after-school chess club I'd led the previous semester. She was alert and shiny eyed, one of only two girls in the chess club, and the only child in the whole school who had ever beaten Latree at chess. She'd actually beaten him twice.

Megan, on the other hand, I didn't know much about. I gathered she wasn't as high achieving as her older sister. Whenever Susie talked about the need for programs for gifted students, she didn't bring up Megan like she did Christine.

I hoped Megan's self-esteem wouldn't suffer as she rose through the educational system. I kind of identified with her. I mean, I'm no dim bulb myself, but compared to my brilliant, Einstein-like older brother, I was always in shadow. It wasn't until I hit my thirties that I began to realize how bright I actually was.

Susie brought me back to the present. She looked up at me and said eagerly, "So what were you doing breaking into Meckel's office? I asked Andrea yesterday, but she wouldn't say."

"That's because I hadn't told her yet." Actually,

I'd asked Andrea to keep everyone in the dark, including our friends. *Especially* our friends.

I checked out Susie's right arm, draped over the steering wheel. It looked pretty well toned, and I knew she worked out at the gym a lot. I tried to picture that arm swinging a trophy at Meckel—and a heavy flashlight at my skull.

"Did you find anything that might help Laura?"

Susie's baby blues looked open and honest. She was a good-looking woman, not Hollywood gorgeous but clean-cut Missouri farm-girl pretty. She even had freckles on the tip of her nose. She seemed guileless, but I knew that couldn't be true—no woman is ever guileless.

Though I suppose that's true of men, too. And I could use some guile of my own right now. I wanted to sneak up sideways on Susie and interrogate her without her knowing it.

"I did find out some stuff," I said. "But I'm not sure if it'll help Laura or hurt her."

"That sounds bad. What did you find out?"

"It turns out Adam didn't meet the criteria for the gifted program."

I eyed her closely, but all I saw was confusion. "What criteria are you talking about?"

Was she just playing dumb? "Meckel called me up and told me about it," I fibbed. "I assumed he called you, too."

"No, he didn't."

"Well, he decided to base entrance into the gifted program on Terra Nova scores."

"You're kidding me."

"You really didn't know?"

She either missed my skepticism or ignored it, and gave her head a disgusted shake. "Figures Meckel would come up with something incredibly stupid like that."

"He set the cutoff at ninety-five. And he did the preliminary scoring himself, so he could get his administrative business done in plenty of time. Anyway, it turns out Adam didn't make the cutoff. The cops think that's why Laura killed Meckel."

"He deserved it. What a jerk."

"Better not say that too loud, or *you'll* be a suspect," I said jokingly.

"Yeah, well, I almost mean it. You know what our kids are going through. Every morning when I take Christine to school, she starts crying. She's so miserable here. And Meckel didn't give a shit."

Still hanging on to the joking tone, I said, "By the way, I hope you have a good alibi for the cops. What is it you told me before, you and Elena were together all morning?"

"No, she and Barry came later. I was in the library with my kids, and Adam."

So far Susie's story matched what she had told me on Tuesday. "And when did Elena get there?" I asked.

"About the same time Barry did. A little before you. I can't imagine anybody would suspect *Elena*."

"Why not?"

"Well, because she's an elementary school teacher. Elementary school teachers don't kill people."

"She's not just a teacher, she's a parent. And her kid didn't make the 95 cutoff either. Did she know about that?"

"She didn't say anything."

"Did she seem . . . flustered?"

Susie looked at me questioningly. "I wouldn't say *flustered*. We were both pretty anxious about what would happen at the meeting."

"Did you know about your kid not making the cutoff?"

Susie's questioning look turned downright hostile. Her arm came off the steering wheel. "What the hell is this, Jake?"

"Susie—"

"You think *I* did it?"

"I have to follow every lead."

"I can't believe you'd try to trick me like this—"

"Look, it's for Laura's sake."

"Get real. I didn't kill Sam Meckel. You're not helping Laura one bit, you're just acting stupid."

Then she rolled up her window and drove off. These Missouri farm girls are tough.

I wondered, how would Susie act if she killed somebody by mistake? Would she be tough enough to fake like it never happened, and several minutes later act essentially normal?

I checked my watch. Eight-fifty. I was supposed to meet my lawyer at Madeline's Espresso Bar in ten minutes.

But maybe I should try to get hold of Elena first, before Susie called and warned her against me. I entered the school and headed up the hall toward Elena's fourth-grade classroom. There were a lot of flowers and candles inside the school, too. Usually at this time of day, before the morning bell rang, the school was filled with laughing, shouting, running children. But not today. Everybody was muted. The kids walked slowly and stiffly, like they'd been taken over by pod people. The hallway monitors stood by awkwardly with their arms folded in front of them, not sure what to do with themselves when there were no rowdy kids to control.

The mood in Elena's classroom was somber, too.

Most of the kids were fidgeting silently in their chairs. Elena was up at her desk whispering softly with a chubby girl wearing a black T-shirt.

I walked over to them. "Excuse me, Elena," I said in a normal tone, and instantly felt weird because "normal" sounded way too loud today.

She waved hello. I relegated my voice to a whisper. "Could we talk for a minute? Privately?"

Elena looked around the classroom. "Sure," she said quietly. "Doesn't look like they'll be acting too wild today." She stood up. "Class, I'll be right back."

She led me down the hall to the teachers' lounge. "It's going to be quite a day," she said. "Assemblies, grief counseling . . ."

We stepped into the lounge, and she shut the door. Except for us, the place was empty. "How's the investigating going?" she asked.

"I'm doing my darnedest," I said, as I tried to think up some way to question Elena without making her mad at me.

Then I got mad at myself for even worrying about that. You never caught S. Spade feeling bad about hurting his suspects' feelings.

"I went to see Laura last night, brought her some Heavenly Hash ice cream," Elena said. "God, she needed it. She was so depressed."

I decided on my approach. "Listen, do you know a kid named Mark Robinson?"

"Sure, he was in my class last year. Why?"

"Tell me about him."

Elena sat down in one of the plastic chairs that ringed the central table. I sat, too. "Okay kid," Elena said. "Not much of a student. But he didn't cause me too much trouble, after I had him sit up front."

"What kind of trouble *did* he cause?"

"Oh, you know. Talking during class, pulling the girls' hair, making loud farts. . . ."

Sounded like the stuff I used to do as a kid. "Did he strike you as ADD or ADHD?"

Elena scratched her head. She was about thirty-five, with long black hair and the thick red lipstick that Cuban-American women often seem to favor. She'd been teaching at High Rock for two years now. I wondered, where would Elena go if she didn't get tenure? Elementary school jobs are hard to come by in upstate New York. She might have to go teach in some inner-city school in Troy, Albany, or Schenectady. Even worse, she might have to move herself and her daughter Luce down to New York City or Poughkeepsie or somewhere.

And then in two or three years, she'd have to deal with the tenure torture all over again.

"That's a tough question to answer," Elena was saying. "ADD is tricky. A lot of kids, if they're not doing well in school, and the work just feels too hard, they start to lose their confidence. And they sort of give up, you know? But which comes first? Do they do badly and then tune out, or do they tune out because they have ADD—and *then* do badly?"

"Good question. So with Mark, you felt he was tuning out?"

"Maybe a little," she said guiltily. "I did my best, tried to give him individual attention and everything. But it was hard. He wasn't one of my slowest students, just below average. Kids like Mark tend to get lost in the classroom. See, Jake, when I've got thirty-six little *muchachos* and *muchachas* in my class, it's not just the gifted kids that suffer. It's everybody."

I nodded intently, still trying to draw her out.

"But some sort of attention-deficit disorder?" Elena

shrugged. "Personally, with a lot of these kids, I think they just drug them up so they'll sit quietly in class. It's easier to throw *drogas* at problem kids than reorient your teaching so you can reach them." She leaned forward confidentially. "Mark's teacher this year—that new girl, Melanie—between you and me, she's no prize."

So Elena agreed with Mark's parents on that. "Did you ever see Mark get violent?" I asked.

She stared at me. "*Violent?* Are you thinking. . . ?"

"Maybe. He's big enough."

"God, how horrible." She shivered. "I hope it's not him."

"So did he ever act violent in your class?"

She shifted uncomfortably. "He used to tease the other kids, and put them down . . . Maybe I saw him pushing kids around at recess sometimes, but that was about it."

"I wonder if he might've gotten worse this year."

"I don't know. If he's having trouble with his teacher, or there's problems at home . . ."

Problems at home—I thought about his parents' endless losing battle against global capitalism, i.e. Kinko's.

"Why don't you talk to Irene Topor, the school psychologist?" Elena suggested. "She might know more about him, if she tested him for ADHD."

Sure, and no doubt she'd feel perfectly at ease violating confidentiality rules and telling a total stranger about a young child who was under her care.

I hoped I'd softened Elena up with questions about Mark Robinson. Now I'd try to slip in the more personal stuff.

"So on Tuesday morning, did you see Mark or any other kids besides, you know, the kids in the library?"

"No."

"I forget. When did you get to the library?"

"Maybe seven-twenty. I was in there chatting with Susie for about ten or fifteen minutes."

Hmm. My antennae went up. I had gotten the impression from Susie that Elena wasn't in the library all that long. Was Elena trying to pad her time in there, to beef up her alibi?

"What about Barry, by the way? Where was he?"

"In the library too, the whole time. Except for when he went to the bathroom for a minute." She eyed me sharply. "You don't suspect Barry, do you?"

"I suspect everybody. Even you," I joked.

The school bell rang. Elena stood up. "Saved by the bell. You won't be able to wring a confession out of me, because I have to get back to class. Or assembly, whatever."

"Hey, not to change the subject," I said casually, "but have you heard the Terra Nova results yet?"

"No, it always takes a while before we get the results back. They're scored by BOCES down in Albany."

I eyed her closely, but didn't see any jaw twitching, eye darting, or other time-honored signs of lying. BOCES—pronounced "bow sees"—was one of many state agencies that had some control over how local schools operate. "Doesn't the school itself, like Mr. Meckel or somebody, do preliminary scoring of the tests?" I asked innocently.

"Not that I know of. But I guess if he was in a hurry for the scores and didn't want to wait . . . Why?"

"I was thinking maybe Meckel planned on using the tests as a criteria. For the gifted program."

"I guess we'll never know what he planned," Elena said. Still no twitching or darting. "Let me know if there's any other way I can help."

I watched Elena take off down the hall. On the plus side, I'd made it through the interrogation without getting into a big angry scene.

On the negative side, I'd learned absolutely zilch. Maybe I'd have been more successful if I'd riled her up.

And maybe I was too darned sensitive for this whole P.I. business.

Once again I thought back to Tuesday morning, replaying every word and gesture. Had Elena's laughter been forced? Had Susie acted more hyped up than usual? Had Barry acted more British? I tried to think about everybody's time line again, but it just made me nutty.

I checked my watch. Nine-oh-two. I hurried out of the school, cajoled my Toyota into starting up, and made it to Madeline's by nine-fifteen. Malcolm was still there. "Thanks for waiting," I said.

"Perfectly alright. After all, you're paying me by the hour. So whose case do you want to talk about first—yours or Laura's."

"Let's be selfish. Talk about me."

"You want it diluted or full strength?"

"Diluted."

"Everything's groovy. You're sitting pretty. The mayor's gonna throw you a ticker-tape parade."

I sipped some java to prepare myself. "How about full strength?"

"You're in deep excrement. Scuttlebutt is, you've ticked off some heavy hitters around town in the last couple of years. Such as the mayor, the police chief, and the judge. I think you're gonna end up doing time."

My throat tightened so much the coffee barely made it through. "But—but the school door was *open*. So was Meckel's office. I didn't break in."

"But you did break out. You ran from the cops. Bad move."

"Okay, I was foolish. I panicked. But I wasn't a criminal."

"Prove it."

"I was stopping a burglary in progress. I was being a good Samaritan."

"That'll be our defense. Unfortunately it sounds like a fantasy."

"So what do you suggest?"

"I wish I knew. You want half of my cookie?"

"How much time are we talking about?"

"Maybe six months. Maybe a year."

"God." By the time I got out, Charizard would probably have forgotten all about Pokémon. I'd miss Latree's fall basketball season.

I felt like a total jerk. I'd allowed my macho law-breaking routine to seriously screw up my family.

"You find the killer yet?" Malcolm asked.

"No. I think maybe I met my match this time."

"Too bad. I'm afraid that's your get-out-of-jail-free card."

"You're saying if I find the killer . . ."

"Then it would be lousy PR to put you in jail."

"What are the cops up to with their investigation?"

"What investigation? Far as they're concerned, the case is pretty much closed. The D.A. wants to move up the trial date."

I closed my eyes. Here I was worried about missing six months. Laura might miss twenty years. Adam could be out of college by the time she got out of jail.

"You sure you don't want some cookies?"

I ate a piece. But I could barely taste it.

I had better get hold of that trophy-wielding assassin—fast.

9

After Malcolm took off, I picked up a copy of *The Daily Saratogian*. On the front page it said that Samuel Meckel's funeral service would be held on Saturday, two days from now. There would be a viewing at Burke Funeral Home.

Personally, I much prefer the Jewish way of burying people, where you lower them into the ground as soon as possible—often the very day after they've died. I mean, good grief, just get it over with. What do you *do* with yourself during all those days while you're waiting around for your loved one to get buried?

I decided to go visit Meckel's family and see what they were doing while they waited around. Maybe they'd be interested in helping me with my quest.

The Meckels, as I learned from the phone book, lived on Robin Hood Lane. This was part of a subdivision west of town called Sherwood Forest that has none of the historic charm its name would suggest. It was carved randomly out of the woods a few years ago. Sherwood Forest is sort of the antithesis of Saratoga Springs itself, with its strong sense of place and old-fashioned picturesqueness. The new downtown Kinko's and Eddie Bauer haven't destroyed that yet.

In its favor, Sherwood Forest does have modern

homes with air-conditioning, central heating, not too many termites, and lots of little kids running around. It's like a baby factory. If we lived there, our boys would never run out of neighbors to play with. Sometimes Andrea and I have fantasized about moving to a place like Sherwood Forest just for that reason.

As I drove down Robin Hood Lane, with its two rows of houses that all came out of the same cookie cutter, it occurred to me that the street resembled Sam Meckel himself—bland, conformist, and avoiding controversy at all costs. Feeling bad about having uncharitable thoughts about somebody who was newly dead, I walked up the Meckels' front walk and rang the doorbell. It chimed cheerfully. A few moments later, Ms. Meckel appeared.

Ms. Meckel—Amy to her friends—was in her mid to late forties with thin, sandy-colored hair, a slightly receding chin, and watery eyes. Wearing a shapeless black skirt and an oversized brown blouse, she looked just as dull as her husband had been.

I immediately felt another pang of guilt for my thoughts. Ms. Meckel was having a real killer of a week. No doubt at other times she shone more brightly.

Behind her in the living room, I caught a glimpse of her two teenage sons. They were watching Jerry Springer. I knew their names and ages from the *Saratogian* article—James and Paul, nineteen and sixteen. They eyed me curiously. The kid who looked older had short brown hair and was wearing black slacks and a button-down shirt. The younger boy had purple hair, and I wondered how many fights he'd had with his school principal father about that. I identified with the kid instantly. If I had to grow up in

WHITING PUBLIC LIBRARY
WHITING. IN 46394

Sherwood Forest, I'd dye my hair purple too. Heck, I'd tattoo my eyebrows, paint my toenails, anything to break out of the mold.

I'd feel a tad uncomfortable with purple hair at my dad's funeral, though. Maybe I'd dye it black for the day.

Ms. Meckel was standing in front of me. "Yes?" she asked.

I arranged my features into a sympathetic expression. "Ms. Meckel, I'm awfully sorry about your loss. My name's Jacob Burns. My sons go to High Rock."

Ms. Meckel narrowed her eyes. "What do you want?"

Not the reception I'd been hoping for. I plunged right in. "As you may know, I've solved a couple of murders here in Saratoga. I'm not convinced Laura Braithwaite killed your husband. I'm hoping you can answer a few questions. It might help me with my investigation."

Her face screwed up with distaste. "Chief Walsh warned me you'd be coming. I know all about that stunt you pulled in my husband's office, trying to destroy the evidence against your friend Laura."

"That's not what I was doing—"

But Ms. Meckel was just warming up. Apparently she was spending her time before the funeral stewing with rage. "Sam used to tell me about you. You and Laura and all these other people, always giving him a hard time."

"We didn't mean to—"

"I hope you're happy, now that he's dead."

"Please, Ms. Meckel—"

"Don't you *please* me." It was good to see this bland-seeming woman had so much passion in her. I just wished it wasn't aimed at me. "Sam is dead now. I don't have to play the principal's wife anymore, always watching what I say. You people made his life hell with your constant whining and complaining. What did you expect him to do?"

"Look, we were concerned about our kids—"

"And you think he wasn't? That's all he ever cared about—how to make things better for the kids. He'd keep me awake nights talking about it. And you all treated him like he was some kind of horrible evil creature."

Had I totally misjudged the dead man? Amy Meckel was close to tears. "I'm deeply sorry if I caused your husband pain—"

"*If* you caused him pain? He couldn't sleep at all last week, he was so upset. And now it turns out that was the last week of his life."

"What was he so upset about—the gifted program?"

"Typical. You think your kids are the only kids in the world with problems," she said disgustedly. "Last week he had to send letters to all the parents whose kids need to be held back next year. He *hated* doing that. These were the kids with *real* problems."

Interesting. "Do you happen to know the names of these kids?"

"Why don't you just break into my husband's office again? Look, you sonufabitch, Laura Braithwaite killed Sam and you know it. You just don't care."

With that she slammed the door in my face.

I walked back to my trusty Camry. I wanted those names. One of them might be Mark Robinson.

That would certainly add fuel to the Robinsons' fire.

Unfortunately, I had to call a temporary halt to my investigation. It was time for me to go to prison.

No, not as an inmate this time, as a teacher. One afternoon a week I taught dramatic writing at the

Mt. McGregor Correctional Facility in Wilton. I didn't get much money from it, but it helped satisfy the old do-gooder yearnings from my hippie days. This semester we were putting together an evening of one-act plays written and performed by the inmates.

With my mind so preoccupied, I wasn't looking forward to rehearsal that day. But as it happened, we had a major breakthrough.

One of our actors, a dark-skinned black guy in his early twenties named Omar, was playing a role where he was supposed to be cowering in terror from two Latino thugs. But for the past three weeks of rehearsals, he'd been doing a crummy job. Either he wouldn't act scared at all, or else he'd overdo it on purpose, camping it up and rolling his eyes and acting silly.

The problem was, it's extremely bad form to ever show fear in prison—especially to someone of another gang or race. You don't want to mark yourself as a punk. So Omar wasn't about to let his guard down onstage, with all his peers watching him.

But today, a couple of the other actors really got on his case. "What's the matter, you too scared to act scared?" one guy needled him.

Brooklyn, the tall, muscular inmate who had written the play, rode him especially hard. "You don't cut this cornball shit, I'm taking the role away from you. I'll play it myself, fool," he threatened.

Finally, on about the tenth run-through of the scene, Omar suddenly shocked us all. Somehow he found the courage to cut himself loose from his macho pose. When the two thugs came at him with baseball bats—actually we used Styrofoam, in keeping with security regulations—Omar let out a scream so primal it chilled me right down to the end of my pinkie toes.

I was worried that the guys would give Omar
some serious shit for acting vulnerable. But instead
they slapped him five and began calling him "Rock,
Junior"—after Charles "Rock" Dutton, the famous
ex-con actor.

When class was over, I hung out with Brooklyn
for a few minutes. He and I had a history together.
This was his third semester as my student, and I'd
developed a healthy regard for his drive and creativ-
ity. Out of all the guys I'd taught, Brooklyn was my
personal candidate for Most Likely to Succeed.

Unfortunately the parole board felt otherwise, despite the passionate letter I'd sent them before their
last hearing. Brooklyn's next shot at parole wouldn't
come for another fifteen months. It seemed insane to
me—especially considering some of the inmates I
knew who *did* get out on parole, and who were clear-
cut candidates for Most Likely to Fuck Up Big Time.

Last semester, Brooklyn had given me advice that
turned out to be very useful in solving a murder I
was working on. Hoping lightning might strike
twice, I laid out the Meckel murder for him.

He heard me out carefully. But when I was finished, he just shook his head. "Can't help you, Mr.
Burns. Don't know nothing about what you're talking about. It's another planet, man. My moms, in a
million years, she never would've had the guts to tell
my principal what to do. And he'd never give her
the time of day anyway. I mean, she's just some rich
woman's maid, what does she know?"

"Maybe a lot." Brooklyn's grammar might not be
the best, but he was a bright guy with a lot of writing
talent. He must have gotten it from somewhere.

Brooklyn wiped a spot of dirt off his prison-issued
pants. "What can I say, Mr. Burns? We didn't have
no gifted and talented program. My neighborhood,

the 'gifted and talented' motherfuckers were the guys who became the big drug dealers. That's hard work, you know, dealing. People underestimate that shit. You got your management skills, your mathematics, your ceaseless vigilance . . ."

"So what about you? Were you a big dealer?"

Brooklyn grinned. "The biggest."

Then the warning bell rang, and the guys filed back to their cells for afternoon count. It hit me that unless I got lucky, I might be doing that myself one of these days. Feeling suddenly chilled, I left the prison.

Thursday was Andrea's late day at work, so I hurried back from prison to meet my kids at the bus stop. As they came down the steps from the bus, Charizard wasn't his usual bouncy self. Latree looked pretty down, too.

"Hi, guys, how was school?" I asked them with fake good cheer as I walked them back home.

"Bad," Latree said.

"Double bad," Charizard agreed.

"What was bad about it?" I asked, expecting Latree to launch into his usual diatribe about school being a waste of time.

But I was wrong. "The other kids are such jerks," Latree complained.

"Why, what did they do?"

"They're dumbos," said Charizard.

"They all think Adam's mom killed Mr. Meckel," said Latree.

Charizard punched the air. "I'm gonna beat them all up. Use a thundershock on them, or maybe a vine whip," he said, naming two of his favorite Pokémon attacks.

"Dad?" Latree asked.

"Yes, honey?"

"Do you know who the killer was yet?"

"I'm working on it."

"What did you find out so far?"

"Yeah, Daddy, what did you find out?" Charizard said.

Should I tell them my suspicions? I had a feeling
the parenting magazines would not approve. And no
doubt they'd spread my suspicions all over the
school if I said anything. "Kids, I really don't think
I should tell you. A good private investigator always
keeps certain things private."

"But we can help you!" Charizard exclaimed.

"Like we helped you with the skateboard," Latree
said loudly, spoiling for a fight.

He did have a point. You never know when a couple of peewee Encyclopedia Browns will come in
handy. "Tomorrow," I said, not sure if I meant it or if
I was just putting them off. "I'll tell you tomorrow."

"Why not now?" Charizard demanded.

Question number thirty-three thousand and one.

I eventually distracted them with a game of basketball out in the driveway. It was a hard-fought strug-
gle, but they ended up beating me, thirty-six to two.

I have a secret, sneaky strategy for when the three
of us play basketball. I never let either of them get
by me on his own; but when they pass the ball to
each other, I act like I can't get back in time to keep
them from scoring. I figure that's a painless way to
promote sibling harmony.

After the game we went inside and had some Pokémon battles. Then Andrea came home and we did
the family dinner thing.

And then finally, with Andrea's okay, I went out
to do some more sleuthing. Andrea, Laura, and Judy
Demarest were forgoing their weekly bowling be-

cause Laura wanted to spend peaceful time alone with Adam. That left Andrea free to take care of our kids and me free to play private dick.

I decided to start with the Robinson angle. Ms. Helquist was bound to know whether or not Mark Robinson was being held back next year. So I walked the two blocks to her house and headed up the front path. Her car was in the driveway and a light was on in one of the rooms, so presumably she was at home.

Then again, I'd thought she was home the last time I came, but she either avoided me or wasn't here after all. So I took a detour off her front path, stepping carefully around some drooping purple flowers, and peeped in the window at the lit room.

The room was Ms. Helquist's study. She was sitting at her desk, with a pretty big-sized computer monitor to her left. It looked like she was cleaning her office. She had all kinds of papers piled up on her desk. As I watched, she ripped up a couple of papers into small pieces and dropped them in her trash can.

I was afraid she'd turn sideways and see me, so I withdrew from my reconnaissance position and rang the front doorbell.

She didn't answer.

I rang again, then knocked hard, then went over to look in the study again, thinking I'd knock on her window. But she wasn't in the study anymore. She must be hiding from me, somewhere in the house.

I eyed that big stack of papers on her desk. And all those papers flowing out of the garbage can. What was Ms. Helquist so eager to rip up and throw away?

Something told me breaking into her house and confronting her wouldn't be such a brilliant stratagem, given my current precarious legal status and

Little Napoleon's pronounced lack of affection for me.

But then I got an idea.

I went over to Ms. Helquist's driveway and checked out her recycling bin. It said "Hudson Garbage and Recycling" on the label. Andrea and I used Hudson, too, so I knew they picked up early in the morning on Fridays . . . meaning Ms. Helquist, like myself, would be putting out her trash cans and recycling bins tonight.

I wasn't sure if stealing somebody's trash off their front curb was legal. There was a case involving Bob Dylan's trash a decade or two ago, but I couldn't remember which way the courts decided.

But as long as the cops didn't catch me, it didn't matter if it was legal or not.

Andrea wasn't overly thrilled about the garbage-grabbing scheme, but eventually she agreed it was a risk worth taking. So several hours later, at one a.m., I kissed her good-bye and left the house. I took her minivan so I wouldn't have to walk home carrying large bags of garbage. I avoided using my Camry, because she's way too loud for secret nocturnal missions. No matter how many times we get her muffler fixed, it never seems to do any good.

Hopefully the Camry wouldn't find out I was two-timing her with our other car.

Our street was deserted. Nothing but parked cars. I turned off Elm onto Oak Street, then off Oak onto Ash, where Ms. Helquist lived . . .

But as I took that second turn, I spotted something: a car behind me, not real close, but close enough to make me wonder. I drove for a few blocks down Ash . . . and the other car stayed right behind. Who could be following me—the killer? The cops? Whoever it was, I decided to keep right on going past Ms. Helquist's garbage cans, which were out front as I'd expected. The other car matched my pace. It was average size, and dark colored.

Should I pretend I was starring in my own private action-adventure movie? Was it time to gun my engine and try to shake my tail? But I'd probably just end up driving into a tree or something. Besides, if it *was* a cop, why give him any excuses to bust me?

So I drove as calmly as I could down Ash to Beekman, then turned left. The car followed at a discreet distance. I turned right on Congress and right again on Broadway. My secret admirer followed maybe forty yards behind me. Squelching an impulse to lean out my window and shout, "Nyah, nyah, I see you," I drove at exactly the speed limit down the almost-empty main drag of town. After about half a mile I turned right into the Spa City Diner, next to the Greyhound bus station. That's the one place in Saratoga where you can get a hamburger or a slice of pie twenty-four hours a day. Most nights they don't have any knife fights or big drunken brawls, so most nights you're perfectly safe there.

I pulled in at the diner and walked right in without looking behind me. I was trying to act like any old ordinary joe who gets a sudden one a.m. craving for blueberry pie, and goes straight to the nearest diner to satisfy it. Except that first I stopped in the foyer, where I was out of sight of the Spa City parking lot, pulled a quarter out of my pants and called home.

Andrea picked up in the middle of the first ring. "Hello?" she asked breathlessly.

"Hey, babe—"

"Oh my God, where are you? Did they catch you?"

"Slow down, everything's cool. I'm at the Spa City Diner."

I heard a sigh of relief, then, "Did you get the trash?"

"Actually, no." I looked around, but there were no cops or murderers within hearing range, just a sour-faced Hungarian waitress who didn't speak English. I knew that from experience, because she doubled as a Greyhound clerk. Trying to buy a ticket from her was like getting trapped inside a bad Abbott and Costello routine.

Since I wasn't afraid of the waitress's caves-dropping ability, I laid out for Andrea what had happened. I finished up with, "So how about *you* get the garbage?"

"Me? You think it's safe?"

"Sure. I can't imagine there were two different cars watching the house. I'll just stay here and have a doughnut and keep the cop or whoever it is occupied."

"I don't know. . . ."

"Come on, you're the big Sue Grafton fan. Pretend you're Kinsey Millhone."

"We'd have to leave the kids alone in the house."

"Just for five minutes. Nothing will happen to them. Come on, this is an emergency."

There was a pause, then: "Okay, I'll do it."

"That's the spirit."

"I just hope I can get your car to start."

"All you have to do is sweet-talk her a little."

"She's a one-man woman. She only starts for you."

"Just promise her you'll still respect her in the morning if she gives you a ride."

I hung up and took a booth by the window. When the waitress came over to take my order, I simply pointed to the one lone doughnut that was underneath a Plexiglas cover on the counter. It was jelly filled, not my favorite, but this way I could avoid linguistic hassles.

I didn't see any medium-sized dark cars in the parking lot. Maybe the guy had parked down the street. Nobody came in the front door, but it could be he was eyeing me surreptitiously through one of the diner's many windows. It felt creepy to sit by a window when somebody might be spying on me, but I figured I was just doing my job—acting as decoy.

Twelve minutes later I got up and called home. No answer. *Oy.* Not only that, the machine gulped down my quarter. I hoped the phone hadn't woken up my kids. If it did, I hoped they wouldn't freak out. They'd never been left alone in the house before.

The waitress came up to my booth. I said "coffee" and she nodded. Coffee is the universal language. What I really wanted was decaf, but that would probably be way too complex for this woman. After five minutes I got up and went to the phone again, then realized I was out of quarters. I contemplated asking the waitress for change for a dollar, then decided to use my calling card instead, even though that would cost me an extra buck or two. I dialed the thirty or so digits you're required to dial, then finally the phone rang once . . . twice . . . three times, and our answering machine came on. Damn, had the cops sent out a second car to our house, and had the car followed Andrea? Was she even now being processed at the police station for felony garbage theft in the first degree? Were our children at home by themselves, crying—

The answering machine cut off suddenly. "Jacob?" Andrea said.

Phew. "So you're not in Chief Walsh's greedy clutches?"

"Nope, I got the trash bags. Just brought them in the house."

"Nice work, Kinsey. I'll be right there. What took you so long, anyway?"

"Your stupid car took ten minutes to start. I really think it's time to buy a new one."

"Did you caress the dashboard lovingly with one hand while you turned the key with the other? Try it next time," I said, and hung up. I paid for my doughnut with two dollar bills, giving the waitress the full fifty cents change for a tip. She hadn't acted quite surly enough for me to stiff her.

I didn't spot any Ted Bundys or Kaczinskis lurking in the parking lot. But as I got in my car and drove home, I noticed my faithful new friend driving along right behind me.

By now I had just about convinced myself it was a cop. Chief Walsh must have set this little trap for me, in case I got inspired to try any more late-night maneuvers—like, for instance, stealing somebody's garbage.

Just in case I was mistaken, though, and my silent accompanist was some crazed marauder, I jumped out of the minivan as soon as I parked it and walked quickly into my house, locking the door behind me. I was still trying to act like I didn't know I was being followed, but at this point I doubt I was fooling anybody.

Andrea was in the kitchen. She had a thousand crumpled pieces of paper of various types and colors on the table in front of her. "What exactly are we looking for?" she asked.

I made sure all the window shades in the kitchen were pulled down all the way and nobody could look in. "Any paper that's been torn," I suggested, remembering Ms. Helquist ripping up paper in her study before she threw it away.

Then we heard a noise in the living room. We both froze. But then, Latree ambled in. Looking a little disoriented, he sat down at the table and began reading one of Ms. Helquist's old credit card statements.

I would have been ticked off at Latree, except I knew he was still asleep. We'd been through this many times before. I sat down and pulled him onto my lap, took the paper out of his hands, and gave him a hug.

Gradually he woke up. I could see his eyes regain their focus. He yawned. "Hi, Daddy."

"Hi, Latree. I'll carry you up to bed."

Now he was fully awake. "Was I sleepwalking? What was I doing?" His somnambulism episodes always intrigued him.

"Nothing too exciting, honey," his mom said, rubbing his back. "Do you want to hit the bathroom before you go back to bed?"

"What time is it?"

"Late," Andrea said. "Come on, I'll take you upstairs." She was trying to sound loving and calm, but she had an edge of desperation in her tone, which any parent who has ever struggled to put a kid to bed would instantly recognize.

Latree wasn't buying her quasi calm for a second. He eyed the clock. "One-thirty? What are you guys doing up? What's all this paper?"

"It's nothing," I said, but Latree, ever the alert reader, saw Ms. Helquist's name on the credit card statement.

"Why's it say 'Hilda Helquist' here? Are you solving the murder?"

Andrea said, "We'll explain in the morning—"

"Can I help?"

"No," Andrea said.

"Why not?"

"Because I said so." When Andrea was pregnant, we both vowed we'd never use that sentence with our kids. But of course, like most of our parenting vows, we break this one repeatedly.

Latree was indignant, on the point of tears. "You *never* let me help. It's not fair!"

"Latree Burns, I'll give you up to three—" Andrea began—

But I cut in. "Honey, maybe we should let him." Andrea shot me an irate look, like she always does when I contradict her in front of the children. "Look, he's wide awake, he's not going to sleep soon anyway," I said defensively. "And he can help us fit the torn pieces of paper together. He's good at puzzles. Better than we are."

Andrea protested, and I had a feeling she'd be giving me heck as soon as the two of us were alone together, but I stuck to my guns. It was a good thing, too. Because half an hour later, it was Latree who gave us a big break in the case.

The three of us had managed to fit together all twelve torn pieces of a yellow invoice from Staples Office Supply in Saratoga. The invoice looked pretty innocuous, though. It was for the purchase of four computers for the High Rock Elementary School library. Each computer was priced at $999, which seemed about right.

"I don't see anything here," I said to Andrea, who was looking over my shoulder.

"Me, neither."

"What is it?" Latree asked.

"Just an invoice," I replied, in the tone grown-ups use when we're signaling kids that something is too complicated to explain to them right now. "Let's see what else we can find."

"What's an invoice?" Latree persisted.

I wouldn't be surprised if Latree asks *sixty* questions a day, not thirty. By that estimate, in the last five years Latree has asked me one hundred ten thousand questions.

Piecing together tiny crumpled pieces of paper at two in the morning had left me short on patience. "Latree—"

"Four Compaqs—High Rock School Library!" Latree read aloud. "That means four computers, right?"

"Right."

"But the library only has three computers."

I looked at Latree, then at Andrea.

"What happened to the fourth computer?" our little logician continued.

Good question. "Maybe it broke," Andrea said.

"We *never* had four computers," said Latree.

I closed my eyes. I was trying to visualize the computer I'd spotted in Ms. Helquist's study at home. It was big and chunky—just like the three computers in the school library.

It sure looked like good old Ms. Helquist had appropriated that fourth computer for herself.

Had her boss found out?

10

The next day, Friday, Andrea got one of her colleagues to cover for her early-morning class at the
community college. Then she came along to High
Rock with me and the kids. She wanted to help me
interrogate Ms. Helquist.

In my previous scrapes with homicide, Andrea had
never shown any interest in helping me interrogate
people. She was happy to leave the dirty work to
me. But I guess last night's garbage bag follies had
gotten her blood up.

And I guess she wanted to do anything she could to
get Laura off the hook. A twenty-year sentence would
definitely disrupt their weekly bowling routine.

I wasn't too excited about having Andrea along. I
was afraid she'd cramp my style. But she wouldn't
take no for an answer, so at eight-thirty that morning
we were sitting together in my Toyota outside the
school. We waited until all the bells had rung, all
the kids were safely stashed away in their various
classrooms, and Ms. Helquist was alone in her office.
Then we walked in on her.

She was sitting behind her desk, slicing open a
thick brown packet she'd gotten in the mail. The return address was from Albany, I noted; probably the
packet contained a motherload of government memos.

Ms. Helquist looked up and frowned. "May I help you?"

For answer, I held up the computer invoice, which we had taped together.

Ms. Helquist squinted at the yellow paper, then gave a start when she recognized it. "Where'd you get this?"

I started to say something, but Andrea surprised me by taking over. "Mr. Meckel found out about you keeping a computer, didn't he?"

"I can't believe this," Ms. Helquist sputtered angrily. "You went through my trash?"

Andrea ignored her and pressed on. "And what happened then? He told you he'd have to fire you?"

Ms. Helquist dropped her aggressive pose and said plaintively, "That's not how it was. Not in the slightest. Mr. Meckel knew all along. It was his idea."

"His idea for you to steal the school's computer?" said Andrea in disbelief.

"It wasn't stealing. He knew I did a lot of work for the school at home. But he knew he couldn't get it approved by the superintendent as part of the budget, so he did it this way."

"You don't really expect us to buy that, do you?" Andrea said. I was taken aback—and impressed—by how hard-nosed Andrea was acting. From now on I'd have to bring her along to *all* my interrogations.

"Look, you have no idea how tight the budget is. Mr. Meckel wanted to give me a raise, but he couldn't. Getting me my own computer was his way of doing that."

"If this whole thing was so innocent," said Andrea, "then why'd you rip up the invoice?"

Ms. Helquist looked abashed. "Because there's gonna be a new principal, and I don't know how he'll react."

I put in my two cents. "I don't suppose you have any proof Meckel was really going along with your little scam."

"What difference does it make, anyway? It's just a computer. If you feel that strongly about it, I'll bring it back to school."

"What we're wondering," said Andrea, "is if you and Mr. Meckel got in an argument about this."

Ms. Helquist looked exasperated. "I told you, Mr. Meckel—"

"And then the argument got physical."

Ms. Helquist's head snapped back like she'd been punched in the jaw. "Are you . . . ? That's insane."

"Ms. Helquist, I'm sure you didn't mean to hurt him," Andrea said. "The cops will understand that."

I piled on with: "You really should go to the cops now, before they figure it out on their own. They'll go easier on you."

Ms. Helquist's voice was shaking. "Look, I was at home that morning. I never came in."

"Can anybody back you up on that?" Andrea said.

"No, but—"

"Then we'll have to go to the cops ourselves," I said. Andrea and I were turning into a pretty good one-two punch.

"How can you do this to me? I've been a secretary at High Rock for twenty years. I've given my heart and soul to this school."

Andrea and I glanced at each other. We felt rotten about ruining this lady's life, but did we have a choice?

Then Ms. Helquist gave us one.

"There *is* one other person who knew about the computer purchase," she said hesitantly. "He can tell you I did nothing wrong."

"Who is this person?" Andrea said.

"Scott Lawrence."

The name rang a bell. "He's on the school board, right? Is that how he found out?" I asked.

"I guess, or else he found out because his son goes to High Rock. Anyway, I know he and Mr. Meckel had a conversation about the computer, because Mr. Meckel mentioned it. If you talk to Mr. Lawrence and he says I'm telling the truth about Mr. Meckel giving me the computer, then you won't have to talk to the cops, right?"

Behind me, two cute little dark-haired girls came into Ms. Helquist's office and waited for her attention. Andrea and I shared another look, wondering what our next move was.

Finally I turned to Ms. Helquist. "We'll talk to this guy Lawrence. Then we'll get back to you."

"And in the meantime," Andrea threw in, "we're going to need a list of all the students in the school who are being held back next year."

"I can't do that."

"Why not?"

"That information's confidential."

Andrea pointed at the invoice in my hand. "If you want us to keep *this* information confidential, then you better make up that list. Fax it to us. Today. Here's our fax number."

Ms. Helquist stared at Andrea, openmouthed, as she jotted the number on a piece of paper. I was staring at her too. Where did her tough-guy routine come from?

Then Andrea walked out. I followed her.

As soon as we got outside I said, "Jeez, you were fierce in there."

"You oughta see me when I catch a student plagiarizing. It's not a pretty sight."

I shuddered to think of it.

*   *   *

The Saratoga Springs School Board is a far from inspiring bunch. At the time of Meckel's death, three of the board's seven members also belonged to an organization called the City Taxpayers Union. The CTU seems to believe that our children would be much better off if we eliminated all school art and music programs, closed the school libraries for most of the day, had at least forty students in every class, and paid our teachers minimum wage, or less.

Two of the other board members were middle-aged Republican types with kids who were already in college. I wasn't clear what their agenda was. Maybe they hoped the school board would be a stepping-stone to higher elective office. But they'd never get my vote. I'd been to a couple of school board meetings, and I'd never seen them come up with any halfway interesting or creative ideas.

The remaining two members were the school board's saving grace, the kind of people who almost restore your faith in democracy. They were both mothers of young school-age children who actually seemed to care about improving the schools. I knew one of these women, a freelance graphic artist named Patty, so I called her now. She wasn't in, so I tried the other woman, whose name was in the phone book. She was standoffish at first, but after I told her I had voted for her last time and gotten all my friends to vote for her too, she opened up some. She informed me that Scott Lawrence worked for H & R Block in town.

We drove downtown and parked outside the H & R Block building, which is hands down the ugliest building on Broadway. It was built about forty or fifty years ago, during a particularly ill-conceived urban-renewal project. Next to the grand old edifices that occupy the rest of the street, the H & R Block building looks short, squat, and Styrofoamish.

All of these adjectives also applied to Scott Lawrence, who rose to greet us with a plastic smile imprinted on his face. Lawrence was one of the leading bozos of the City Taxpayers Union. You'd think that with a kid in elementary school, he'd realize the CTU's ideals were incompatible with good public education. But I guess he found some way to delude himself.

"Pleased to meet you," Lawrence said, beaming. "Sit down, sit down. Your names are . . . ?"

"I'm Jacob Burns and this is my wife, Andrea."

Lawrence lifted his eyebrows. "You're the screenwriter, aren't you? Loved your movie. Bet it complicated your financial life, though, right?" He was off and running. "I do taxes for several other writers in town, so I'm well aware of the unique issues writers face—"

"Actually, we're not here about taxes. We're here about this." I showed him the invoice from Staples.

Lawrence took it and checked it out for a couple of moments, then gave us a puzzled look. "I don't understand. This is an invoice of some sort."

Andrea said, "We're trying to confirm something Hilda Helquist told us. She says you were aware of a certain computer purchase the school made."

Lawrence threw out a little laugh. "As a member of the school board I do try to keep close tabs on where the taxpayers' money goes. I consider that an important responsibility. But I don't keep track of every single equipment purchase. That would be a little extreme, even for me." He examined the invoice more closely. "Where did you get this, anyway? And why is it all torn up?"

"It's a long story."

"I see." He handed the invoice back. "Well, sorry I can't help you."

Andrea and I got up. "Thank you for your time," Andrea said.

Lawrence put on his big fake smile again and shook our hands. "Any time. And if you ever need help with your C form, let me know. Do you take a home office deduction?"

"We'll talk later," I said, and eased on out of the room.

On the sidewalk, Andrea asked me, "So who's lying—him or Helquist?"

"I'll say him, because I dislike him more. Though I can't imagine why he'd *want* to lie."

"Or how he would've found out. He's right—the school board members can't get involved in every little purchase."

"So any ideas where we go now?"

"You tell me, you're the sleuth."

"Hey, you've been looking pretty smooth yourself," I said.

Andrea kissed me. "I enjoyed sleuthing with you."

"The family that sleuths together stays together."

She checked her watch. "Unfortunately, I'm late for my office hours. So you better just drive me back home, and I'll get my car."

On the way home we threw out ideas, but none of them seemed any good. "Okay, Jake," Andrea told me as we were saying good-bye, "I expect you to solve the crime before I get back."

"No sweat."

After Andrea drove off, I went in the house and checked for phone messages. There were none, but there was a fax. From Ms. Helquist.

I picked it up. This was the list of High Rock kids

who had been held back. There were nine names on
it. I scanned them quickly. Mark Robinson's name
wasn't among them.

I scanned the list again, slower this time. When I
came to the third name from the bottom, my eyes
stopped cold.

Megan Powell. Susie's younger daughter.

Sam Meckel had decided that Megan would have
to repeat first grade.

I wondered how Susie Powell felt about that.

Probably not too good.

I wish Andrea was still with me, I thought as I
drove up to Susie's house. I wouldn't have minded
sticking her with this job. My last little chat with
Susie had been none too pleasant.

She lived in a development west of town that was
similar to Sherwood Forest. The houses were a little
bigger and the roads a little windier. Susie's corporate husband must be making high five figures by
now, maybe even low six. I rang the front doorbell. It
chimed cheerfully. But Susie didn't look too cheerful
when she opened the door and saw me.

"Now what?" she said.

"Susie, I don't know how to say this. . . ."

"Just say it."

I tried the light touch. "Well, I just found out about
another little murder motive you had."

As soon as the words left my mouth, I realized
they didn't sound nearly as light as I'd intended.
In fact, they sounded about as light as an Al Gore
campaign speech.

Susie knew exactly what I was getting at. "You
heard about Megan getting held back."

"Yes."

We both stood there in the doorway. She didn't

invite me in; I guess she wasn't feeling too warmly toward me. Not that I really wanted to go in, anyway. Accusing people of murder always makes me feel socially awkward.

"Look, I met with Meckel last week, after I got his letter. We worked it out."

"How'd you do that?"

"He was amazingly reasonable. We agreed Megan would get special tutoring this summer, and then she could go to second grade next year."

"Was anybody else aware of this arrangement?"

Susie flushed. "Just me and Meckel, as far as I know."

Well, well, well. So now both Susie and Ms. Helquist had told me stories that couldn't be confirmed or denied, since Meckel was dead. If Susie's story were true, that would have decreased her desire to kill the man. But should I believe her? The woman had depths inside her that I had never suspected. "I don't understand. Why didn't you tell me or Elena or Barry or *somebody* what was going on with Megan?"

"Because we're always talking about our gifted kids. I didn't really feel like sharing about my low-achieving kid."

"That's a little weird, Susie. I mean, we're friends."

"I can't help it. It would've felt disloyal to Megan." Susie's voice was pained. "I keep hoping her problems are just temporary, and she'll have an intellectual growth spurt or something. Just get into reading all of a sudden, like some kids do."

"How long have you been concerned about her?" My question arose partly out of friendship, but mostly out of fishing around to see how distraught she'd been. Distraught enough to bop somebody with a spelling bee trophy?

"I've known something was wrong since last September. I kept telling her teacher, Ms. Merritt. But she kept saying no, everything's fine, Megan'll catch up."

A school year's worth of pent-up frustrations were boiling over now. "But I saw what all the other kids in class were doing. They were reading actual *books* and all Megan could really do was recognize letters. So I told Meckel I wanted to get an assessment. They're required by state law to do it, you know. So he promised he'd have her assessed.

"But then the reading teacher went on maternity leave. And it took them more than a month to find a new one, and she was only here two days a week, and she was swamped. And things kept getting put off and put off. . . . Until finally I get that goddamn letter from Meckel. Saying the same thing I'd been saying all year, that Megan needed special help. Except I couldn't get anyone to *listen* to me."

"That sounds like a horrible experience," I said. "But at least now she's getting help. I'm sure she'll be alright."

"Yeah. No thanks to Meckel or Merritt or any of the rest of them."

I looked at Susie, with her freckled nose, clean white T-shirt, and trendy running shorts.

She didn't look like a killer.

That and sixty cents will get you a chocolate bar.

I drove the old Camry back down Broadway. I really wanted to return to Ms. Helquist's office. That way I could confront her with Scott Lawrence's denial that he knew anything about the computers.

I also wanted to ask Ms. Helquist about this supposed agreement between Susie and Meckel. Susie thought no one but Meckel knew about it, but I was hoping that Ms. Helquist knew. Secretaries know everything.

Unfortunately, I wouldn't be able to mine Ms. Helquist for knowledge just yet. Much as my Camry groaned in protest, I had to go back to prison for another rehearsal. Opening night for the inmatewritten one-acts was next week, so we had an extra rehearsal today.

As soon as I walked into class, I knew something was wrong. Brooklyn was cussing and gesticulating and acting generally frenzied. I walked over and put a hand on his shoulder. "What's up, Brooklyn?"

"I'll tell you what's up. Omar can't act in my play anymore. The motherfuckers in administration transferred him to Greene."

"You're kidding." Greene was another mediumsecurity prison, down below Albany.

"No, I ain't. Sonufabitch left this morning. And he was just getting good, too."

I shared Brooklyn's frustration. This business of students getting transferred out in midsemester had been happening way too frequently in the past year or two. I'd start a semester with twenty students, and wind up with eight or nine by the end.

All the statistics show that giving prisoners an education is the single best way to keep them from going back to a life of crime after they get out. But the powers that be didn't seem to care about that. They treated these guys' education like it didn't matter.

"I guess we better go to Plan B, Brooklyn. You got the part."

"Yeah, I know," he grumbled. "I was hoping to sit in the audience and just *watch* my play."

Once we made it through that crisis, and a couple of more minor ones, we had a decent rehearsal. Brooklyn was terrific, like I knew he'd be. We had a semi-retarded guy in one part who kept forgetting his cues, but the other guys covered for him so well that his screwups were unnoticeable. The semi-retarded guy's mom was coming up from the Bronx next week to see the show, and his fellow inmates were already focused on making sure he looked good in front of her. It was sweet to see.

After rehearsal, I did my usual routine of hurrying out of there so I'd be in time to pick up my kids at the bus stop. Working in jail always makes me treasure my kids even more.

The kids and I went out to the driveway to play a little b-ball. I did better this time, only losing thirty-two to eight.

Andrea came home during the game, and I was planning to head over to Ms. Helquist's house as soon as the game was over. But when I went inside to wash up, there turned out to be a message on my machine from the woman herself. "Mr. Burns," her voice said, "this is Hilda Helquist. I need to talk to you about something. I'll be at my bridge club until nine. Could you come over after that? Thanks." *Beep.*

Was Ms. Helquist going to confess to the murder? Dubious at best. Maybe she had come up with some kind of evidence against somebody else. I called her at home, but there was nobody there.

I checked my watch. Nine o'clock was three and a half hours away. How would I while away the time? Maybe I should cook supper. God knows Andrea wouldn't mind if I took care of that for once—

But my cooking plans were interrupted by the next phone message. "Jacob, this is Gretchen," the voice said. "Just calling to remind you we're announcing the poetry prizes tomorrow. So you need to call me first thing in the morning with the winners. Okay? I really appreciate it."

Oh phooey, I'd forgotten all about that darn poetry. I erased all my phone messages, but that didn't

erase my responsibilities. Maybe I should just pick
the winners at random, like I'd threatened to. I could
be a Dadaist judge.

But my conscience wouldn't allow me to do that.
So while Andrea gave the kids a snack I went upstairs, found the stack of poems in the drawer of my
night table where I'd stashed them a few days ago,
and began reading. The first poem was entitled
"Corn."

> Corn, I love you, you're so great.
> For a week, you were all I ate!
> Oh corn, sweet corn, I love you, I do.
> You'll be my favorite food until I'm through.

Well, nobody could ever argue this poem didn't
have a clear, well-thought-out point of view. And it
rhymed. I turned to the next poem, "Spring."

> Spring,
> Birds flying everywhere!
> Flowers and beans are growing too.
> The most beautiful season of all,
> Especially for kids named Paul.

You can probably guess the first name of the kid
that wrote this poem. I smiled and picked up another one.

> Bad men walk the earth.
> They're mean from their very birth.
> They yell at kids and they steal their stuff.
> It's time to say we've had enough,
> And if we have to, we'll get tough.

Hmm, kind of a change of pace. Not the most
rhythmic piece of writing, but it had a nice shit-

kicking quality to it. This kid could grow up to be the next Abbie Hoffman, or Che Guevara. I checked the signature at the bottom. Then I did a double take.

This ode was penned by none other than Mark Robinson.

"They yell at kids and they steal their stuff. . . ." That must mean Mark's skateboard.

"It's time to say we've had enough,/And if we have to, we'll get tough. . . ." Interesting.

Maybe Ms. Helquist would have some insight into the whole skateboard incident, in addition to whatever else she was planning to tell me. At nine twenty-five, as soon as we put the kids to bed, I took off for her house. I was afraid the cops—or whoever—might be doing surveillance on me again, so I slipped out the back door and cut across some backyards. Then I doubled backward and around to see if anybody was following me. Nobody was. Feeling pretty slick, I went up to Ms. Helquist's house and knocked on her door.

No answer. I knocked again, but still no go. Was Ms. Helquist staying late at her bridge club? But it looked like there were a couple of lights on at the back of the house. Maybe she'd had second thoughts about inviting me over, and was hiding from me again. I turned the doorknob, thinking that if it was unlocked I'd step into the hallway and call out Ms. Helquist's name.

The knob turned, alright, and I went into the hallway. But before I could call out her name, I tripped over something. Something large and solid. I fell headlong to the floor.

Right next to Ms. Helquist's prone body.

It was a little hard to make out in the dim hallway, but I was pretty sure that's what it was. I let out a strangled scream. Then I jumped up . . . and slipped on something wet, and tripped over Ms. Helquist's left foot. I went down again.

I crawled far enough away from Ms. Helquist's body that I felt safe, then got up again. This time I was able to stay up.

I looked down at the body. I wasn't certain it was Ms. Helquist, or that she was really dead. Carefully avoiding bumping into the body, I eased my way along the wall back to the front door. I closed the door, felt around for a light switch, and finally found one. I turned it on.

It was Ms. Helquist. And she was dead, no question about that. There was a big red hole in her chest, and a gun nearby on the floor.

And that wetness I'd stepped in was Ms. Helquist's fresh blood.

I was about to give in to the horror of it all and begin puking or fainting or something when I heard a police siren blaring. It was coming closer. Had some neighbor called about the gunshot? Oh, God. Just what I needed—a murder rap. Terror took over from horror, and I ran for the back door. Then I remembered something—the blood I'd slipped on. I went back to the front hall. Sure enough, my shoe prints were in the fresh blood.

No doubt I was one of the usual suspects that Chief Walsh would look at first for this murder. When he matched those prints to my shoes, he'd be in hog heaven.

I ripped off my old orange polo shirt. I swirled it around in the blood, just enough to obscure my shoe print. As I did this, I silently asked Ms. Helquist for forgiveness. Then I dashed once again to the rear door.

When I got there, another thought struck me. I looked down at the floor. It was just as I had feared: my bloody shoes were still making prints.

That cop car must be parked by now. The cops were probably hurrying up the front walk.

I kicked off my shoes, then raced back toward the body, swabbing shoe prints as I went. Then I swabbed quickly at the light switch, where I'd maybe left fingerprints. It was possible I was swabbing the murderer's fingerprints too, but I couldn't help that.

There was a knock on the front door. I ran to the back door, reaching down to grab my shoes. Another knock. The door was still unlocked—they'd be coming in any second. I wrapped the bloody shirt around my right hand so I wouldn't leave fingerprints, and opened the back door. Then I slipped out and closed the door behind me.

Wearing my socks and pants, I ran through Ms. Helquist's backyard. My feet were attacked by thorns from her rosebushes. I vaulted over her back fence.

Then I made my circuitous way home, once again availing myself of the West Side backyards. I didn't want anybody seeing me running down the street carrying my bloody shirt and shoes. That's the kind of thing that can get misunderstood.

When I came in the side door to our house, Andrea was at the sink doing dinner dishes. She dropped her sponge when she saw me.

"*Jacob,*" she said. She was so alarmed she looked comical, but I didn't laugh.

I spoke rapidly. "Andrea, here's the deal. A, I didn't kill anyone. B, I want you to take this shirt and these shoes, put them in a bag, and get rid of them."

"Now?"

"That would be good."

"What about the cops? If I try to drive out of here, don't they have us under surveillance?"

"Don't worry, I'm sure they're all over at Ms. Helquist's house."

"Why would they be at Helquist's house?"

"She's dead. Please, go."

Andrea gave me a look. I thought she was going to ask for more explanations, but all she said was, "Better give me your pants, too."

I looked down. The knees were all red. I must have crawled through blood. "Good point."

I washed my hands quickly to get a few remaining spots of blood off them, then removed my wallet and key and gave Andrea the pants. She put all the stuff in a big black garbage bag and took off.

I went to the side door, where I had entered the house, and found a little blood there. I rubbed it off with some toilet paper, then flushed that down the toilet.

I went upstairs and took a shower. Despite the hot water, I began shuddering uncontrollably at the memory of Ms. Helquist's body. Finally the tremors subsided, and I got out of the shower. I sat down and picked the thorns out of my feet.

By the time the police arrived, I was decked out in blue-and-white-striped pajamas and looked fresh as a daisy.

11

"To what do I owe the honor?" I asked Foxwell and Balducci, who were standing on my doorstep.

"You mind if we come in?" said Foxwell.

"Yes." I quickly stepped outside and closed the door.

Balducci eyed my wet hair. "You just get out of the shower?"

"You came here to inquire about my bathing habits?"

"You always take a shower at night?"

I nodded. "You should try it. It's a wonderful way to get rid of that workday stress."

"Where were you tonight?" Foxwell asked.

"I thought we already established I was in the shower. Come on, guys, what's this all about?"

"You were seen leaving your house about forty-five minutes ago," Balducci said. "Where did you go?"

Oy. Had I really been seen sneaking out my back door? If that was true, I was in major trouble.

But I gambled that Balducci was talking through his hat. With barely a split second's hesitation, I responded, "I haven't been out of the house all night. What, did somebody break into the school again?"

Foxwell and Balducci exchanged a quick look. I realized with relief that they were uncertain whether or not to believe me. Then Balducci stepped toward me and put his face about six inches from mine. His acne scars danced before my eyes as he growled, "Look here, Burns—"

But just at that moment the door behind me opened. Latree and Charizard stood there in the doorway gazing up worriedly at me and the cops.

My little protectors threw Balducci off his game. He stopped in midgrowl and glared at the kids, then at me. Finally he said, "You better watch yourself," and strode off down the path to the cop car. Foxwell went with him.

"Is everything okay, Dad?" Latree asked.

"Sure," I said. And as long as the cops didn't find my fingerprints on Ms. Helquist's front doorknob, or her bloody floor, or anywhere else in her house, then maybe things would continue to be okay. "Let's go back inside."

"How come the cops hate you so much, Daddy?" Charizard asked.

"They don't hate me, Charizard, they just . . ."

". . . hate you," Latree said.

"I think they're jealous, because they know you're gonna find the murderer and they won't," said Charizard.

If only I were as all-powerful as Charizard thought.

And if only I'd gone to Ms. Helquist's house right at nine o'clock instead of nine twenty-five. Maybe I could have prevented her murder.

Who did the evil deed, anyhow? Maybe the murderer found out Ms. Helquist knew something, and she was planning to tell me about it. So the murderer decided she had to be silenced before she spilled the beans.

But what information did Ms. Helquist have?

I kept coming back to one thing: her claim that Lawrence knew about her computer, and Lawrence's denial. I had gone to see him that morning; Ms. Helquist left me a message that afternoon; and she was killed that night. Was there a connection?

I sure hoped so. If Scott Lawrence turned out to be involved in the murders, I wouldn't be too broken up.

Whoever killed Ms. Helquist, one thing seemed certain: her killer wasn't somebody who just grabbed a convenient object and commited murder by accident. I was up against a cold-blooded killer.

Fun, fun, fun.

Shortly after the cops left, Andrea came back. She had dumped the bloody clothes in a Dumpster behind Price Chopper.

I was in the middle of telling her all about my adventures at Ms. Helquist's when we got a frantic call from Laura. The police had arrived at her house, and they were taking her in to the police station for questioning about the new murder.

So Andrea left the house again, this time to take care of Adam while Laura went off with the cops. I called Malcolm and woke him up, and he went off to the police station to head the cops off at the pass.

As for myself, I went to bed. I never expected to get to sleep, but I surprised myself.

I was beat.

The next morning Laura made it back home, thanks to Malcolm's intervention and the cops' lack of evidence. Andrea made it back to our house in time for a quick change of clothes before she headed off to teach. Meanwhile I dropped the kids at school and then took off to see Patty Nichols, my friend who was a colleague of Lawrence's on the school board. Patty kept office space at a place on Broadway called the Creative Bloc. The Bloc was a second-story four-room office shared by eight or nine local artists and writers. Combined rent was only $800 per month, so the Blocheads were able to get by pretty cheaply.

When I entered the Bloc, I was greeted warmly by Joe, a nationally known cartoonist, and Bonnie, a choreographer/writer/amateur boxer whom I once stabbed in the arm with a pitchfork—for good reason, I might add. But that little episode was forgotten now. Bonnie gave me a big hug that almost crushed three vertebrae. She'd been off the steroids for over a year, but she still didn't know her own strength. Joe gave me a handshake, which I vastly preferred. I find social hugging and kissing too complicated—how tight do you hug, do you just kiss the air, if not, which cheek do you kiss, etc.

Joe and Bonnie sprayed me with questions about Meckel and Ms. Helquist. Word of the secretary's murder had spread through town, and Joe and Bonnie seemed to think I'd know something about it. I did, of course, but I was in no mood to let on.

Eventually they gave up on pumping me for homicide info. "So, Jake, what are you doing in this neck of the woods?" Joe said.

"You ready to join the Bloc yet?" Bonnie asked.

"Not quite," I replied. I liked Joe and the other Blocheads, and I liked the idea of being part of this little community here. It would be nice to have a definite place to go to each morning. But since I wasn't doing any writing these days, there didn't seem to be any real point to it.

Bonnie laid an earnest hand on my arm and gave me what she no doubt thought was a gentle squeeze. It would probably leave a welt. "You really should join," she said. "Just being around all this wonderful energy will inspire you."

"I'm looking for Patty," I said in a not-too-subtle change of subject.

"She's in there," Joe said, pointing to one of the inner offices. I broke away from Bonnie and went in.

Patty looked up from her drawing. "Jake, hi, sit down. Did you hear about Hilda Helquist?"

"Actually, that's why I'm here. But first, what can you tell me about Scott Lawrence?"

She groaned. "Scott Lawrence? Why do you want to know about *him*?"

"Humor me."

"He's a picayune twerp. Our meetings have been twice as long ever since he joined the board."

"How come?"

"He's always bringing up inane side issues and obscure rules of procedure and points of order. He has a persecution complex or something. We can't even make it through the daily minutes without him raising his hand five times and complaining he was misquoted. But what's this about?"

I proceeded to tell Patty the whole story about the computer. She frowned in thought. With her prematurely gray hair and permanently worried expression, she looked like she took life far too seriously. Fortunately her art was much less dour than she was. "But why would Lawrence lie about this? And how could it have anything to do with the murder?"

"You got me. But Ms. Helquist seemed sure that Lawrence knew. So what I'm wondering is, would a school board member have access to information about computer purchases?"

"Not ordinarily."

"Does H and R Block do any work for the school, helping them fill out tax forms or whatever?"

She shook her head no. "Why do you ask?"

"Because that's where Lawrence works."

"I didn't know that. He must've switched jobs."

I got a premonition. "Where'd he used to work?"
I asked.

"Staples." My face split into a mile-wide grin.
"What's so funny?"

I stood up. "If this guy feels persecuted," I said,
"he ain't seen nothing yet."

"Good to see you again," Scott Lawrence greeted
me when I walked in. There was anxiety in his eyes,
which he tried to hide with an ingratiating smile. "So
you decided you need tax help after all?"

"How long have you been at H and R Block?" I asked.

"Long enough," he promised. His short, compact
frame was encased in a shiny brown polyester suit.
He looked like an undercooked hot dog. "I'm fully
dedicated to serving my clients' needs."

"Three months? Four months?"

"Something like that," he admitted. "But that's to
your advantage. You want a lean, hungry, aggressive
accountant who will work overtime to save you
money."

"And on January twenty-nine of this year, you
were working where?" I said.

Lawrence's face clouded over.

"You worked at Staples, didn't you? In fact, you
filled out this invoice, right?" I said, showing it to him.

He scratched his ear, perhaps hoping that would
stimulate some ideas. But I guess it didn't help, because he remained silent.

"Why didn't you tell me?"

He gave me that sickly looking ingratiating smile
again. "Because I didn't want to speak ill of a dead
man. Whatever Meckel did, it's over now."

"How did you figure out something fishy was
going on?"

He shrugged modestly. "It was easy. Hilda Helquist called up and ordered those four computers. Then I was in the library a couple weeks later for the school open house, and I noticed there were only three computers there. So I asked Meckel about it."

"And what did he say?"

"He hemmed and hawed for a while, then finally he explained his reasons for giving his secretary a home computer. Personally, I thought he was wrong, but I decided not to make an issue out of it."

"That's hard to believe," I said.

Lawrence stared at me.

"From what I hear, you'd make a federal case out of it if somebody borrowed a pencil from the school and forgot to bring it back."

"Hey, you can believe whatever you want—"

"If you exposed a school principal for misusing funds, your little taxpayers' group would turn you into an instant local hero. You'd be so famous around here your tax business would double."

"Maybe you should leave—"

"Maybe you should tell me the truth."

"I already did." He lifted his palms and attempted an innocent, pleading look. "Mr. Burns, you gotta remember, I have a fourth-grade kid in that school. I don't want to make waves, give anybody a reason to treat my kid badly."

Horse manure. This guy loved to make waves. But how could I break him? "Who's your kid's teacher?" I asked.

"Elena Aguilera."

Good—maybe Elena could give me some dirt on this guy. I stood up. "One last thing."

He gripped the edge of the table nervously. "Yeah?"

"What did Hilda Helquist have on you?"

"Nothing," he squeaked.

"Then why'd you kill her?"

Lawrence just sat there and stared at me, his eyes popping. Then I walked out of the room.

I told myself I'd asked him that last question so I could gauge his reaction. But to be totally honest, maybe I just enjoyed terrorizing the guy.

Sometimes I wonder what kind of person this sleuthing business is turning me into.

I had the tables turned on me about five minutes later when Dave Mackerel cocked his head and asked me, "So why did you kill Hilda Helquist?"

The bad news was, Dave Mackerel was a cop. The good news was, he was my friend and he was just razzing me.

We were sitting in the cozy back room of Madeline's Espresso Bar, sipping cappuccinos. I wasn't surprised to run into Dave there, because he was engaged to Madeline herself. He spent a lot of time in that back room.

Dave was the one cop in Saratoga I really liked. He was also the only black cop in the department. I think his outsider status gave him a healthy perspective and a dollop of extra sympathy for people.

In addition to introducing Dave to Madeline, I've also solved a murder for him once or twice. Unlike Chief Walsh and the others, he had actually acknowledged my help. I figured that gave me the right to ask him stuff, so I said, "What's the thinking at HQ? Strictly on the QT, of course."

"Sorry, I can't divulge that information."

"Come on, Dave, is this any way to treat the man who introduced you to your future bride?"

Dave sighed. "You always say that. How long are you going to keep using that line on me?"

"As long as it works."

"Well, I gotta tell you, the primary suspect in this new murder is Laura Braithwaite. We find anything at all tying her to Helquist, she's gonna get her bail revoked. Even it we don't find anything, Walsh is gonna try to stick her back in jail, make sure she doesn't go for victim number three."

"You guys are wasting your time with Laura," I said. "She's more likely to fly to the moon than shoot somebody in the head."

"Her alibi is nonexistent."

"So's her motive. Look, Dave, while you guys screw around and ignore other suspects and threaten to put her in jail, her kid is going through major trauma. His dad died of a drug overdose a while back. I wish you guys would think about that when you make these accusations."

"Fact is, Chief Walsh and all the rest of them would love to bust *you* for the murder. They just can't seem to think of a motive for you, either."

"How about, Meckel and Ms. Helquist and I were involved in a particularly sordid love triangle?"

"Sounds good. I'll run it by them."

"Tell me, have the cops been doing surveillance on me?" Dave hesitated, so I said, "I just want to know if some crazed killer has been on my tail."

"Don't ever tell anyone I told you," Dave said, "but yes, we've been tailing you off and on. Manpower permitting."

So I'd been right about my late-night pal who accompanied me to the Spa City Diner. I shifted gears. "They find any fingerprints on the gun, or other exciting stuff?" I wanted to ask if they'd found any shoe prints, but I refrained. My trust for Dave went only so far.

"All we have on the gun is smudges, like somebody wiped it off on their shirt or something."

"Hmm," I pondered. "I wonder if the killer also wiped prints off the trophy, after killing Meckel."

"We can't be sure the same person killed both of them."

"True. Have you traced the gun?"

"Sure did. It belonged to Helquist herself."

"You're kidding. Somehow I can't picture old Hilda as a pistol-packing mama."

"Hey, a single woman living alone. . . ."

"So what do you figure happened?" I pictured the scene in my head. "Somebody knocks on her door, and she answers it with a gun in her hand. Then whoever it is grabs the gun, shoots her, and leaves her for dead in the front hall."

Dave brought his cup down from his lips, spilling some cappuccino on the table. "How'd you know she died in the front hall?"

Whoops. "You must've told me."

"No, I didn't."

"Then I must have read it in the *Saratogian*," I said with feigned casualness.

"That little detail wasn't in the *Saratogian*. We kept it back."

"Then Foxwell or Balducci must've mentioned it last night when they were interrogating me."

Dave's nose narrowed a little, like he had just encountered an unpleasant smell. He didn't believe me for a second, and he was still trying to decide whether to press me on it when Gretchen Lang walked up. We had made a date to meet at Madeline's so I could give her the winning poems.

I excused myself from Dave's table and walked off with Gretchen. Dave watched me from underneath quizzical eyebrows.

"So was I right or was I wrong?" Gretchen was

saying as we sat down at a corner table. "Weren't the poems marvelous?"

"I got a tad weary of reading about how pretty flowers and butterflies are."

"You're just saying that. Admit it, you loved the poems."

Actually it was true, I did enjoy them. I opened up my folder full of prize-winning literature. "And the grand winner for Grade 1 is . . . drum roll, please . . . Gabe Carlson!"

I handed the poem to Gretchen. She read aloud,

> If all the snowflakes
> Were cookies and lemon cakes,
> I wouldn't care about freezing and sneezing,
> I'd lay outside
> With my mouth open wide.

"That is *fabulous*," Gretchen said happily. "Great choice. I knew I could count on you."

I gave her the rest of the winners, and she chirped with pleasure. The way she acted, you'd have thought Saratoga Springs was a veritable hotbed of young T. S. Eliots.

Then she checked her watch and got up to go. "I have to run down to the *Saratogian* and tell them who the winners are, so they can put it in tomorrow's paper."

I glanced over at Dave's table. He was still dawdling there, and I had a feeling that as soon as Gretchen left he'd come over and talk to me some more about Ms. Helquist's death. Not that Dave would be trying to bust me exactly, but he might get a little too curious.

So I said to Gretchen, "I'll walk you over there,"

and left the espresso bar with her. We headed down Broadway toward the newspaper office.

Saratoga Springs has a pleasingly old-fashioned lay-out. You can live there for years and almost never go to a shopping mall, just hang out downtown. Within a block or two of Broadway you can get anything you want—groceries, hardware, Xerox copies. . . .

As we passed Grand Avenue, where L & S Copies was located about two blocks up, I interrupted a monologue from Gretchen about the ethereal sweet-ness of children's poetry. "Some of their poems were anything *but* sweet. They were fierce," I said. "Like there was a poem from Lou Robinson's kid that I almost gave the prize to, it was so raw."

"Funny you should mention that," Gretchen said. "Lou Robinson came to see me yesterday. Wanted to withdraw his son's poem from the contest."

"Really. Did he explain why?"

"Something about the poem not being appropriate. But when I told him I already gave it to our contest judge, he said never mind and took off."

"Did you mention that the judge was me?"

"Yeah, he seemed kind of flustered by that, to tell the truth. What's going on between you two, anyway?"

I didn't feel right telling Gretchen I suspected Lou Robinson's wife—and his son, too—of murder. Or murders. So I said, "Just school politics. Listen, I have to go to the bank, I'll catch you later."

Gretchen effusively thanked me again and moved on down the street. I walked up the marble steps to the Saratoga Trust Bank, then went inside to Barry Richardson's office.

He was on the phone with his wife when I came in, so he waved me to a seat. They were discussing the groceries he would buy on his way home. My mouth watered as I listened to the guacamole ingredients.

I looked around the room, and focused on the family photos on the bookshelf. Barry's wife, Ronnie, was a bleached blond from Stony Creek, a sneeze-you-miss-it town northwest of Saratoga. They met on a bicycle trip ten or fifteen years ago, and had been together ever since. Barry had taken a job at the Saratoga bank so they could live near Ronnie's family. They had two children—Justin, the second-grader who had made the Terra Nova cut, and Wendy, a three-year-old. In the photos, they looked like a very happy family.

I wasn't all that impressed by Ronnie, to tell the truth. She talked a lot and didn't seem all that intelligent, a deadly combination. But she couldn't be *too* dumb—she did work as a nurse, at the Saratoga Hospital. And it sounded like she made a mean guacamole.

Barry said, "I love you, too," to his wife and hung up. Myself, I always feel a little funny saying "I love you" to Andrea on the phone when there are other men in the room. Seems too private somehow. Andrea teases me about it, and sometimes when we're on the phone and she knows there are other men around, she'll try to get me to say the magic words.

"Hey, Jake, what's up?" Barry said. This quintessentially American greeting sounded funny in his British accent. "You heard about Ms. Helquist?"

"Yes, I did."

"What the devil is going on here? People are getting killed right and left."

"Listen, I have a couple more questions about that shouting you heard."

"I was afraid of that," Barry said with a tired sigh.

"If I'd known somebody was about to get knocked off, I'd have listened more carefully. You gotta remember, I was making noises in the bathroom myself."

I asked my question anyway. "Do you think the shouting could have come from a boy, instead of a woman?"

Barry stared at me. "What a horrid thought. You think one of the students killed Meckel?"

"I'm considering the possibility."

"Who are you suspecting?"

"I'd rather not say."

Barry sat there and fiddled with a pencil. "I suppose it could have been a boy. I mean, to be honest with you . . . if I had to testify in court, I couldn't absolutely swear it wasn't a man."

My jaw dropped. "You're kidding." My field of potential suspects had just doubled.

"I still *think* it was a woman. But when people scream and yell, don't their voices go up a little higher? Even if they're men?"

"Yeah, they do." Especially if the man was someone like, say, Lou Robinson, whose voice was relatively high to begin with despite his burly frame.

"I'm sorry, Jake. I've been laying awake at night, replaying the sounds I heard in my mind."

"Have you remembered anything new? Any specific words?"

"Not really."

"Like 'skateboard'?"

Barry shook his head.

"Or 'ADHD'?"

Barry kept on shaking. But there seemed to be a little shiftiness in his eyes.

"No words at all?" I prodded.

He finally said, "Listen, maybe I'm imagining this . . . but I feel like I might have heard the woman, or whoever, shouting the word 'back.' "

"Back?"

"Or maybe Jack, I don't know."

Back, Jack, black, Zack . . . Reading all those rhyming poems had gotten my mind going. But I couldn't think of any Jacks or Zacks who might be involved in this. "Maybe somebody said, 'Get back!' "

"I'm telling you, Jake, I don't know. I probably shouldn't even have said anything."

" 'Back,' " I said thoughtfully. The word was tickling at my brain, but why? "Why would somebody shout that word? Get off my back. Jump back. Don't come back. Don't hold back." I stopped. "*Held back.* Somebody yelling about a kid getting held back?"

Barry gave a start. "What makes you say that?"

"Why the sudden reaction?" He looked down. "Come on, old chap, spit it out," I said.

Barry was so tense he split his pencil in two.

"You better tell me, before you break any more of those."

He put the two pencil ends down. "This probably has nothing to do with anything. But last week I came into school to teach Justin's class a little bit about investing and interest and so on." He paused. "I mean, it always amazes me how much credit card debt you Americans have. It's never too early to teach kids about these things."

I nodded impatiently. "Anyway," Barry continued, "I was in Ms. Helquist's office, signing the visitor's sheet, when Sam Meckel's door opened and Susie Powell came storming out. She slammed the door behind her. She was so upset she didn't even see me standing there, just walked right by me.

"Then after she left, Ms. Helquist and I were just kind of looking at each other awkwardly. And she said, 'It's hard to deal with, when your child gets held back.'

"So I said something like, 'What are you talking about?' And Ms. Helquist clammed up all of a sudden. But I figured it out. Susie's daughter—it had to be Megan, not Christine—was getting held back. And the only reason Helquist said anything in the first place was she figured I must already know, because Susie and I are friends. Though I sure as hell don't feel like I'm *acting* like her friend right now."

"Barry, don't feel bad about this. The truth is, I already knew about Megan."

"How do you do it without going crazy, Jake? Don't you feel like you're trying to screw your closest friends?"

I didn't want to go there. In the past I'd had to deal with my sleuthing efforts being responsible for destroying the lives of people I liked—even loved. I told myself it wasn't really my sleuthing that destroyed them, it was their own actions. But still.

I shook off these unpleasant musings and asked, "What day last week did this happen?"

"Thursday afternoon."

It sure sounded like Susie had lied about working things out with Meckel last week. On Thursday afternoon she was still hopping mad at him.

And on Tuesday morning of this week he was killed.

INT. SAM MECKEL'S OFFICE—DAY
Susie Powell screams at Meckel:

    SUSIE
    You can't do this.

MECKEL
(placating)
Look, Susie—

SUSIE
You can't hold my child back!

MECKEL
It's not the end of the world—

SUSIE
You bastard!

She grabs a trophy off Meckel's desk and swings it at his head. It connects. He grunts, gives a surprised look, and falls. . . .

A little melodramatic. But possible.

An angry mother is capable of anything.

Speaking of mothers. . . . "Where was your wife that morning, anyway? If you don't mind my asking."

Barry gave a wry grin. "Don't worry, it wasn't my wife. *Her* screaming I would recognize. Anyway, Ronnie was working the seven-a.m.-to-three-p.m. shift at the hospital. She's got a solid alibi."

Then he picked up a broken pencil piece and pointed the sharpened end at me. "But you'll probably check it anyway just to make sure, won't you?"

"I probably will," I said, standing up.

"You're a real hard-ass sonufabitch," Barry said, trying to make it sound like he was joking. But he wasn't. Not really.

Weird. In the old days, back when I was a full-time *artiste*, nobody ever would have referred to me as a hard-ass sonufabitch.

To tell the truth, it felt kind of good.

12

My illusions about being a hard-ass sonufabitch were quickly shattered, however, when I got to Mt. McGregor Correctional Facility. Walking alongside the swaggering guards past the surly inmates reminded me who the *real* hard-asses were.

We were doing a dress rehearsal for our one-act festival that day, and it was quite a ruckus. The actors forgot their lines, the techies forgot their cues, and the playwrights ran around yelling at everybody.

Dress rehearsals of new plays are always like that, of course. But in prison, as I was about to learn, the usual nuttiness can get unusually dangerous.

During the intermission, I pulled aside a promising twenty-year-old playwright and multiple murderer named Chino. I recommended to him that he cut half a page of dialogue because it was deadly dull and repetitious.

I guess I should have put it more diplomatically, because Chino took umbrage, to say the least. He got up in my face. We were off in a dark corner of the auditorium, behind some stage flats, and there were no guards around to protect me. Maybe some of the other inmates would have stood up for me—maybe not—but they weren't nearby either.

"My play is only boring to you 'cause you a stupid cracker and you don't know shit," Chino said, snarling. "You ain't making me change my motherfucking play."

I stared at him, which was difficult to avoid since his face was only a few inches away. My heart was pounding so badly, I was sure he could hear it. How should I respond? He looked like he was thinking about punching me, or worse. I thought back to all the horror stories I'd heard about homemade shanks.

But as I stood there, fearful though I was, I somehow was able to remember how *I* used to feel when one of my plays was in rehearsal and the director would suggest a major revision. My first impulse was always a fierce urge to strangle the director, then drop him in a vat of boiling oil for good measure.

Those painful memories gave me enough empathy that I could say to Chino, pretty evenly, "Nobody is going to make you change your play. I'm the director and you're the writer. That makes you the boss."

Chino stood there, stunned that I was giving in so easily. I stood there too, not backing down, to make clear I wasn't giving in out of fear.

Then I said, "But I still gotta tell you, Chino, you'd have a better motherfucking play if you cut half of a motherfucking page."

With that I walked away.

Come to think of it, maybe I did have a little hardass in me.

I stayed at the prison for an extra hour and a half. God knows the show needed every last bit of rehearsal time we could muster. Andrea was picking up the kids today, so there was no need to rush back to the bus stop.

On my way home, I decided to stop at the Y and work off my prison tension. I figured I'd spend a cheerfully mindless half hour running on one of the Y's two treadmills.

But when I hit the gym, my plan to be mindless didn't pan out. Elena Aguilera was on the other treadmill. She had it cranked up high and she was running fast and sweating freely, like she had some serious tension of her own she was getting rid of. Over against the wall, her daughter Luce was drawing brightly colored pictures of what looked like female matadors. In addition to being academically gifted, Luce was one heck of an artist.

I eased onto the second treadmill. "Howdy, fellow revolutionary," I said.

Elena began running even faster. "Don't talk to me about revolution. I have no heart for it today."

"Hey, we can't let a couple of murders stop us. The school board meeting about special programs is tomorrow. We should go."

"I can't believe they'll be doing business as usual."

"According to the paper, there'll be a tribute to Meckel and Helquist, then they'll do their regular agenda, or at least some of it."

"I don't care what they're doing. All I want is a nice quiet weekend. No *muertos*, nobody getting arrested, no school politics. . . ."

"So who decides on your tenure, now that Meckel's gone?" I asked, as casually as I could.

"You got me. Maybe the superintendent, or maybe they'll hire an interim principal."

I nodded, and ran for a few moments without saying anything. Then I tried, "Too bad Meckel was killed. I'm sure he would've given you tenure."

I glanced sideways to gauge her reaction. But she didn't give me much. All she said was, "We'll never know."

But what if Elena *did* know? Maybe Meckel had decided to reject her, and Elena found out, and she hit him with the trophy in a fit of rage.

And maybe Ms. Helquist knew what Meckel had decided, and somehow she connected that with the murder . . . so Elena ended up killing her, too.

"So do you have any idea who killed Ms. Helquist?" Elena asked.

"I was thinking maybe you," I said in a joking tone, again gazing sidelong at her.

She rolled her eyes. "You're *loco*."

I changed tacks. "I want to ask you about one of the kids in your class."

"Mark Robinson again?"

"No, this year's class. Scott Lawrence's kid."

Finally, I got all the reaction I could have wanted—and more. Elena looked over at me for a split second too long, and didn't notice her running had slowed. She banged her feet against the back of the treadmill, then tripped and fell off. *"Aiee!"* she yelled.

I managed to get off my treadmill without tripping, and Luce jumped up from her drawing. We helped Elena back up.

"Are you okay, Mommy?" Luce asked scared.

"Sure, honey, I'm fine. Just broke a couple of bones, that's all."

"You want to walk it off?" I suggested.

"I'm fine." She went back to her treadmill. "I gotta do five more minutes of running, so I can eat *chorizo* tonight with a good conscience." She began running again, and I did too. Meanwhile Luce drew a big purple sword for her matador.

"Why do you wanna know about Mike Lawrence?" Elena asked.

"I'm curious. I met his father."

"Kid is nothing like him, thank God. Sweet little

boy like Mike, I always wonder if he'll grow up to be a *mal huevo* like his dad, or will he get lucky and avoid that tragic fate."

"What do you have against his father?"

That brought her up short. For a second I thought she'd fall off the treadmill again.

"Nothing. Guy's an asshole," she said.

Then she turned off the machine. Quickest five minutes I ever saw. "*Vámonos*, Luce," she said. "Time for a shower, a nice dinner, and two days of doing nothing."

With that, Elena and Luce hurried off.

Why did Elena get so riled up about Scott Lawrence?

I was so busy puzzling over this question that within ten seconds I found myself sprawled on the floor, bemoaning a twisted ankle.

Like most red-blooded, patriotic Americans, I generally look forward to Friday afternoons. Although I'm not a nine-to-five guy myself, that time of the week still feels uniquely peaceful.

But this particular Friday afternoon was different. When I got home, Latree and Charizard had only gotten there a minute earlier, because their bus was late. Much more worrisome than the late bus was the state of Latree's right eye. It was turning black and purple, and he was crying hysterically.

"God, what happened, Latree?" I said in alarm. I'm no good in medical crises, I just freak out. Luckily Andrea was on the case. We were all in the kitchen, and she was getting ice.

"I got punched," Latree squalled through his tears.

"Who punched you?"

"Mark Robinson."

I was so intrigued by this news I almost forgot to

be upset. Andrea brought over some ice cubes wrapped in a kitchen towel. "Here, honey, put this on your face."

"Ow, that's cold!" Latree yelped.

"It'll make you feel better," Andrea said.

"It's too cold. Do I have to?"

Latree seems to have inherited my extreme distaste for physical pain.

While Andrea and Latree got the ice situation straightened out, Charizard said, "I *hate* Mark Robinson. I'm gonna go right up to him and kick him where it hurts."

"You better not," Latree warned. "He's big."

"I'll kick him and then run away real fast."

"Where did this happen?" Andrea asked.

"On the bus. He was on it today because he was going to a friend's house."

"Did you tell the bus driver he hit you?" I said.

"No, the bus driver was busy."

Andrea put her hands on Latree's shoulders. "If something like this ever happens again, I want you to tell him anyway. I don't care how busy he is."

"Why did he hit you?" Charizard asked, beating me to the punch.

"Because he's a jerk."

"Why else?" I pressed.

Latree's banged-up eye was covered with the towel. The other eye looked at me anxiously. "You promise you won't get mad at me?"

"Of course."

"Because I know you don't like it when I do too much murder investigating."

"Is that what you were doing on the bus?"

"You promised you wouldn't get mad," Latree said.

"I'm not mad, just tell me already!"

"Okay, okay. I was asking him questions, that's all. Like, how'd he get his skateboard back from Mr. Meckel, did he steal it? And when did he get to school on Tuesday, stuff like that."

"And what did he say?"

"Nothing. He basically just punched me."

"We should call the bus garage and tell them," Andrea said.

Charizard stuck with his Plan A. "We should kick him in the you-know-where."

"We could tell the principal about it, except he's dead," Latree said.

I had my own plan. "I'm going over to the Robinsons' house."

"Why?" Andrea asked, frowning.

"I think Lou should know what his son did. Don't you?"

"Don't get in any fights with him. For all we know, he's the killer."

"Yeah, Daddy, don't let him murder you," Charizard said.

"Dad, just forget it. It's not that big a deal," Latree said. "My eye doesn't even hurt anymore."

"Guys, you don't have to worry about me," I said as I grabbed my jacket and headed for the door. "Nothing's gonna happen."

"We'll come with you, Daddy," Charizard said. "I'll kick him in the you-know-where."

The kid was obsessed.

I had to admit, though, Charizard's version of justice did have its appeal. If only all of life's problems could be solved by kicking the bad guys in the balls.

I eventually shook off my wife and kids and headed for the Robinsons' house. In retrospect, it might have been a good idea to accept Charizard's offer of help. Lou Robinson wasn't just big, he was fast. Too fast.

I rang his doorbell, and he answered it. "Lou," I began—

Before I even saw what was coming, he shoved me in the chest—hard. I fell off the steps onto the ground, retwisting the same ankle I had twisted in the gym.

Lou came down the steps and stood over me, all two hundred pounds of him. "You bastard, stop trying to frame my son!"

"Ease up, Lou," I said from the ground. "I'm not trying to frame anybody."

"Now you got your kid doing it too. Giving my son the third degree. You have no right to do that!"

I rolled away and stood up carefully. Lou better not come after me again, because with my ankle like this I was in no shape to run. "Lou, your kid punched my son. Gave him a black eye."

"Serves him right."

"Jesus, Lou, what are you so scared of? Do you think your kid killed Meckel? Is that why you didn't want anybody reading his poem?"

"I'm gonna kill you," Lou said, and came after me.

Busted ankle or no, I hauled ass. Luckily he didn't follow me into my Camry. And luckily she started with a minimum of fuss.

I guess she knew I was desperate.

But once the car and I got rolling, we didn't go very far. We drove into the school parking lot right across the street.

It wasn't five o'clock yet. The school psychologist was at High Rock two days a week; if today was one of those days, maybe she'd still be here. And maybe I could get her to talk about Mark Robinson.

I knocked on her door. When I heard a "Come in," I entered.

I had encountered Irene Topor twice before, when my kids were being evaluated to see if they were ready to enter kindergarten. She was a crisp woman in a power suit, with a sharp pointy nose that looked like it was better suited to some obscure species of deepwater fish.

"What can I do for you?" she said briskly, moving away from her computer keyboard. She didn't exactly have a calming, nurturing manner, and it was hard to picture her helping troubled kids.

But maybe that didn't matter. Despite her job title, giving therapy to kids didn't seem to be a major part of her job description. She spent most of her time giving tests, scoring tests, writing memos on tests, and referring kids to places where they could take still more tests. Terra Nova tests, CAT tests, reading tests, psychological tests. . . . Sometimes it seemed like our school was more about testing than teaching.

"Ms. Topor, I'm Jacob Burns. My sons Latree and Charizard go to school here."

"Latree and Charizard?"

"Excuse me. I mean Nathan and Daniel. I'm here because I'm fearful for their safety."

Her eyes narrowed. "Their safety?"

I nodded solemnly.

"Why?"

"Do you know a boy named Mark Robinson?"

Irene pursed her lips. "Yes."

"Mark beat up Nathan on the bus today. Gave him a black eye."

"I'm very sorry to hear it. That kind of thing happens more often than we'd like. I would talk to the principal about it."

And not to me, she was saying.

"We don't have a principal now," I pointed out.

"I'm sure we'll have a temporary one by Monday or Tuesday."

"I'm worried about my own safety, too," I said. "Mark's father just finished beating *me* up."

"How did this happen?"

"I went over to his house to talk to him, and—"

"That wasn't a good idea. You shouldn't physically confront the other parent."

How could I get through to this woman? I tried to come up with some tricky angle, but my brain drew a blank. In the absence of any good lies, I tried the truth.

"Look, Ms. Topor, let me put my cards on the table. I suspect Mark and Lou Robinson—and Sylvia, too—of killing Sam Meckel and Hilda Helquist."

She looked at me like I had just barfed on her desk. "What, you think the three of them marched into Sam Meckel's office and—"

"I think *one* of them did, I'm not sure which. I need you to tell me what's going on with these people. What are we dealing with here?"

"Why would any of the Robinsons want to kill Mr. Meckel?"

"As you know, there was a great deal of outrage about the ADHD diagnosis."

Irene looked down. She picked up a pen and began doodling. I do that too sometimes, when I need to relax. "This seems rather far-fetched."

"Maybe you don't realize how much the diagnosis upset them. They felt you were all a bunch of drug dealers who were doing tremendous damage to their child."

She kept doodling. "Have you gone to the police with these suspicions of yours?"

"I need more before I go to them. That's why I'm here."

"My contacts with Mark, and the tests I did on him, they're all confidential."

"You had extensive contact with the parents, too. That's *not* confidential."

"I'm not so sure. Listen, I'm beginning to feel very uncomfortable with this whole conversation."

"And if Mark or Sylvia or Lou goes out and kills a *third* person, how comfy will you feel then?"

"Mr. Burns, I'm going to ask you to leave."

Whoa. "Why are you so uptight? This is about more than just confidentiality, isn't it?"

"Maybe you don't appreciate how important confidentiality is—"

"Are you scared of a scandal? If people believe your diagnosis led to murder?"

"Mr. Burns—"

"Just tell me what I need to know, and I'll try to keep you out of it."

She reached for the phone. "If you don't leave right now—"

"Never mind. I'm going."

I stood up, readying a snappy exit line. But then I sat down again. I had just noticed what Irene was doodling.

A skateboard.

"Why'd you draw that?" I asked, pointing at it.

She brought the piece of paper toward her, trying to hide it from me. "No reason."

"That's Mark's skateboard you just drew. Why's it on your mind?"

"Look—"

"He stole it back from Meckel, didn't he? And Meckel told you that."

The phone rang. Irene hesitated, then answered it and started talking to somebody about some memo or other. Maybe she figured the pause in our conversation would give her time to figure out how to deal with me.

But the pause also gave me time to look around. On the far corner of her desk, I saw a weekly appointment calendar. I looked closer. What was that word underlined in blue, on the section of the calendar devoted to this past Tuesday?

I reached out and grabbed the calendar. Irene put out her hand that wasn't attached to the telephone and tried to grab the calendar back. We had a brief tug of war, but I won.

I examined the calendar. Sure enough, the underlined word was "Robinsons." And next to it was the word "Meckel" and a time: "4:00."

Irene had scheduled an appointment with Sam Meckel and the Robinsons for Tuesday afternoon at 4:00.

She hung up the phone. "Give that back."

"No problem," I said. I handed the calendar back. "But why were you and Meckel meeting with the Robinsons on Tuesday?"

"If you don't leave right now—"

"Let me guess. You and Meckel were gonna lay down the law to Mark's parents. You were gonna tell them the skateboard theft was further proof of his problems."

"Mr. Burns, you leave me no choice. I'm calling 911," she said, and true to her word, she began dialing.

"That won't be necessary, Ms. Topor," I said getting up to go. "I've got everything I need."

Maybe I didn't quite have *everything*. But still, it wasn't a bad way to start the weekend.

13

On Friday evenings it's a Jewish tradition to say a prayer over a cup of wine. Translated into English, it goes, "Blessed art Thou, Lord our God, King of the Universe, Who created the fruit of the vine."

Andrea and I aren't big wine drinkers, though, so we pray over a glass of grape juice. Meanwhile, Charizard prefers apple juice and Latree goes for milk. So we've invented our own family prayer, which goes: "Blessed art Thou, Lord our God, King of the Universe, Who created the fruit of the vine, the tree and the cow."

That Friday evening, Laura and Adam Braithwaite were breaking *challah* with us. Laura had iced tea and Adam just wanted water. So our prayer that night blessed "the fruit of the vine, the tree, the cow, the bush, and the water faucet."

It was a cheerfully goofy way to begin the Shabbat meal, and we were almost able to forget all the recent death and destruction. Laura and Andrea discussed the finer points of bowling and the future of the women's pro tour. Latree, Adam, and Charizard tried to decide which Pokémon would be the best basketball players, and what positions they would play. Charizard stoutly maintained that Pikachu, even if a little on the short side, would be every bit as good as Michael Jordan.

I chowed down on Andrea's delicious eggplant parmigiana and drifted lazily between conversations, musing over which Pokémon would make the best bowler. But our dinnertime idyll was interrupted by the doorbell ringing. I tensed up instantly. Had the cops found some way to link me to Helquist's murder?

Or maybe they had come to pick up Laura. I wondered, if she had to go to jail for an indefinite time, where would Adam live? Probably with us.

I opened the door. Unless any of the local men in blue had taken to dying his hair purple, that was no cop standing there. It was Paul, Sam Meckel's sixteen-year-old son. He shifted his feet nervously, and there was a scared-rabbit look in his eyes.

"Hi, Paul."

"I only have a minute, I'm supposed to be back home. I just wanted to tell you that—"

He stopped and looked around my shoulder. Behind me, Charizard, Latree, and Adam were all standing there staring. And behind them were Andrea and Laura.

"Guys, take off," I said.

"But we want to hear too," Charizard complained.

Andrea came to my aid. "Kids, get back in the dining room."

"Is it about the murder?" Charizard asked.

"You mean *murders*," Latree corrected him.

"That's what I said," Charizard protested.

Paul looked skittish, like he was about to bolt. "Latree and Charizard, I'll give you up to three. One . . ."

"*Dad* . . ."

"Two . . ."

"Okay, okay," they said, and ran out of there with Adam. It always amazes me that the counting-to-three ploy still works. What terrible fate do my kids imagine is in store for them if I count to three and they're still there? I wonder how old they'll have to be before they start ignoring my counting. I guess that's when I'll know their preadolescence has officially begun.

Paul was still standing there. "Do you want to come in?" I asked.

He shook his purple hair vigorously. "I have to get back home for the wake. Look, you remember the other day, when you came to my house?"

"Yes."

"And you asked my mom if she knew anything that might help you?"

I nodded.

"Well, there was something she didn't tell you."

After a pause, I said, "What was it?"

"My dad was . . . he was . . ."

I waited. Paul was fidgeting so much I wanted to reach out my arms and steady him.

"He was accused of sexual harassment."

Huh? "By who?"

Now that the cat was finally out of the bag, Paul started talking fast. "I'm not sure, but I heard my mom and dad talking on Monday night. They were in their room, but they were so upset they were talking loud, and I could hear some of it. My dad said somebody at the school was making a complaint against him. He claimed it wasn't true. But my mom was, like . . . not so sure." Paul's face reddened. "I just thought I should tell you, because . . ."

"No, you're doing the right thing. But are you positive you have no idea who it was?"

"I think a teacher. My dad said something like, she was just accusing him of harassment because he wasn't going to rehire her."

Rehire her? Most of the teachers at the school were already tenured. "Was it Elena Aguilera?"

"I don't know."

"Did your dad ever have any affairs?" Paul's face turned the color of an unripe cherry. "If you don't mind me asking."

"I don't think he did. I never really thought about it. I'm sorry, I don't know anything else. I really should go. My mom will be wondering where I was."

With that he hurried back to his Honda Accord—actually, it was probably his dad's—and got in.

I hated to ask him my next question, but I had to. Before he had a chance to drive off, I followed him down the path and tapped on his car window. He rolled it down.

"Forgive me, Paul, but . . . where was your mother on Tuesday morning?"

His eyes widened. "Getting me out of bed. Jeez."

Then he took off.

I went back into the dining room, where ten ears eagerly awaited my news. "Somebody accused Meckel of . . ."

Then I stopped. I didn't want to talk about sexual harassment in front of my kids.

"Of what, Daddy?" Charizard asked.

"Some stuff," I said.

Latree said, "I think that guy said something like 'sexual harassment.'"

The darn kid's ears are amazing. Ask him to put down his book, and he's deaf . . . but whisper something at the other end of the house that you don't want him to hear, and it comes in loud and clear.

"What's that?" Adam asked. Latree and Charizard looked puzzled, too.

"Listen, I have to go out. Ask the moms to explain

it to you." I was glad to leave that job to somebody else.

"Does 'sexual' mean, you know, that sex stuff?"
Latree asked, frowning. Andrea and I had conscien-
tiously informed our sons about the birds and the
bees, but they weren't too impressed by the whole
business. They thought it was gross.

"Who did he harass?" Laura asked.

"I'm not sure *if* he did, and *who* he did. But my
money's on Fidel Castro's compatriot." I was using
a little bit of code here, because I didn't want the
children to know Elena was a suspect.

Laura put her hand to her mouth. "My God." I
understood perfectly what was going through her
mind: *hope* that we would get her off the hook by
nailing Elena for the murder, combined with *fear* that
we would nail Elena.

I turned to my wife. "Listen, Andrea—"

"Go," she said, reading my mind. "I knew a peaceful Shabbat dinner at home was too much to hope
for."

Elena and Luce Aguilera lived in a small apartment on the third floor of an old nineteenth-century
mansion turned whorehouse turned apartment building. It was located in Franklin Square, a recently reju-
venated part of town just west of Broadway. I could
smell the garlicky Cuban cooking before I even
reached her floor.

It smelled like I'd be busting up yet another peaceful Friday-night dinner.

Elena didn't look too surprised to see me when
she answered the door. But she didn't look too
pleased, either. Behind her, Luce was eating some
kind of delicious-looking stew.

"Now what?" Elena asked. "I'm getting a little

weary of this, amigo. You ask more questions than my daughter."

"I'm getting a little weary of people I thought were my friends lying to me."

Back at the table Luce made a choking sound, like some stew had just gone down the wrong way. After checking to make sure it was nothing fatal, Elena gave me a little push, edging me out into the hallway.

She closed the door behind us. "What is your problem?" she said, waving her arms angrily.

"So you were sexually harassed by Sam Meckel?"

Her arms stopped moving, and so did the rest of her. "Where'd you hear that?"

"What happened Tuesday morning, Elena? He came on to you again? And you had to defend yourself?"

"You've got it all wrong—"

"Don't be stupid, Elena. Eventually the cops will find out about this—"

"No, they won't—"

"Sure, they will. *I* did." I piled it on as thick as I could, trying to harangue Elena into making a mistake. "Play it straight and you've got a legit self-defense case. Especially if you already filed a harassment complaint. That'll back up your story—"

"Jake—"

"How can you even look Laura in the eye, for God's sake? She's facing life in prison."

"Meckel never harassed me—"

"Bullshit."

"Bullshit, yourself. He was harassing Melanie Wilson."

That stopped me. Melanie Wilson was Mark Robinson's sexy young fifth-grade teacher.

But was Elena just trying to throw me off track? "How do you know this?" I asked.

"Melanie told me. She was bringing a complaint, and she wanted to know if anybody else had been harassed, too. I told her, not me. If Meckel tried to mess with me, I'd've kicked him right in the *cojones*."

Evidently Elena agreed with Charizard's views of justice. "Why didn't you tell me this before?"

"Why should I? Melanie asked me not to. She may not be the world's most brilliant teacher, but I don't want her to get fired just because Meckel acted like a pig and she gets caught up in some big political mess."

"Listen, Elena, if you truly want me to keep Laura out of jail—"

"I do."

"—then you have to trust me enough to tell me *everything*."

"I don't trust anybody that much. Not even my priest when I go to confession."

"Do you think Melanie might've killed Meckel?"

Elena sucked in her breath. "She certainly hated the *hijo de puta*." I didn't know what *hijo de puta* meant, but I doubted it was anything too favorable. "But then again, so did I. And believe it or not, I didn't touch him. So if you'll excuse me, I spent two hours cooking Ajiaco stew and I intend to eat it while it's hot."

Then she went back inside and shut the door in my face. But that was okay. It wasn't her I wanted to talk to now, it was Melanie Wilson.

Melanie also lived in a recently renovated apartment, though hers was on the east side of town. She rented the bottom floor of a two-story house that was decorated in the traditional Saratoga style, with purple, white, and green paint and fancy Victorian trimmings.

When Melanie answered my knock, she was decorated with some pretty fancy trimmings herself. Even in the relative darkness of the front hall, her golden earrings sparkled. She wore a shiny necklace with a ruby pendant that hung down to some serious cleavage. But she didn't have a wedding or engagement ring, I noted.

Melanie was in her midtwenties. Her dress was tight, black and strapless, and seemed to hold on to her body by sheer magic. She wore high-heeled leather sandals.

I felt a quick rush of sympathy for Sam Meckel. Now don't get me wrong. I'm a sensitive left-wing kind of guy, I've listened to Anita Hill's book about Clarence Thomas on audiotape, and I understand sexual harassment can be a devastating thing. I know sexual harassment is supposedly more about power than sex.

But having said that, I'm still glad I don't have to work at close quarters, day in and day out, with any insanely sexy women. I'd find it stressful as hell. Sometimes I wonder how people do it.

After all the domesticity I'd been part of, first at my own house and then at Elena's, it was kind of a shock to my system to find myself thrust back into the singles world. I couldn't help picturing myself dating this hot babe.

Ah yes, to be free and single again. I wouldn't be here trying to bust Melanie for murder, which is rather a lousy way to start a relationship. I'd be picking her up for dinner. Then we'd hit a romantic movie . . . coffee at some classy artists' hangout . . . and then we'd come back to her place . . . I'd find

out once and for all how that dress of hers managed
to stay up—

"Yes?" Melanie said a little petulantly, her hand
on her hip, cutting off my reverie. She looked like
she'd been expecting to find somebody else at the
door, somebody much more interesting than me.

"Ms. Wilson, my name is Jacob Burns." I was a
little unnerved by my useless attraction to her, so I
fought it by acting a little more formal than usual.
"I'm looking into the murders of Sam Meckel and
Hilda Helquist."

"Yeah, you're, like, the guy the police arrested,"
said Melanie.

"That's me, alright." I gave what I hoped would
be an infectious smile, but she wasn't infected. She
just stood there, her eyes wary. They were bright
blue and her cheekbones were high. I'd seen her at
school, and I'd noticed she was good-looking. But not
until tonight had I realized how lovely she truly was.

"I'm kind of busy. What do you want?"

"I understand Mr. Meckel was sexually harassing
you," I said.

Her mouth hung open in surprise, making her look
even less intelligent than usual. The sad truth was
that, despite her beauty, she didn't look all that
bright. I don't know what it was, maybe something
missing from her eyes. Or maybe I'm just eager to
find fault with gorgeous blonds, trying to make them
seem less perfect. They're so darned unattainable.

"Where did you hear that?" Melanie asked.

"I'd like to hear it from *you*."

"You won't. Because it, like, never happened."

"What are you afraid of?"

"Nothing. This is so totally ridiculous."

Maybe it was. Elena could have been misinformed,
or simply lying. "Look, Sam Meckel was killed. Ev-

erything about his life is going to come out. Why don't you just tell me what went on, and I'll try to help you."

"I don't have time for this tonight." With a toss of her thick yellow mane, she stepped back and started to shut the door.

Feeling a little clichéd, I stuck my foot in the way. "Then I'm going to the police."

"Just try it. I'll sue you for slander or libel or whatever they call it."

"And if you're telling the truth, you'll win. But I don't think you are."

Melanie stood there uncertainly, pouting her lips. "It's not fair," she said. "If people find out about this stupid thing, you know who's gonna get hurt. Me. Everybody will think *I* did something wrong, even though it was him."

Hurray! We were almost there. I tried not to jump up and down with excitement. "Melanie," I said, oozing sympathy, "what did he do to you?"

She gave me a scared, helpless-little-girl look. Whether it was a conscious ploy or an honest reaction, I wasn't sure. Even after ten years of marriage, women are still a mystery to me. "You promise you won't tell the police?"

"I swear I'll do my best to avoid it."

She shut her eyes for a second, like she was having a bad migraine. "Well, I guess you better come in," she said, not sounding too thrilled about the idea.

She led the way into the living room and we both sat down. She was in a pink love seat, and I occupied a white armchair opposite. I could see into the dining room, where the table had been set for two. There were long white candles, red roses, and wineglasses much more elegant than the ones my wife and I had drunk out of earlier. Some guy was going to get awfully lucky tonight.

Melanie crossed her legs at her ankles. I doubt she was trying to be provocative, but it turned me on anyway. I tried to find a part of her body that I could look at without getting horny. I focused on the little space between her eyebrows.

She rubbed that space with her fingers, then launched into her story. "Yeah, Meckel harassed me, alright," she said. "It started out, he'd just give me these weird little winks whenever I went into his office for something. Then he'd come into my room after the kids were gone, when I was grading homework or whatever. He'd be, like, 'I know this is your first job, are you happy here, are you lonely, is there anything I can do to help you out...?' At first I thought maybe he was being sweet. But then he started making all these dumb jokes. Like, how I was probably giving the fifth-grade boys their very first erections."

Melanie eyed me carefully to see how I reacted to this lascivious tidbit. I guess she wanted to know if I'd laugh at Meckel's crude humor. I tried to keep my mouth from twitching.

"So I quit staying late at school," Melanie went on. "I graded the homework at home. But he would call me into his office whenever I had a free period. To discuss some student, he'd say. Yeah, right. I didn't know what to do." She kneaded her fingers together nervously. "This is my first teaching job. If he fired me and gave me a bad recommendation, I'd have trouble getting another job. I have all these huge loans to pay off . . . I mean, I went to college for six years. I don't wanna end up in McDonald's or someplace, like my sisters."

I spoke up, to keep her monologue on track. "The situation must have gotten pretty bad, if it got you upset enough to file a complaint."

"Yeah, well, he pretty much said if I didn't screw him, he wouldn't rehire me. So that's when I filed."

"What's the process, anyway? Who did you file it with?"

She checked her watch. "Look, I'm expecting company and I haven't finished making dinner. I don't have time to go into every stupid detail."

"I'd like to be able to verify your story."

Melanie recrossed her legs, but I was glad to see it didn't turn me on this time. One less distraction. I guess all this talk about harassment had kind of taken away the erotic edge. The whole thing was much more sordid than sexy, and my sympathy for Meckel had faded.

"I never exactly filed it," Melanie said. "I just wrote something up and gave it to Meckel. I told him I'd file for real if he didn't stop."

Something wasn't quite right about this. It took me a moment, but I got it. "Wait a minute. You *threatened* Meckel that you'd file a complaint against him?"

"Well, yeah."

"If he didn't rehire you?"

Her hands played with her necklace. "No, no, it wasn't like that—"

"Sure it was. You were blackmailing him."

She stomped her foot on the rug. "Stop it. You're twisting everything around!" Then she regained control of herself and said, with a trace of a whine, "I just wanted him to stop *bothering* me, that's all. It wasn't right. Why should I have to put up with that?"

"You were pretty angry at him."

"Yeah, I was furious. You're a man, you don't know how it feels."

"Were you furious enough to hit him with a spelling bee trophy?"

Melanie shook her head back and forth several times rapidly. "That wasn't me."

Since I'd already played this scene with Elena, it wasn't hard to think up my next line. "What happened, he came on to you again? And you fought back?"

But unlike Elena, Melanie had an alibi—or claimed she did. "I wasn't even there. I was with somebody."

"Who?"

"I can't tell you."

"Then your alibi's worthless."

"I don't care. I didn't kill him, and you can't prove it!"

"Who was it, the same person who's coming over tonight?"

Melanie opened her mouth to say something, but before any words came out, the front door of the house opened. Someone called out, "Hey, sweetie!"

The voice was a surprise.

It was a woman's voice.

And when the woman came into view, that was a surprise too. It was Irene Topor, the school psychologist.

Like Melanie, she was all dolled up. She didn't have Melanie's curves, but in her tight blue jeans and embroidered peasant shirt, she actually looked pretty cute. She'd done something to her hair, and it made her nose fit her face better. Instead of looking pointy, it looked . . . what's the word . . . *aquiline*.

Moving my eyes from Irene to Melanie and back, I couldn't resist a grin. This little twist brought my

dating days back to me in a hurry. When I was in
my early twenties, I had the nasty habit of falling in
love with lesbians. I even lived with one for a couple
of years before she "left me for another woman," to
quote an old Woody Allen movie.

I didn't go for gay women on purpose, it just
seemed to sort of happen. And here it was happening
again. Hadn't I learned *anything* in the past twenty
years?

I suddenly found myself very glad to be safely
married and finished with the dating game.

Irene stared at me, then at Melanie. "What's *he*
doing here?"

I figured now wasn't the time for small talk.
"Where were you on Tuesday morning at seven-
thirty?" I asked.

Irene gave Melanie a questioning look. Melanie gave
her back a shrug, as if to say, *go ahead and tell him*.

But Irene said, "How should I know where I was?
I was probably getting out of bed. Why?"

"Were you alone?"

Melanie broke in. "She was here, with me."

Irene said, "Melanie—"

"Look, we have to tell him. He thinks I killed
Meckel."

"He thinks *what*?" Irene said, raising her eyebrows
as she turned to me. "God, what an idiot."

"I've been called worse. Were you here that
morning?"

"I thought you were after the Robinsons."

"Were you?"

Irene glowered at me, then finally said, "Yeah, I
was. So what?"

"Does anybody else know you were here?"

"No. We try to keep it secret, as you can imagine."

"Only problem is, Melanie could use another

backup for her alibi besides you. Lovers have been known to lie."

"Melanie would never *kill* anybody, come on."

I regarded the two of them. I wasn't completely sure Melanie and Irene really were together on Tuesday morning.

But I *was* sure of something else. Even if these two women had nothing to do with the killings, I still had them by the short hairs. "Tell me about the Robinson family," I said to Irene.

"I told you before, that's privileged information."

"And so's your sexual preferences. But if you don't answer all my questions, I'm gonna blow *your* privileged information right out of the water."

Hatred and fear spilled into Irene's and Melanie's eyes. I felt like a heel using their private lives against them. I mean, I don't think somebody's sexuality has anything to do with whether they're a good teacher. But hey, we were talking murder here.

"You can't do that," Melanie sputtered.

"Sure I can. Why don't you go in the other room and finish making dinner while I chat with your friend." But Melanie didn't move, and Irene looked like she would keep resisting, so I kept on bullying. "Look, this isn't exactly San Francisco. You think the school district wants a gay psychologist working with the kiddies? You think the new principal will rehire a fifth-grade teacher who's a lesbian?"

I know, I know, I was being brutal. But sometimes you catch more flies with vinegar than with honey.

Melanie stood up. "You shit," she said. Then she left for the kitchen. Hopefully she wouldn't come back with a bread knife and stab me.

Irene spent a few moments hurling more epithets at me, then finally sat down and bowed to the inevitable. It was time to talk turkey.

"You were right about the skateboard," she told me grudgingly. "Meckel found out Mark snuck into his office and stole it back. So he called a meeting with me, Mark, and his parents. We were going to meet this week, on Tuesday."

"So you could pressure them into putting Mark on Ritalin?"

"I wouldn't say that. . . ."

"What *would* you say?"

"We wanted to make them realize the seriousness of the situation. Mark is flunking half of his tests at this point, and he's getting more and more unruly. Melanie will tell you, he just sits in class and pulls the other kids' hair. Now he's escalated to stealing. His parents need to start exercising more control."

"By putting him on Ritalin."

"If that's what it takes, yes."

"Who made the call to his parents, yourself or Meckel?"

"I did."

"Who did you talk to?"

"The mother."

"How did she react?"

"Look, parents give all sorts of responses when their kids are in trouble. I don't take them too seriously. It's just heat-of-the-moment stuff."

"I take it Sylvia wasn't too pleased."

"No."

"What did she say, exactly?" Irene didn't answer. This was like pulling teeth. I stood up and stepped toward her. "Damn it, I'm sick and tired of everybody stonewalling me. Doesn't it bother you just a teensy little bit that Sylvia Robinson may have committed murder—and you're, in effect, covering up for her?"

Irene opened her mouth, and finally said, "Sylvia was pretty wacky on the phone. Screaming about conspiracies and we had it in for her son and all kinds of stuff. It scared me a little."

I nodded. "Thank you. That wasn't so hard, was it?"

"You're a prick."

"Only when I have to be. Here's what I don't get. If Mark was in such big trouble, why wasn't he being held back?"

"Honestly? Because none of the fifth-grade teachers wanted to deal with him next year. And neither did Meckel." She stood up and made like she was going to the kitchen. "If you're finished, I'd like to try and salvage what's left of my night."

I put up a hand to stop her. "One more thing. Susie Powell's kid, Megan. What did you think of Meckel's decision to hold her back?"

"Nice kid. I felt bad for her. I was glad he changed his mind."

I stared at her. "He did what?"

"He talked to Susie. They agreed Megan would get private tutors this summer and then go on to second grade."

"You sure about this?"

"Meckel told me."

But according to Barry, he heard Susie and Meckel having a screaming fight about Megan on Thursday afternoon. "When did they make this agreement?"

Irene scrunched up her face in thought. "I saw Susie in his office, let's see, last Friday."

"You sure it wasn't Thursday?"

"Actually, I saw her both days last week, Thursday *and* Friday. Those are my two days at High Rock."

So Barry's story checked out. But evidently, after

Thursday's screaming fight had come a *rapprochement* the very next day. That would seem to decrease Susie's motivation to kill the man.

What about Irene Topor's motivations? I stuck an I-feel-your-pain expression on my face. "That must have been really weird, having to work closely with Meckel when here he was, sexually harassing your girlfriend."

"It was different, that's for sure."

"Did he realize you were going out with her?"

"No." Irene nailed me with her eyes. "Now I've told you everything. You better keep your end of the bargain and shut the hell up about me and Melanie."

This woman was pretty intense. I wondered, if I threatened Irene's affair with the lovely Melanie, and her career as well, would she be angry enough to grab something and hit me with it?

Could that be what happened in Sam Meckel's office that morning? And did Hilda Helquist somehow figure it out?

14

The next morning, Saturday, Latree and Charizard went to the birthday party of Justin Richardson, Barry and Ronnie's kid. My guess is, my sons just barely made the invite list. Latree and Justin weren't all that close, even though they were the same age and I was friendly with Justin's dad. Latree found Justin bossy. Latree can be kind of bossy himself, so they weren't the best match. The main time they had play dates together was when Andrea and I—or Justin's parents—were going out on a Saturday night and couldn't get a baby-sitter. Then whichever couple wasn't going out would take care of the other couple's kids.

Given that the Richardsons did invite Latree, I was grateful they invited Charizard, too. Otherwise he'd have felt left out. I resolved to like Barry's wife Ronnie more, since I assumed she was the one who was in charge of the invitations. That's the kind of detail work women always get stuck with.

The party was being held at a laser tag place on South Broadway. If you've never played laser tag, I highly recommend you try it. The way it goes is this: you don a suit of armor and grab a large "laser machinegun." Then you fire away at your opponents with a "deadly" red light. You can kill six or seven people in a minute. It's highly therapeutic.

When we handed over our kids to Barry and Ronnie, they invited us to stick around and play laser tag, too. "It won't cost us anything, we got a package deal," Barry said, putting a hand on my shoulder.

"I'd love to, but Andrea and I are hitting the school board meeting."

"What for? So you can hear endless eulogies of the great leader Sam Meckel?"

"I guess it could get kind of tedious," I acknowledged. I turned to Andrea. "Honey, how about we play just one game? That way we'll miss the eulogies."

So we stuck around and put on our suits of armor, then attacked each other and our kids with abandon for the next forty-five minutes. It was like eating potato chips—we couldn't stop at just one game.

It's amazing and rather scary how good it feels to have a gun in your hand. For the first half minute or so we kind of joked around, pointing our guns at each other's toes and not really trying to "destroy the enemy," to use laser tag lingo. But soon all our circumspectness and pretense at civility ceased. We charged around obstacles and took deadly aim at our enemies' chests.

I blasted Latree repeatedly, paying him back for all those times he'd kept me waiting and failed to even hear me while he read a book. Latree blasted Andrea for all the times she yelled at him to hold his spoon the right way. Andrea blasted Charizard for being stubborn about going to the bathroom right before bed, even though he sometimes peed in his sleep if he didn't. And Charizard blasted me for not buying him Pokémon cards whenever he wanted them.

All in all, it was good clean family fun.

It reminded me of something I heard once: a healthy family is one where the love overcomes the psychological torture.

In the middle of it all, the Richardsons' dog Miata, a large brown Doberman pinscher that you wouldn't want to mess with, wandered in. He took one look at all the crazy humans charging around in the strobe-lit darkness, attacking each other with red laser rays, and ran out yipping like a chihuahua.

Who could blame him?

Eventually Andrea and I tore ourselves away from the carnage and drove down to the junior high school, where the school board was meeting in the auditorium.

In the car we practiced the two-minute speeches we were going to make at the meeting. The school board would be taking audience comments on the budget, and Andrea and I wanted to hit them with our most eloquent shots when we asked for more bucks for the gifted and talented program. We were pushing for a full-time coordinator who would work with teachers and the gifted students themselves to create individualized programs for these kids. Also, we were plugging for special pull-out programs for gifted kids at least three hours a week.

"How about this for a speech?" Andrea said. " 'Ladies and gentlemen of the school board, I'd like you to imagine the most horrible job you've ever had. Cleaning toilets for eight hours a day. Telemarketing.

" 'Then imagine you were stuck at this job for the next twelve years. Twelve years of getting bored half to death. And there's no escape, because you're not allowed to quit. Sounds like torture, doesn't it?

" 'Well, ladies and gentlemen, that's what life is like every day for highly gifted children in our schools.' "

Andrea turned to me. "What do you think? Good speech?"

"It makes me nervous."

"Why?"

"Because it's perfect. How am I ever gonna follow an act like that?"

"You'll think of something. You're the writer."

"Yeah, but you're forgetting my writer's block."

"Something like this oughta be able to get you unblocked."

"I've got it," I said, and cleared my throat. "Ladies and gentlemen of the school board, you better treat my kids right or I'll grab a gun and make you sit there for five hours while I read you *Berenstein Bears* books."

"Well, at least it's heartfelt," Andrea said. "But maybe we better keep you away from laser tag from now on."

As it turned out, though, all our speechmaking preparations went for naught. We got there just as the eulogies were ending and the business part of the meeting was beginning. We soon learned that the budget was not part of today's agenda, after all.

The president of the school board, a forty-five-year-old guy with a white shirt and blue tie who looked like an accountant, and in fact *was* an accountant in his day job, stood behind the podium and adjusted his glasses.

"Fellow school board members, and members of the public," he began, "we have a surprise change in the agenda. I am happy to announce that this week the superintendent's office received the official results of this year's Terra Nova tests."

Instantly the entire audience stopped coughing, undoing candy wrappers, and shuffling in their seats. Everyone realized we were about to hear . . . drum roll, please . . . The Test Results.

It's amazing, the hold that these standardized tests have on the psyche of America. All over the country, everybody from conservative politicians to inner-city mothers use these scores as a measure of how well our schools are doing.

I hate these tests, and not just because George W.'s demagoguery about them helped him get elected president—or should I say, selected. For about one month every spring, our children's school gets fanatical about preparing for the darn things. The kids take practice tests at school and get practice test questions for homework. We parents get inundated with dittos and Xeroxed pages from the teachers and the principal advising us how to get our kids ready for Test Week.

But the reality is, these tests do absolutely *nothing* to help my kids. No matter how dull their teachers and how worthless their classes, my kids will always pass these tests. They're a waste of time for them, and a distraction.

And in fact, standardized tests are useless for *most* kids. They don't measure how exciting or fun or truly valuable the school experience is. They're only useful for making sure the lowest common denominator for a certain kind of knowledge doesn't go below a certain level. The tests don't measure the ability to think creatively. They measure the ability of students to do well on multiple-choice tests, and the ability of teachers to "teach to the test."

As I listened to the school board prez describe the results, I realized an even bigger reason why I hated the tests: they encouraged people to get complacent. Like the prez was demonstrating right now.

"Once again," he said, a smug smile playing on his lips, "the Saratoga Springs public schools have shown their continuing excellence. All of our elementary schools, across the board, have either stayed the same or improved since last year. The complete statewide scores are not yet in but it's fair to predict, based on last year's statewide scores, that our schools finished above the sixtieth percentile in every grade. In reading, our first-grade students scored approximately sixty-eight percent. At the second-grade level, we reached the sixty-ninth percentile. . . ."

The prez went on to rattle off statistics and pass around handouts to all the parents. Most of the parents read their stapled pages with rapt attention. I just jammed them into my jacket pocket.

I guess I was happy that most of the Saratoga kids were scoring above average. And I felt a small surge of pride when I heard that High Rock had finished slightly ahead of all the other local elementary schools this year. As the prez pointed out at great length, Sam Meckel would have been proud.

But mainly, I wished I could burn all those stapled pages. Those pages, and pages like them throughout the country, doom our schools to mediocrity. And it wasn't just my kids who would have to endure years of deadly dull classes; Andrea and I would have to deal with it, too. Sometimes I wished my kids weren't quite so bright.

Unfortunately, private schools weren't really an option. The only ones in Saratoga are Catholic schools and a Waldorf school, and neither choice appealed to us.

The prez kept on rolling with his mighty stats, and the parents kept on reading those heartwarming pages. Andrea and I looked at each other and, by mutual consent, stood up and walked out.

When we got back to the laser tag place, Barry was standing out front with Miata. "The dog and I needed a break from all the heavy violence in there," he said. "So how was the meeting? You put in your two cents?"

"Not exactly." Andrea went inside, and I told Barry how the standardized tests had taken over the meeting.

"Sounds exciting," Barry said.

I snorted in response. Then I told him what Irene Topor had said about Susie—namely, that Susie and Meckel had worked out an accommodation about her younger daughter.

Barry just sat there rubbing Miata under her left ear. He was oddly silent.

"Barry," I said, "you're oddly silent."

He bestirred himself. "So the killer isn't Laura, it's not Susie—"

"I haven't ruled Susie out. She still could've bopped Meckel on the head because she was mad about her *older* daughter."

Barry let go of Miata's ear and started rubbing his own. "Listen, Jake, I have a confession to make."

"Confess away."

"Well, I was in there playing laser tag with the kids. And I was listening to them shouting and screaming, you know?"

He paused. "Uh-huh," I said encouragingly.

"And it hit me all of a sudden. The way they were shouting . . ."

I began to sense what was coming. "Uh-huh," I said, not so encouragingly this time. Miata gave me a questioning look.

"Well, it sounded a lot like the shouting I heard that morning."

"Jeez, Barry. First you think it's a woman, then maybe a man, then a kid. . . . Remind me never to use you as a witness."

"I'm really sorry, Jake, I was just trying to help."

"Next thing you'll be telling me there was no screaming after all, just a mouse squeaking."

"Look, maybe I could get hypnotized or something, do you think that might help?"

"Skip it."

"I'm serious. My wife knows a doctor at the hospital who was telling her about some guy—"

I stood up. "If you think it'll help, try it. Listen, when Andrea comes out, tell her I took off for a little while. She can go ahead and drive the kids home."

"Where are you going?"

"To pay a friendly visit to Mark Robinson and his illustrious parents."

"Are you sure that's safe? Didn't Lou get rough with you the other day?"

"Let's hope he got it out of his system," I said, and walked off.

It was a short five-minute trek down Broadway and up Grand to L & S Copies. The sky was blue, the daffodils were blooming, the girls were wearing miniskirts, and I was on my way to track down a double murderer.

As I passed Kinko's, I looked in. The joint was jumping. Skidmore College students, housewives, elderly folks. . . . There were ten or twelve customers packed in at the gleaming new self-service Xerox machines, and more customers at the big long service desk, manned by fresh-faced young employees.

But when I went up to L & S Copies, it was forlorn and empty. The peeling sign on the window claimed that the store was open from ten to five on Saturdays—unlike Kinko's, which was open twenty-four seven—but nobody was visible inside, not even Lou and Sylvia.

I pushed the front door anyway. It opened. I went in.

At first I couldn't hear anything, except for mechanical buzzing and groaning from the machines, most of which were of early '90s vintage. But then I thought I heard voices coming from the back. "Hello?" I said tentatively.

No answer.

I stepped past the machines toward the back room of the store. Now I was able to identify the voices. They belonged to New York Knicks announcers. Somebody had a television set on.

I rounded the corner and immediately came face-to-face with all three Robinsons. Lou and Mark were sitting on a worn-out sofa watching the game. Except now they were watching *me*. Sylvia sat in a nearby chair that had some stuffing showing. She was watching me, too.

Decidedly unpleasant.

But now was no time to be shy. Or scared. If only one of them were in the room, and that one was a murderer, then I'd be in trouble. But I couldn't imagine all three of them would whack me together. That would be too weird.

I waded in, aiming imaginary lasers at their souls. "I know everything," I said.

Lou turned to Sylvia. "Can you believe this guy?"

"I know about Mark stealing the skateboard. I know they were leaning on you hard to give him Ritalin. And it was all coming to a head on Tuesday."

"You're getting on my goddamn nerves," Lou said.

"I know Mark killed Sam Meckel. There's a witness who heard Mark yelling at him that morning in his office."

I was stretching, of course. But they didn't know that.

The three of them just stared at me in shock. Seconds passed. On TV, the Knicks were losing by fifteen.

Lou came out of it first. "Sylvia," he said. "I hear a customer."

I hadn't heard anything, myself. But Sylvia went out of the room. Then Lou stepped behind me, quick as Latrell Sprewell driving to the hoop, and slammed the door shut.

Now there were three of us alone in here. The room suddenly felt extremely small. There was a greasy smell, like somebody had been eating a burger and fries. I felt like choking.

And Lou felt like choking me. "You're full of crap," he said. "Nobody heard my son screaming. Mark wasn't there."

I looked at Mark. He said nothing.

I spread my palms wide, trying to look conciliatory. "Lou, the sooner you come clean, the better. I'm sure Mark wasn't *trying* to kill Meckel. They just got in an argument—"

I barely saw Lou's fist coming. It hit me smack in the forehead. I staggered back against the doorknob and fell to the floor. Then he kicked me in the ribs.

Repeatedly. And he was wearing boots.

I tried to protect my sides with my arms. He was screaming at me, cussing, going berserk. Listening to him, it flashed on me that his screams were higher pitched than his regular voice, which was pretty high already. Maybe Barry had been wrong yet again about that yelling. Maybe it was Lou.

And maybe Lou was about to commit his third murder.

His son wasn't doing anything to stop it, that's for sure. He just cowered there rooted to the spot.

I wasn't doing much to stop it, either. My arms

were protecting my ribs from getting kicked, but then he started aiming at my head.

And my head was in no mood for this. It had been only four days since my concussion. One of Lou's kicks landed pretty hard, and my ears started ringing. My brain got fuzzy. The ringing . . . the screaming . . . the Knicks. . . .

Some barely alert part of me noticed a boot coming straight at my eyes. I moved my head just in time and the boot flew by me. It hit some of my naturally curly hair but nothing else.

The close call seemed to knock my brain back into semi-normality. I rolled away from Lou and tried to get up.

But he came at me again, with a primordial yell. He reared back his boot, aimed at my face, and cut loose.

I snapped my face back out of the way. This time, as his boot whizzed by, I swept my arm underneath it and caught it on the backswing. I shoved Lou's foot as hard as I could, and he lost his balance. He tripped and fell.

I jumped up. If only I could make it out the door. I lunged toward it.

But Lou got up, too. He roared and matched my lunge. Now I couldn't open the door and get out, because opening it would take too many precious milliseconds. Lou would be all over me.

But then, magically, the door opened by itself—or that's what I thought until I saw Sylvia right behind it. She must have heard all the screaming.

I didn't waste any time. I threw Sylvia out of the way and ran, holding my side. Lou chased me to the front door, yelling some rather rude remarks. But when I made it out to the street, he didn't follow.

I ran a couple of blocks, then slowed to a walk.

With the danger subsiding, my body began to register all my new pains. I felt like my head was split open and my ribs were broken. Or maybe the other way around. Not the pleasantest way to spend a Saturday afternoon. I stumbled the block and a half to Broadway and made it into Madeline's Espresso Bar.

Dave, the cop who was going out with Madeline, was sitting at the front counter eating a sandwich. Brie and sliced pear on a baguette. I doubt he ever ate anything remotely resembling that before he met Madeline. I went up to him. "Hey, Dave."

He looked up and saw the big bruise forming in the middle of my forehead, thanks to Lou's first punch. "What the hell happened to you?"

"I ran into several doors. You think you could give me a lift to the emergency room?"

He put down his baguette and got up. "No problem."

"Sorry to interrupt your lunch."

"Like I said, no problem. I'm sure you've got one hell of a story."

On the way to the hospital I told it to him, as coherently as my addled brain would allow. "So I'm thinking of pressing charges," I said after I'd finished. "Maybe that will stir things up. The cops will start investigating the Robinson family for the murders."

"Which Robinson are you betting on?"

"Before, my money was on the kid, but now I don't know. Lou certainly proved he was capable. He almost killed *me* just now."

"But maybe he just flipped out all of a sudden because you were getting too close to nailing his kid."

I squirmed uncomfortably and undid the seat belt. My ribs were killing me. "Whoever killed Meckel and Helquist, I need you fearless cops to look into it, not me. My health can't take much more of this."

"I just wish you had more hard evidence against the Robinsons."

I pointed to the bump on my forehead. "Doesn't *this* count as hard evidence the guy's at least worth checking out?"

"Hey, it's not me you have to convince. The chief is still stuck on Laura Braithwaite."

"For Helquist's murder, too?"

"Yup. Sorry to tell you this, but the D.A.'s going to see the judge on Monday about revoking bail."

"Oh, Lord."

"What do you expect? She was found standing beside the dead man with the murder weapon in her hand. And it's pretty tough to believe Lou or his kid or anybody else could've snuck into Meckel's office that morning with nobody seeing them."

I had thought about that a lot. "There was a good twenty minutes when Meckel was in his office and that front hallway was empty. Except for the gifted and talented parents coming through with their kids. I figure there was a total of maybe one minute during that twenty-minute period when someone was actually in the hallway. It would have been easy for the killer to go into Meckel's office, get in a quick screaming fight, give him one fateful wallop with the trophy, and then run out."

Dave sat there looking doubtful.

"Look, it was only seven-twenty in the morning," I said. "The school wasn't exactly bustling."

"The problem is, Jake, Laura's not the only one with legal problems," Dave said as he pulled into the emergency room entrance. "You remember the judge saying if you kept investigating, your bail would be revoked?"

"Don't bother me with petty details."

"You questioning the Robinsons is a pretty clear case of you violating the judge's order. I'm not sure you want to call attention to that. Unless you want to spend some time in county."

Good grief. "So what do you suggest I do?"

Dave didn't answer. But unfortunately I already knew the only solution: I had to get so much evidence that Little Napoleon would feel stupid messing with me.

I stepped gingerly out of Dave's car, heading for my least favorite place in the universe: the hospital.

No, that's not quite true. My least favorite place is jail. But hospitals rank right up there.

I went up to the triage nurse. She determined I wasn't dying, only in severe pain, so it wouldn't matter if I sat and suffered indefinitely in a molded plastic seat in the waiting room. I asked her for aspirin, but she said she wasn't authorized. The hospital could get sued if I had an adverse reaction. I considered vaulting across her desk and searching her cabinets, but decided it would take too much effort.

Dave came in and sat with me for a while, spreading gloom and pessimism about the murder cases. I eventually asked him to go to my house and baby-sit my kids so Andrea could come to the hospital and keep me company instead.

By the time Andrea got there, I had finally been admitted into the examination room. The doctor, a friendly young Pakistani woman, was poking and prodding me in ways I would have enjoyed under other circumstances.

An X-ray technician took about a hundred pictures of my ribs. I couldn't help remembering that when I was a kid, my father made a big deal of not letting the dentist take too many pictures of my teeth, because he said X rays cause cancer.

I seemed to have mortality on my mind that afternoon—an unfortunate side effect of being in a hospital. "Should I be worrying about all these head injuries?" I said. "Am I going to end up like Muhammed Ali?"

Andrea folded her hands together and switched into sympathetic mode, like she always does when I go hypochondriac on her. "Muhammed Ali made a living out of getting banged on the head. That's different."

"Is it? Seems to me, every time I get involved in a murder, I end up with a concussion."

"That only happened one other time."

"You sure?"

"Yes."

"See, I don't remember that. Probably a sign my brain is already shot."

"Hey, if your brain got rearranged a little, it might not be such a bad thing."

I rolled my eyes. But the old eye sockets didn't appreciate the effort. "Andrea, would you mind going out to Rite-Aid and copping some aspirin for me?"

"Don't they have some here?"

"It's contraband."

So Andrea took off on her mission of mercy. That left me alone in the room when Sylvia Robinson walked in.

I immediately got a visceral fear that Sylvia was going to strangle me with a stethoscope or something and finish off the job her husband had started. But she wasn't holding any weapons in her hands as she perched on the doctor's stool opposite me. She was wearing faded blue jeans and an old yellow T-shirt. Her shoulders were hunched up. Focusing on her up close, she looked a lot older than I'd remembered, like she'd aged ten years in the past week.

"How are you feeling?" she said anxiously.

"Couldn't be better."

"Lou feels terrible about this."

"Yeah, so do I."

"I don't know what came over him."

"I do. He's upset his son killed somebody."

"That's not true."

"Then he's upset *he* killed somebody. Your husband and your son both have slight problems with impulse control, don't they?"

She gazed steadily at me. "I understand what you're trying to do. You want me to get all upset and say something stupid."

She was right. While I sat there and tried to figure out my next ploy, she continued on. "Look, between Kinko's and that horrible teacher, my family has been going through hell. I've been after Lou to see a therapist, and after what he did to you today, he's finally agreed. All three of us are gonna see a therapist. But I want you to know, I've never seen Lou hit anybody before. He's been a little verbally abusive to me and Mark, but he's never been physical. He's a good man."

While I digested that little speech, and tried to decide whether I bought it, Sylvia said, "I don't like what you're doing to my family. But I understand you're just doing what you feel you have to do. Why don't you just tell me what you want to know, and I'll do my best to answer you."

Why was Sylvia being so accommodating all of a sudden, after spending the whole week stonewalling me? Was she simply suffering from a sudden attack of the guilts, after her husband's assault?

Her next comment explained everything—or at least seemed to. "All I'm asking in return is, please don't tell the police what my husband did today. I swear, he's not really *like* that."

I didn't make any promises, instead just launched into my questions. I had plenty of them. "Are you going to admit you knew about your son stealing the skateboard?"

She dropped her eyes. "Yes."

"And the meeting with Meckel on Tuesday—you figured he would push you about the Ritalin."

"We were afraid of that, yes."

She seemed to want to say more. I waited. Finally it came. "What you have to understand is, Lou and I have both been through terrible substance-abuse problems. We lost years of our lives to alcohol and coke. That's where we met, at an AA meeting. So we both get affected pretty strongly when these so-called professionals recommend some kind of mood-altering drug. We feel like we'd be starting Mark down the same road that almost killed us."

Everything she was saying added to Lou's motivations to pop Meckel. And her own motivations, I noted.

"But maybe your son really needed this drug," I said, trying to keep Sylvia riled up so she'd say more than she meant to.

She gave a grimace. "I'm aware our son needs extra attention. He gets frustrated sometimes. He can have trouble staying on task. But if he's really into something, if he's *engaged*, then he's not a problem. Like, he can spend three hours at a time putting together one of those Lego sets. Or he'll play math games on the computer *forever*. He doesn't need drugs, he needs *help*."

I sighed. Yet another kid who'd been failed by the schools. My side was hurting, so I shifted a little. "You guys must have been totally furious at Meckel."

"We were way past furious. We've given up on public schools. We're enrolling Mark at Spring Hill next year."

Spring Hill was the local Waldorf school. They subscribe to an educational philosophy that's a little too weird and cultlike for my tastes.

Actually, three years ago we did send Latree to nursery school at Spring Hill, because it was nearby and the hours were convenient. But then one day Latree came home from school, gazed earnestly into my eyes, and said, "I feel the breath of God upon me."

"What?" I asked.

"I feel the breath of God upon me," he repeated, robotlike.

"Oh, really."

"Mother Mary watches over us all," he explained.

Hmm.

But Spring Hill was a warm, nurturing place in many ways, and might be a good fit for Mark. One major drawback: the tuition had to be at least six or seven K per year, and Lou and Sylvia weren't exactly dot-com millionaires. "How are you going to afford Spring Hill?" I asked.

"We'll manage somehow. Dip into Lou's 401(k) from his old job if we have to. Jacob, you have to understand, we love our child."

"I'm sure you do. But what I'm also hearing is, you hated Meckel. He was gonna turn your only child into a drug addict—and if you said no, then he was gonna force you and your family into the poor-house."

Sylvia's hands turned into fists and her eyes blazed. I was afraid maybe I'd pushed too hard, and she was about to spring out of her chair and attack me. Where was that cute Pakistani doctor when I really needed her?

But Sylvia managed to stifle her rage. "Who are you accusing of murder?" she said through gritted teeth. "Me, my husband, or my son?"

"I'm still working on that."

"I was at the store by seven-thirty that morning, working. And Lou and Mark were together, at home, waking up."

"Then I think either you killed him on your own, or Mark and Lou did it together." Once again Sylvia looked ready to tear me apart. "I'm sorry, Sylvia, I'm just calling it like I see it. And I'll tell you something else. Whoever killed Meckel, they really ought to go to the police and confess. Obviously, this death wasn't intentional. It was a tragic accident."

"And what about Ms. Helquist's death? Was *that* a tragic accident?"

Sylvia had a point there. Meckel's killer might catch a break from the cops. But not Helquist's.

"Do you think one of us killed Ms. Helquist, too?" Sylvia asked.

My head was swimming from Sylvia's questions and her husband's punches. She kept on going. "Why would me or Lou or Mark want to kill *her*? That doesn't make sense. Admit it."

"She must've known one of you killed Meckel. So one of you went over there to shut her up."

"How would she know if we killed Meckel? She wasn't at school that morning. She couldn't've seen anything."

I thought back to the phone message Ms. Helquist left for me shortly before she was killed. She knew *something*. But as Sylvia was pointing out, what kind of incriminating evidence could Helquist have had against the Robinsons? Maybe she knew about the whole skateboard affair. But would that knowledge really have scared any of the Robinsons enough to kill her?

Sylvia's face turned pleading. "I don't blame you for being mad at Lou. I'm mad at him too, for what he did to you. But please, sleep on it before you go to the police and destroy my family. If this stuff gets in the papers, Spring Hill won't even let Mark in. He'll be stuck in that horrible middle school."

I understood her desperation. Saratoga Springs has a middle school for sixth- and seventh-graders that's more like a warehouse than a school.

Twenty or thirty years ago, it was the national fashion to build huge middle schools to dump pre-teens in for two or three years. Nowadays nobody in the education biz thinks these institutions are even halfway sensible, but because of inertia and economics, kids are still stuck there. The best thing you can say about them is they're better than hospitals or jails.

But not by much.

Sylvia was still talking. For someone who was ordinarily quite taciturn, this was impressive. "And the publicity would totally kill our business. Wouldn't you feel like a jerk if it turns out we're innocent?"

"Look, Sylvia—"

"Don't you have other leads to follow? What about Mark's teacher? I'll bet *she* wanted to kill Meckel."

Whoa, how did Sylvia find out about Melanie Wilson's sexual harassment complaint? "You mean you knew...?"

"Yeah, I'm the one who told Meckel in the first place."

Very strange. "*You* told him? How did he respond?"

"He was shocked. He said he'd talk to her, and I got the impression he might fire her."

"He threatened to fire her for filing a complaint? That must be illegal."

Sylvia blinked at me. "Filing a complaint? What are you talking about?"

I blinked back. "What are *you* talking about?"

"Her cheating."

Huh? "Cheating on who?"

Sylvia looked at me like I was an idiot. "On who? You mean, on what."

"Look, why don't you start over from the beginning."

"Don't you know about Melanie cheating on the Terra Nova tests?"

Andrea better get back with that aspirin soon— real soon. "No, I don't."

"Melanie spent, like, a month giving her students pretests. Just like all the other teachers did. Only Melanie's pretests included questions from this year's *actual tests*."

"Really."

"And Mark said, during the test she went around the room. And if she saw somebody had circled a wrong answer, she'd point to it and say something like, 'Why don't you think more about this problem.'"

Sure sounded like cheating, all right.

"And then some of the questions, she was supposed to read them and the multiple-choice answers out loud. So what she did, she'd always say the correct answer in a different way, with a special, you know, inflection, to make it obvious it was the right answer."

"Why did she do all this?"

"Are you kidding? So her kids would get good scores. And she'd look like a good teacher and get rehired. It was a total hustle. That's what I told Meckel."

"When did you talk to him?"

"When he was hassling me about that stupid skateboard."

I nodded, and my aching head instantly regretted it.

Sexual harassment, sexual orientation, a cheating scandal. . . .

Sam Meckel and Melanie Wilson had some pretty serious issues to deal with.

Had Melanie found a uniquely decisive way to solve them?

15

My tête-à-tête with Sylvia was interrupted when the Pakistani doctor came in with the X rays. "Hi," she said. "Is this your wife?"

"Not exactly. This is the lady whose husband beat me up."

"It was a misunderstanding," Sylvia said quickly.

"I see," the doctor said. "Well, anyway, good news for everybody: your ribs, collarbones, hip bones, et cetera, are all miraculously unbroken."

Sylvia and I both heaved simultaneous sighs of relief. My headache lifted. I felt like hugging the doctor, but my ribs, however unbroken, weren't up to it.

I've noticed an interesting thing about me and doctors. Whenever they give me good news, I always think they have a good bedside manner. But whenever their news is bad, their bedside manner also seems bad.

In any case, the doctor left a little bit later, as did Sylvia. I promised her I wouldn't go to the cops just yet.

Then Andrea came with the aspirin. I took a couple for good luck, and Andrea and I bid the hospital farewell. I wouldn't miss it.

"The kids got pretty worried when they heard you were in the hospital," Andrea said as we headed for her minivan. "They'll be thrilled to see you."

"We're not going home just yet," I said.

"Why not?"

"Because we're going to Melanie Wilson's house." Then I told Andrea all about Melanie's cheating.

Andrea shook her head, disgusted. "Those standardized tests make people insane."

I gave her directions, and we drove over to the East Side and onto Melanie's street. The salutary effects of hearing good news from the doctor began to wear off, and the aspirin hadn't kicked in yet. "Andrea, you feel like taking the lead with Melanie? My head hurts, and she likes women better, anyway."

"She won't like me when I'm done with her."

"I don't doubt it."

Andrea pulled up to the curb outside Melanie's house. She started to get out, but then I noticed a little red car across the street pulling away. A familiar perfect profile was behind the wheel.

"Andrea, wait." She turned and I pointed. "That's Melanie. She's taking off."

Andrea slammed the minivan into gear and burned rubber as she did a screeching U-turn.

"Hey, don't go crazy," I said. "We can always catch Melanie later—"

But Andrea was a woman possessed. "No time like the present," she said as we tore off. I had no idea our Honda Odyssey could move like that. I mean, it's fine for driving kids to little-league practice, but the thing only has four cylinders.

Andrea taxed every one of those cylinders to the max. She blew past a slow-moving SUV and squealed around the corner, closing the distance between us and the little red car. There were still two cars and a motorcycle separating us, but Andrea made short work of them. In a cloud of exhaust fumes, and with various horns beeping at her, she left those other vehicles in the dust.

I was so astonished, I forgot to scream. Since when had my wife turned into Nicholas Cage?

Ahead of us Melanie sped up, doing her own imitation of an action-adventure hero. She roared down Nelson Avenue, going through two red lights. Andrea blasted through right behind her, leaning on the horn. The pedestrians at the corner of Nelson and Union stood there and gaped. One grizzled old guy gave a pinched frown, and even though we were buzzing by at sixty miles an hour, I could tell exactly what was going through his mind: *Bunch of crazy New Yorkers. This town is going to the dogs.*

I finally got my equilibrium back and was about to yell at Andrea to stop. But just then, Melanie stopped. Screeched to a halt, in fact, right in front of us. These airbags sure as hell better work, I thought as I gasped—

But Andrea slammed the brakes, and we stopped an inch short of Melanie's car.

There were a few seconds where nobody moved. I guess we were all thinking about our near brush with death—or at least with major car repairs.

"Andrea, you are a total lunatic," I said when I got my breath back.

"I did kind of overdo it," she agreed, breathing pretty uncertainly herself.

But when Melanie stepped out of her car, and we did too, Andrea immediately got back into her Kinsey Millhone persona. She needed it, too, because Melanie was on the warpath.

"Are you out of your mind?" Melanie shouted. Her gorgeous face was disfigured by anger and fear. "You almost killed us all!"

"You shouldn't have run away," Andrea said coolly.

"I ran away because you scared the shit out of me. What would you do if some idiot came charging after you like that!"

"I don't believe we've been introduced. My name's Andrea. I think you've met my husband—"

"Yes, I have, and fuck you both. Stay out of my fucking life." This woman had a mouth on her. She stomped back to her car.

"You cheated on the Terra Nova tests," Andrea said.

Melanie stopped and glared at her. But she didn't say anything, just opened her car door and started to get in.

"And Meckel found out. He told you he was firing you. That's why you killed him."

"He wasn't gonna fire me," said Melanie. "He was gonna hold it over my head, unless I slept with him."

Then Melanie stepped away from the car and got in Andrea's face. "But the whole thing's a lie, anyhow. I never cheated on those tests. Sylvia Robinson made that up to get back at me."

"Yeah, right," my wife said. "I'm sure we can find other parents who'll confirm what Sylvia said."

"Why are you people out to get me?" Melanie said, giving her hair an angry toss. And then, as I watched her blond hair tossing, I suddenly saw something else, too.

The late-afternoon sun was angling down toward Melanie's little car, and over her shoulder I caught a shiny metallic glint in her front seat. No, not in her front seat actually, in her glove compartment. It must have sprung open when Melanie braked her car so abruptly.

The two women kept jawing at each other like

guests on the Jerry Springer show, but I no longer heard all their words. I moved toward Melanie's car, stooped down, and looked in the glove compartment. Sure enough, that glint belonged to a flashlight.

And not the two-dollar plastic kind that you can find in half the glove compartments in the world. This was a big, hard, metal flashlight.

The kind that, if somebody swung it at your head, could cause a pretty nasty concussion.

I opened Melanie's car door. "Hey," she said. I reached down and grabbed the flashlight by the handle as Melanie snapped, "Get out of there."

I ignored her and examined the head of the flashlight. "What are you doing? Give me that!" she yelled, and came at me.

I put the flashlight behind my back. She reached around and tried to grab it away. Then I held it up high where she couldn't reach it. But she shoved me back against the car and grabbed again.

Throwing all sense of chivalry to the winds, I aimed a forearm at her perky nose and drove her backward. Then Andrea came up and gave her a hard shove in the stomach, pushing her back even farther.

Melanie put her hand to her side. *God, she's reaching for a gun.*

But no, she was just putting her hand on her hip, trying to give herself some attitude. It didn't work. Her eyes were too scared.

Now that Melanie was far enough away from me that she couldn't snatch the flashlight—especially with Andrea as my bodyguard—I lowered it down to eye level so I could examine it again.

"What happened to your flashlight?" I asked.

Melanie didn't respond, just stood there panting.

"Looks a little banged up."

And indeed it did. One side of the flashlight head was dented. No doubt that happened when the flashlight was putting a dent in my own head.

I inspected the flashlight carefully. "What's this little red speck?" I said. "Could it be blood? *My* blood?"

Melanie curled her lips, and her hands balled into fists. She reminded me of a trapped animal, a large cat of some sort. Is there such a thing as a blond jaguar?

Now the truth is, there *was* no red speck on that flashlight. But hopefully Melanie didn't know that. "Guess I'll bring this to the cops," I said. "I'm sure they can match the DNA."

"You sonufabitch," said Melanie.

Now Andrea got into it. "You practically kill my husband, and you have the balls to—"

"Look, I *had* to hit him," Melanie said.

Aha! Now if we could just get her to keep talking. "Why'd you have to hit me?" I asked.

"Why do you think? Because you were about to catch me. Hey, it was dark in Meckel's office that night. I didn't know who you were, I thought maybe you were gonna kill me. I was just protecting myself."

"Why were you there in the first place?"

"Oh, hell." Melanie looked suddenly tired, and her face drooped. "You know why I was there."

"Yes. To cover up for your murder."

Her face jumped back into full alert mode. "No, I didn't kill him!"

"It's time to give up, Melanie," said Andrea softly. "It's all over. You know that."

"I didn't kill anybody. Yeah, I broke into Meckel's office that night, but that's *all* I did!"

"Why'd you break in?" Andrea asked.

"It's like I told you. He wrote up a report about me cheating, and threatened to go to the superintendent with it. I just wanted to get it back. I knew it was in his desk somewhere."

"But Meckel was already dead. He couldn't hurt you anymore. So why'd you want it back so bad?"

"I didn't want the new principal seeing it. Or the police."

"Why the police?"

"I don't know. 'Cause cheating is, like, illegal."

"Get real," Andrea said. "You wouldn't break into the school after midnight and risk arrest because you were nervous about some little cheating scam. It was the murder you were scared about."

Melanie shook her head vigorously. "I just wanted to take that stupid report home and burn it. That's all. What if the new principal gave it to the superintendent? It would go on my record. I'd never get another job."

Andrea and I looked at each other. "Sounds like an excellent murder motive to me," she said.

"Me, too."

"Oh, for Christ's sake," Melanie said.

"Why didn't you just go into Meckel's office during the day, instead of sneaking in at midnight?" Andrea asked.

"Because I knew I'd never get in there. That old witch, Ms. Helquist, she was always there."

"You didn't like Ms. Helquist?" I asked.

"What, now you want to frame me for that one, too? Look, I'm sorry I hit you on the head, but except for that I never hurt *anybody*."

"If that's the story you wanna go with, fine," I said. "Come on, Andrea, let's hit the police station. Melanie, we're 'borrowing' your flashlight."

"It's not fair," Melanie said. "I didn't cheat, I

swear. You can't believe anything the Robinsons say. They're, like, pathological liars."

Melanie was following Andrea and me to our car. I got in the driver's side, still yakking, still trying to coax a confession out of her. "We'll let the cops sort it all out," I said. "Too bad you weren't smart enough to get rid of the flashlight."

"What about that friend of yours, Elena Aguilera?" Melanie said bitterly. "*She* cheated. Why don't you tell the cops about *her*?"

Andrea and I both stared at Melanie. "Elena?" Andrea asked. "*Elena* cheated on the tests?"

Melanie realized she was onto something. She curled her lips triumphantly. "That's right. You sic the cops on me, and I'll rat on Elena. There goes *her* teaching career down the toilet. Especially when the cops find out everything else she did."

I was sitting in the car with the door still open. "Okay, I'll bite. What else did Elena do?"

"She gave one of her kids a higher grade on his report card than he deserved. Because Meckel pushed her into it."

"Which kid was this?"

"Mike Lawrence."

Holy tamale. I turned to Andrea, who was still standing outside the car by the passenger side. "His father is Scott Lawrence, the jerk on the school board."

"Why would Meckel push Elena about this kid's grade?" Andrea asked.

Melanie shrugged. "I guess his dad had some kind of pull."

I figured I knew exactly what that pull was. Lawrence was blackmailing Meckel about the computer purchase.

Melanie pointed a finger at us. "If you guys really

want to catch the murderer, you should go after Elena, not me. She's the one who was there at the school that morning."

"But you were the one who clobbered me with a flashlight."

"I just wish I'd hit you harder," said Melanie. "Hey, go to the cops if you want. They'll investigate me, and I'll get run out of town for being gay. So will Irene. If you feel good about that, go ahead."

Then Melanie turned on her heels and went back to her car.

Andrea got into the passenger seat. "We should tell the cops anyway," I said. "This is too darn complicated for me."

"You know we can't do that. We'd be ruining too many lives—Elena's included."

She was right, of course. Andrea is almost always right. It can get downright annoying.

"So what do you suggest, O wise one?" I asked, as we watched Melanie drive off.

"Run down the time line for me again," Andrea said.

I obliged. "Meckel was found dead by Laura at about seven thirty-five. The cops say he was killed some time after seven, but that's the best they can do."

"So he went to his office, then stepped out for a while at the same time Laura came along and dropped off her trophy."

"That sounds right, Kinsey."

"And when did Barry hear the yelling from Meckel's office?"

"He says he hit the john sometime between seven-fifteen and seven twenty-five."

Andrea frowned, then asked, "Meanwhile Elena was out of anybody's sight for how long?"

"I'm not totally clear on that. Neither is Susie."

"And Susie got to school before any of the other parents."

I nodded. "So she could have had time to drop off her kids in the library, then drop the trophy on Meckel's head."

"And how long was Barry supposedly in the bathroom?"

"According to Susie, maybe a minute. Now you also have to remember, Melanie could have come in early to grade papers or whatever. So it really could have been her."

"Or one of the Robinsons. Or the gas man." Andrea sighed.

I started up the car. "We don't have time to sink into the slough of despair. Let's go and interrogate Elena."

"Stop at Ben and Jerry's first."

"Why?"

"We'll bring her a pint of Cherry Garcia. That's her favorite flavor."

It seemed a trifle unorthodox to me, bringing a pint of gourmet ice cream to somebody you're trying to nail for murder.

But I didn't object. After all, Andrea is usually right.

16

On the way from Ben and Jerry's to Elena's, we had to wait as a large flock of cars went cruising by with their headlights on. Sam Meckel's funeral procession.

The lead car was occupied by Meckel's immediate family. Through the side window I saw a shock of purple hair. Paul was looking out the window as he passed me, and we locked eyes for a moment.

Andrea and I thought about heading for the cemetery ourselves, but decided the best way to pay our respects to the dead man was by finding his killer. So a few minutes later we pulled up in front of Elena's apartment building.

The tinkling of "Three Blind Mice" being played on the piano greeted Andrea and me as we headed up the stairs to Elena's apartment. I rang the doorbell.

Elena opened the door and glared at me. Then she eyed Andrea—or more precisely, the carton of ice cream Andrea was holding out. Her face turned perplexed. "What's up?" she asked.

"Peace offering," Andrea replied, handing over the goods.

Elena stood there turning over the carton in her hand, then said, "Well, come on in the kitchen. I don't usually do Cherry Garcia in the middle of the day, but today I'll make an exception. Luce, say hi to Jacob and Andrea."

Luce looked up from her piano. "Hi," she said, then went back to her playing. Only now she switched out of "Three Blind Mice" to some complex classical piece, Mozart maybe. She played it flawlessly. I stopped and listened for a few moments before following the women into the kitchen. Besides being smart as a whip, Luce was a veritable musical prodigy.

Elena was working on scooping the stiff, frozen ice cream into bowls while Andrea got out spoons. "That's quite a Vladimir Horowitz you got out there," I said.

Elena nodded. "So I'm assuming this ice cream means I'm no longer a suspect?"

Andrea and I shifted our feet. But Elena went on, oblivious. "Have you figured out who did it?"

I waited for Andrea to say something. Meanwhile she waited for *me* to say something. I guess our detecting duo routine still needed a little work.

Elena waved her ice cream scooper for emphasis. "Come on, your secret is safe with me."

"The truth is," I finally said, "you *are* still a suspect."

She did a double take. "Then why'd you bring me the Cherry Garcia?"

"Don't blame me, that was Andrea's idea."

"Did you lace it with truth serum?"

"I want us to still be friends," Andrea said plaintively.

"Right. Will you come visit me in jail after you frame me for murder?"

From the other room came the ethereal Mozart. "Look, Elena," I said, "we understand you cheated on the Terra Nova tests."

She slammed the scooper down on the counter. "I did *what*?"

"Cheated," Andrea said, finally getting into the act. "On the Terra Nova tests."

"You got some *cojones*, coming in here and giving me this shit."

"Elena," Andrea said.

But Elena cut her off. "I did not cheat. My kids got good scores, yeah. But they got 'em fair and square. Who told you this lie?"

I didn't want to start a war between Elena and Melanie. "Let's just say I got it on good authority."

"Tell your good authority to go piss in a hat. I drilled those kids for the Terra Nova for five weeks straight." She picked up the scoop and began serving the ice cream again. It looked like she was trying to calm herself. "Look, I'm not proud of drilling them like that. I hate wasting the class time. But it's not *cheating*. All the teachers do it. Everything depends on those stupid test scores: tenure, bonuses, staying on the administration's good side. . . ." She had one bowl filled and started another. "Maybe I cheated my kids by holding them hostage to a test. But that's the *only* cheating I did."

I continued our attack. "Why'd you give high grades on Mike Lawrence's report card?"

That threw her. She was in the middle of dropping a scoop into the third bowl, and she missed. The scoop hit the edge of the counter, then fell to the floor.

Elena ignored the mess. Her thick lips tightened. "I gave Mike straight threes." At High Rock that meant B's. The highest grade you could get was a four. "Which is exactly what he deserved."

"Elena, we know all about Meckel pressuring you," Andrea said.

"And do you know all about me refusing him?"

"No, but we'd like to hear."

Elena finally put down the ice cream scoop for good, and sat down on a kitchen chair. Andrea, evidently feeling uncomfortable standing over her friend, sat down too. Myself, I stayed standing. I'd grab any psychological edge I could, friendship or no friendship.

"That bastard Meckel comes to me, asks for a 'favor,' " Elena said. "He tells me Scott Lawrence is a very influential member of the school board. Anything we can do to keep him happy would be beneficial. Maybe he'd vote a few more million dollars into our budget.

"I said, Sam, what exactly do you have in mind? He says, what grade were you planning on giving Lawrence's kid? I tell him, threes. The kid's a very average student. Meckel says, would it kill you to give him fours? He says, I'll remember it in June."

She gave us a look. "June, that's when tenure decisions get made." Andrea and I both nodded.

Elena shoved a spoon into her bowl, but didn't eat. "So what the heck, I said, sure, Sam, I can give the little twerp a bunch of fours, no sweat off my back.

"But then I went home. And the more I thought about it, the more pissed off I got. I couldn't sleep. I don't like people trying to tell me what to do. Nobody gets away with that, not my ex-husband, my father, nobody.

"So two weeks later—this would be last week—I go into Meckel's office. Tell him I've reconsidered, I'm giving Mike Lawrence threes after all."

Here Elena stopped. She stared down at her bowl, perhaps hoping the pattern of cherries in her ice cream would give her inspiration.

"So what did Meckel say?" Andrea asked.

"He made some not-so-veiled threats and told me to re-reconsider. So I came in the next day, told him I'd *re* and *re-reconsidered*, and the kid was still gonna get threes. Meckel starts screaming, and threatening me all over again. I tell him if I'm going to lose my job over this, then he can take the job and shove it. I'd rather be a teacher's aide in Poughkeepsie than bow down to Meckel's bullying."

"And is that what you told him on Tuesday morning?" I asked.

Elena threw me a puzzled look. "I'm not positive which days I met with him, but I think it was a Wednesday and a Thursday."

"I'm talking about *this* week. The Tuesday morning when you killed Meckel," I said.

"For God's sake, how many times do I have to tell you—"

Suddenly Elena stopped. The piano music from the other room had stopped without our noticing, and now Luce came into the room. We all looked at her. I felt guilty as hell. Here I was, trying to put her mommy away in jail.

"Mom, what's wrong?" Luce asked.

Elena forced a smile. "Nothing, honey. We're just arguing about silly stuff. Why don't you go back to the piano?"

"What are you arguing about?" Luce had inherited her mother's deep dark eyes, and right now they were wide open and heartbreaking.

"Grown-up things. Go do that sonata again. It was beautiful."

"But Mom—"

"I said *go*."

Luce went.

Then Elena turned back to us. "Alright, you want the truth?" she whispered angrily. "I'll give you the truth. Come on."

She stormed out of the kitchen. Andrea and I looked at each other, then followed her.

We ended up in her bedroom. Elena shut the door behind us. What was she up to? Was she about to confess to murder, and she didn't want her daughter to hear?

Elena reached into the top drawer of her bureau. She pulled out a tiny microcassette recorder and an even tinier microcassette. Then she inserted the tape into the machine and said, "Last week, when I went to see Meckel the first time, I recorded it. The second time, I played the tape for him."

And now she played it for us. Andrea and I listened to Sam Meckel's irate voice:

"Christ, Elena, don't be so self-righteous. Think about the greater good of the whole Saratoga school system—"

"I'm sorry, Sam, I've made up my mind."

"Maybe you better think hard about your own future, Elena."

"Is that a threat?"

"Call it a statement. Look, what am I supposed to tell Lawrence when he comes here next Tuesday? I promised him his kid would get fours."

I put up my hand. "Stop the tape."

Elena stopped it. "So you can see I had no reason to kill the *come mierda*, I had him by the short hairs. If he tried to fire me, I'd spread the word he wanted me to cheat on a kid's grade."

But I was focused on something else. "What was that on the tape about Lawrence having a meeting with Meckel on Tuesday?"

Elena looked at me. "I hadn't noticed that," she said quietly.

I turned to Andrea. "When I talked to Lawrence, he never said anything about any meeting."

"And you know what else?" Andrea said. "It's kind of weird Meckel showed up at seven-oh-five for a seven-thirty meeting. Every other meeting we had, he showed up a few minutes late. Maybe this time he had an earlier meeting with Lawrence."

Elena spoke up. "So you're thinking Lawrence comes to this meeting, and Meckel springs the news his kid isn't getting fours after all. So Lawrence gets all worked up . . ."

I continued the thought. "And there's this trophy sitting conveniently on the desk . . ."

Andrea added, "Meckel is calling Lawrence a blackmailing scum, Lawrence is calling Meckel a lying crook . . ."

"I like it," I said. "And Ms. Helquist comes in on Wednesday and realizes that Meckel and Lawrence had a morning appointment scheduled for the day before. So she calls and asks me to come to her house, so she can tell me about it."

Andrea picked up the thread. Our dynamic duo act was back on track. "Only Lawrence figures out that Helquist knew about the appointment. So he goes to her house first, maybe just to talk to her, but she's got a gun and one thing leads to another and now she's dead too."

I turned to Elena. "Do you have a copy of this tape?"

She shook her head no. "Why, did you want to play it for Lawrence?"

"Not right now. Just don't lose the tape," I said. "Hey, how about we all sit down to some Cherry Garcia before it's totally melted?"

So we all trooped into the kitchen and shared a convivial sugar rush, joined by Luce, who was relieved that the wacky grown-ups had finally stopped their quarreling. Elena and Andrea laughed giddily and made jokes, the tension of the murder accusation forgotten.

It wasn't until later, when Andrea and I were back in the car on our way to H & R Block to grill Lawrence, that a more sinister explanation for Elena's actions surfaced in my mind.

I interrupted Andrea in the middle of chattering about how relieved she was that Elena didn't do it. "You know," I said, "if that was Elena's only copy of the tape . . ."

"Yes?" said Andrea, and then when I kept quiet for a moment, she added, "Spit it out."

"I'm just thinking. Maybe she didn't play Meckel the tape last week, like she said. Maybe she played it for him on Tuesday morning. And they got into a fight . . . it was her only copy . . . he tried to grab it out of her hands . . ."

"And died in the attempt."

"Exactly."

Andrea groaned.

"Sorry to throw Elena back into the pot—"

"Just shut up and drive," Andrea said, discouraged.

I shut up and drove.

We got to H & R Block just after five o'clock. It being a Saturday, we weren't too optimistic about finding Lawrence still slaving away at people's taxes. But we got lucky. All the secretaries had gone, and so had everybody else, but Lawrence was still there, bent over some figures in his office in the back.

He didn't hear us come in. "Hey, big guy," I said, and he jumped three feet in the air.

"Don't scare me like that," he said when he came back down.

"So you're staying late, huh? Crunching numbers?"

"What do you want?"

"You take numbers pretty seriously, don't you?" I was giving him the kind of knowing sneer that the homicide detectives on *Law & Order* always give, trying to keep the bad guys off balance.

"Look, I was just on my way out—"

Andrea interrupted him. "You especially like the number four."

He stared at her. She had a pretty good sneer, too. "What?"

"You like the number four a lot more than the number three," I said.

"If you're still hassling me about that extra computer Ms. Helquist ordered—"

"Don't play dumb," I said.

"We're hassling you about your son's grade," Andrea said.

"You felt life wouldn't be complete unless little Mikey got straight fours," I said.

"So you told Meckel he better make damn sure that happened," Andrea said.

Lawrence just stood there, in shock. I said, "What was the deal, you wanted straight fours so you could get him into some private school in Albany?"

"Or was it just an ego thing?" Andrea said.

"You people are so out of line," Lawrence sputtered.

"Are we really?" Andrea said. "We have a tape recording of Meckel ordering your son's teacher to raise his grade."

"I don't believe you," Lawrence said, but then he looked us both over and realized we were telling the truth.

"Look," he said, "I don't know anything about this. I never once talked to Meckel about Mike's grades."

"Nonsense. Meckel was pretty clear on the subject," I said.

"Then all I can say is, maybe Sam had some kind of twisted idea I'd be more laid back about financial irregularities if my son was doing well."

"Your story doesn't hold up," Andrea said. "We know you had a meeting scheduled with Meckel for Tuesday."

"The Tuesday he was killed," I elaborated.

Lawrence's eyes darted around the room, like he was looking for a way to escape.

Or maybe he was looking for a spelling bee trophy or some other weapon to attack us with. Hopefully he wouldn't find one.

"We also know," Andrea said deliberately, sounding very much like the English teacher she was, "that Meckel had just learned your child would be receiving threes, after all. That's what he told you on Tuesday morning. Just before you began yelling at him."

"And just before you killed him," I said, beating Andrea to the punchline.

The room was silent for a moment. Then Lawrence said, "You've got it all wrong."

"Enlighten us," Andrea said.

"You're not gonna believe this," said Lawrence, "because you're both dyed-in-the-wool bleeding-heart liberals. You think people like me who believe in conservative values are just idiots."

Lawrence got up from his seat and began pacing. I watched him warily, hoping he wasn't working himself up into a homicidal rage. "But I don't care, I happen to think fiscal responsibility is important. *Honesty* is important. It bothers me that my taxpayer money is being used to buy somebody a personal computer. Doesn't it bother you?"

Before Andrea or I could reply, Lawrence said, "And I believe firmly in holding our schools accountable. The best way to do that, objectively, is with standardized tests. So we have to keep those tests fair and accurate."

Andrea and I gazed at each other, raising our inner eyebrows. Where was Lawrence going with this? Then we got our answer. "On Monday, everybody on the school board got an e-mail from the superintendent. The BOCES office in Albany had finished scoring the Terra Novas from Saratoga County, and the superintendent was forwarding us the results. He asked us not to tell anybody until the big school board meeting—you know, the meeting we had this morning—because that way we'd get maximum publicity. And he definitely wanted the maximum. Because as you know, the results were really good.

"And like you heard this morning, the results from High Rock were better than just good. Seventy-second percentile. Highest in the district. Which is a little weird, don't you think? The poorest kids in Saratoga go to our school. We've never been first before, we've always been last or next to last. So what the heck is going on here?"

Lawrence answered his own question. "I'll tell you what I *think* is going on. Hanky-panky. Meckel knew his reputation would go up if the tests did, and maybe he'd get a merit pay increase, so he rigged the results. I'm betting he changed a lot of the students' answers before he sent the tests off to BOCES to be scored. And that's what I was going to confront him about—Tuesday afternoon, not Tuesday morning. Our meeting was scheduled for two o'clock."

"Why haven't you brought this up before?"

"The man's dead. I'm not sure I'm right. I don't want to besmirch his reputation without proof."

I turned to Andrea. "Just for argument's sake, let's say this guy"—I pointed my thumb at Lawrence— "is telling us the truth. How could Meckel's cheating on the tests lead to his murder?"

Andrea asked Lawrence, "When you made the appointment with Meckel, did you mention your suspicions?"

"Yes, it came up."

"And what did he say?"

"He flatly denied it."

Andrea frowned thoughtfully. "Okay, suppose you're right, and somebody *futzed* with the tests. But what if Meckel himself didn't do it? What if somebody else did the *futzing*, and after you made the appointment with Meckel, he investigated and found out?"

"So Meckel confronted this other person on Tuesday morning—and got bonked on the *conkus* for his troubles," I said. "I like it."

Lawrence was watching me and Andrea, his head bouncing back and forth between us like he was at a Ping-Pong match. "But who else might have done the cheating?" he asked. "Helquist?"

My prime suspects were Elena and Melanie, but I didn't mention that. "Look, I've already seen the general results for the Terra Novas. But do you have a more specific breakdown?"

Lawrence blinked at us, no doubt taken aback at this new turn of events that had us all working together like colleagues. I was pretty taken aback myself. Then he shrugged. "Sure, I got a breakdown in my desk here."

He went over and pulled out a sheaf of papers

stapled together. "The High Rock results are on pages two and three," he said, handing them to me.

I turned to the fourth-grade results and found Elena's class. In math, they were in the seventy-eighth percentile. In English, they were in the eightieth.

Then I found Melanie's class. Their high scores were even more pronounced—eighty-first in math, eighty-second in English.

There were only twelve classes in the whole school. So Elena and Melanie's classes accounted for a lot of the dramatic High Rock increase. Had Elena and Melanie both cheated? Of course, maybe they just had smart kids in their classes, or maybe they did an especially thorough job of test preparation and drilling because they were concerned about tenure. But it seemed questionable.

Andrea was reading the scores over my shoulder. She asked Lawrence, "If one or more of the teachers was cheating, is there any way we could prove it?"

"I don't know," Lawrence said. "Maybe if you looked at the actual tests themselves, you might find something. Like, if the teacher erased wrong answers and put in correct answers, you might find some kind of pattern. Or in the math section where it's not just multiple choice, you might find some answers in the teacher's handwriting instead of the kids'."

"So where are these tests?" I asked.

"After they're scored by BOCES, they get returned to the schools."

"Which means they're probably at High Rock somewhere," said Andrea. "Sitting in the principal's office, maybe."

Suddenly my mental neurons began firing on all cylinders. For the first time in five days, I got that high you get when a puzzle finally starts to come together. "Andrea," I said, "do you remember when we went to see Ms. Helquist in her office? And she was in the middle of opening that big brown package?"

Andrea's face lit up. "You think the tests were in there?"

"The return address was from Albany. I didn't see anything else—but I'm betting it was from BOCES."

Andrea frowned in thought. "So she opens the package, finds the Terra Novas . . . And then later that day she calls you up, says she's gotta tell you something."

"Something she found in those tests. Something that would help solve the murder. That's what she was gonna tell me—except she got killed."

"We have to get ahold of those tests," Andrea said. "Maybe we can figure out whatever it was that Ms. Helquist figured out."

"Any way I can help you get the tests?" Lawrence asked.

I thought about that for a second—but only a second. My adrenalized mind had already come up with a plan. I was going to get those tests by methods that weren't really legal, strictly speaking. Or even loosely speaking. Lawrence had turned out to be a big help, and perhaps a better guy than I had given him credit for . . . but I didn't think he'd be the best guy to accompany me on my upcoming mission.

"No thanks, we'll take care of it ourselves," I said. "We appreciate your help. Andrea, let's roll."

And with that, we headed out into the Saratoga sunset.

Walking back to our car, we debated my grand plan, which was this: I wanted to go back to the school tonight and break into Helquist's and Meckel's offices. I figured there was a good chance the package with the Terra Nova results was in one of those two places. Either Helquist stuck it in her own desk, or else she put it on Meckel's desk so the new principal would be able to deal with it.

Andrea wasn't all that interested in my reasoning. "Are you *nuts*?" she said. "Look what happened the last time you tried to play cat burglar."

"How else do we get hold of that package?"

"We don't even know the package is still there."

"We have to at least try."

"Why don't we go to Chief Walsh?"

We went back and forth on that for a while. We could tell the chief all about our suspicions of Elena and Melanie, and ask him to go into the school and search for the Terra Novas.

But then word would leak out that Elena and Melanie were suspected of cheating. We weren't eager to spread those kinds of rumors even if they were true—and they might not be.

The other problem was, Chief Walsh was ornery enough that he might refuse to act on our suggestion. Or if he did, he might not act on it right away. And in the meantime, with all the dirt we'd kicked up lately, the killer might decide to sneak into Helquist's or Meckel's office and grab those tests before we got a chance.

"Maybe that's what Melanie was really doing that night when she broke in," I suggested. "Maybe she thought the tests were already there, and she was searching for them."

"But fortunately the tests didn't get delivered till the next day." Andrea bit her lip. "I hope the killer hasn't snuck off with them already. If it was Elena or Melanie, they could've just gone in and gotten them during the middle of the school day."

"It's possible. But security's been pretty tight in there this week." The cops had somebody hanging out at school all week long, to reassure the kids. And I was pretty sure they'd kept Meckel's office locked.

By this point in the discussion we were back in the minivan again, pulling onto our street. "So you're really hungry for another B and E, huh?" Andrea asked. "Not scared of getting another concussion?"

"Hey, I'm a hardheaded guy."

"What if this time you get attacked with something more lethal than a flashlight? And another thing— the tests could be at Ms. Helquist's house. Maybe she took them home with her."

"That's a good point. Guess I'll have to break into both places."

"Oh, God."

"Look, Andrea, you're not going to talk me out of it."

"I'm painfully aware of that. So you know what?"

"What?"

"I'm going with you."

"There's no need for that."

"You're afraid I'll get hurt, aren't you?"

"Well . . ."

"So now you know how I feel."

Andrea parked in front of our house and got out of the car. "Look, Andrea, you can't do this."

"Why not?"

"Well, for one thing, who would take care of the kids? We can't very well ask Dave to baby-sit again while we go out and commit a burglary. He's a cop."

"Then we'll ask one of our other friends."

I would have argued further, but just then the kids came racing out the front door of the house, with Dave behind them. "Mommy! Daddy!" they yelled.

"The Knicks won!" Latree shouted as he put his arms around me.

"Dave bought me a new Pokémon deck!" Charizard yelled joyfully.

"They're winning the series two games to one!" said Latree.

"I got a Japanese Raichu with ninety HP!" said Charizard.

"And the next game's a home game!"

"And a Kangaskahn and a Snorlax and . . ."

And needless to say, it was a while before Andrea and I could get back to the business of murder.

17

But we did eventually get back to it. I called Barry and asked if our kids could do a sleepover at his house. It turned out, though, that he and Ronnie were going out tonight. They didn't think their baby-sitter, a twelve-year-old girl, would be up for taking care of our kids, too.

I asked Barry if he could come over himself around midnight, just for an hour or two, but he also nixed that idea. "Sorry, old chap," he said, "but the little woman and I are going to have that rarest of all treats for married couples: a romantic evening for two."

So I got off the phone and called Judy Demarest. I wasn't too enthusiastic about that, because I knew she'd pepper us with pointed questions and would get ticked off when we didn't answer them. Newspaper reporters are funny that way.

Judy was at home, and after our requisite banter-ing and sparring, she agreed to come over. So at the stroke of two a.m., with the kids sound asleep up-stairs, Judy stood in the front hall watching Andrea and me don dark jackets and pull dark baseball caps down low over our eyes. We thought about using our kid's watercolors and going in blackface, but it felt too politically incorrect.

Judy shook her head, amused. "Now I get it. You're planning to break in somewhere, aren't you?"

"No way. We're going stargazing," I said.

"Five to one you're back in jail before the night's out," Judy said.

"Hey, this time he's got me with him," Andrea said. "It'll be a piece of cake."

"Famous last words."

But we ignored Judy's negativity and marched out the door. I reached into my Toyota and grabbed Melanie's flashlight.

Just in case there were any cops or killers keeping tabs on us, we stuck to the shadows as we headed down Elm Street, turned right on Long Alley, and then came back up Ash to Ms. Helquist's house. There was no wind and all the dogs were asleep, or at least silent. Except for our own footsteps, the only noise came from the occasional buzzing streetlights. Easing down Ash, our hearts stopped when we thought we saw a dark figure lurking alongside a house half a block away. But then we decided it was just a bush.

We stepped past Ms. Helquist's panoply of flowers onto her porch, and I pulled out my AAA card. Getting the door open took maybe five seconds. I felt like a pro.

Unfortunately, the cliché "no pain, no gain" turned out to be an accurate description of our search of Ms. Helquist's domicile. We found plenty of seed packets and gardening magazines, but no envelopes from BOCES and no standardized tests.

"I hope whoever killed Ms. Helquist didn't take those tests away," Andrea said as we stepped out of the house onto the porch.

"And I hope whoever buys this house takes care of her flowers."

Still sticking close to any cover we could find, we oozed on down the street, took a couple of rights, and found ourselves on High Rock Avenue. We saw our first moving car of the evening, which turned out to be a cop car. We ducked down behind a parked SUV and waited for it to pass by.

A couple of blocks away loomed the object of our criminal designs, High Rock Elementary. Across the street from it was the Robinson house, and Andrea and I both noticed at the same time that the lights were on in their front downstairs window.

"You think they're awake?" Andrea said.

"Let's reconnoiter."

We edged up the street, then hid behind a row of bushes in front of the house next door to the Robinsons. We stood there for about three minutes and didn't see any signs of activity.

"Looks okay to me," I whispered.

"We should look in the window and make sure. I don't want them jumping us from behind."

"You women are always so cautious," I said, but didn't mean it. A little extra caution wouldn't be such a bad idea here.

We slunk up the Robinsons' driveway toward their house. I almost tripped on some object, which I then realized was a skateboard. Probably Mark's. I shook my head. He'd made such a point of stealing it back from Meckel, and it had gotten his whole family into such a mess, and now here he left it just lying around on the driveway.

Andrea and I moved around the front wall of the house and looked in through the windowshades, standing a couple of yards back from the window so nobody in the front room would be able to see us.

But the room was empty. Andrea and I watched

for a while, then withdrew. I was careful to steer clear of the skateboard this time.

Then Andrea and I headed across the street to the school. We walked up to the front door. This time it was locked.

"Do not fear," I said, "Triple A is here."

I took out my card and set to work.

Then I set to work some more.

But nothing happened. The magic was gone. "I'm so embarrassed," I said.

"Let's try the other doors."

And we did. We went around the school and tried every single one. But nothing gave. My AAA card let me down again and again. I was seriously pissed. Maybe next year I'd let my membership expire.

"How about if we just break a window?" Andrea suggested.

"I'm worried about the noise, but I guess we'll have to," I said. Then I got a minor brainstorm. "Wait a minute. Let's try the window to Meckel's office. Me and that cop might've damaged it when we were pushing our way out."

So we went over there. Sure enough, the window was open slightly, maybe a quarter of an inch. I was able to work the tips of my fingers in there and pry it open a littler farther. Now it was open maybe an inch.

"You try opening the bottom of the window," I told Andrea, "and I'll get the side."

So we wedged our fingers in and pulled. I groaned, Andrea grunted . . . and suddenly the window slid wide open.

"Cool," Andrea said.

"Way cool," I agreed.

The windowsill was about five feet off the ground. I gave Andrea a boost, and she dropped into Meckel's office. Then I scrambled up to the sill, and dropped in myself.

We made sure the windowshade was all the way down. Then we turned on Melanie's flashlight and began exploring.

Almost immediately we found a huge pile of mail on Meckel's desk, addressed to either "Samuel Meckel" or "Principal, High Rock Elementary School." Evidently the mail was sitting there waiting for the next principal to come along.

I went through the pile quickly, and within seconds found a familiar large brown envelope at the bottom of the file. It was about twelve inches wide by fifteen inches long, and filled with papers. I turned the envelope over and read the return address: BOCES in Albany.

"Jackpot," Andrea said.

"Hopefully."

I removed the envelope's contents and Andrea shone the flashlight on them. It sure looked like a jackpot. Just as we'd anticipated, these were the High Rock students' Terra Nova answer sheets, as graded by BOCES. The three hundred or so answer sheets were divided into twelve manila folders, one for each class.

Andrea and I started with the answer sheets from Melanie's class. We checked the first test, from a girl whose name I didn't recognize. At the top of page one was her official score for the English portion, which was an eighty-four. The page looked like something from a college SAT test. It had all of those little ovals you're supposed to fill in with a number-two pencil.

Shining the flashlight closely, we noticed that several times someone had erased one oval and filled in a different one. But we didn't find reason to believe anyone but the student herself had made these changes. In fact, about half the time the change resulted in the student getting the wrong answer.

"I don't see any evidence Meckel or Melanie or anybody else cheated on this test," I said.

"Let's check the math section."

We turned to the math, where the student had scored a ninety-one, and found two pages that didn't have any ovals on them. Here the student had to write down actual numbers instead of circling multiple-choice answers. Also, there was an empty space for her to do calculations before she wrote her answers.

Andrea and I checked the answers, and found hardly any erasures. Then we checked the answers against the calculations. They matched. No obvious chicanery here, either.

We examined an answer sheet from another student of Melanie's, and again came up goose eggs.

Then we tried four or five more. Still *nada*. Was Melanie clean?

"Let's try Elena's tests," I said.

"I hope we don't find anything," said Andrea, still loyal to her friend.

Outside the wind was starting up, rattling the windowshades in Meckel's open window. We were leaving it open in case we had to make a sudden escape, like I'd made the last time. I checked my watch: five minutes to four. "Whatever we find, we better find it fast," I said.

But the first test in Elena's batch didn't yield anything interesting, and neither did the second, third, or fourth. It was enervating. Soon it would be getting light outside, and we'd have to take off with nothing to show for all the risks we'd taken.

I put Elena's folder back down on Meckel's desk.

I picked up a couple of other folders and flipped through them, feeling dispirited.

But as I flipped, something suddenly caught my eye. I looked again. It was still there.

Meanwhile Andrea was saying, "Maybe we should just head back home—"

"Wait." I stared at the answer sheet I was holding in my hand.

"What?"

"Holy tomato juice."

"What *is* it?"

I pointed to the top of the answer sheet. "Eighty seven. He got an *eighty-seven* in English."

"Who?"

"Justin Richardson."

I flipped to the math portion and read the official math score. "And he got an eighty-six in math."

Andrea frowned. "I thought you said he scored over ninety-five in both."

"I *did* say that, 'cause that's what it said on the other thing—the page of preliminary scores I found in Meckel's office that night." I was talking fast, because I was excited. "The scores Meckel did before he sent the tests off to BOCES for official tabulation."

"So what are you thinking?" Andrea asked. "That Meckel scored the test wrong?"

I had a flash of inspiration. "Wait a minute, I bet Meckel didn't score those tests himself—Ms. Helquist did it for him. That would explain everything."

"Slow down and explain it to *me*."

"Try this out. After Ms. Helquist scored the test, Barry got hold of the score sheet. And he changes his kid's preliminary score because he wants him to get into the gifted program." I snapped my fingers. "I'll bet Barry didn't even realize those scores were just *preliminary*. The way Ms. Helquist did it, it looked official."

"But how could Barry have gotten hold of the score sheet? You think he snuck into Meckel's office at some point?"

"Or Helquist's office. Hey, he volunteered in the school. And he hung out sometimes to talk to Meckel about stuff. He probably saw the scores lying around one day and took advantage. He figured, I'll just change these scores before Meckel sees them."

"So you're thinking Barry might've . . ." She stopped.

But I didn't stop, I kept going. "I think Meckel realized the numbers were changed and figured out it must be Barry. So on Tuesday morning, he sees Barry heading for the john, and he goes, 'Come in my office.' So Barry does. And Meckel accuses him: 'Somebody changed these scores. It was you, wasn't it?' So Barry denies it of course, and Meckel gives him a hard time, and Barry starts yelling, and Meckel says no way in hell will your son ever get in my gifted program, you sonufabitch. And then somebody pushes somebody, Barry grabs the trophy, and he doesn't mean to kill Meckel . . ."

"But he does."

"And we can prove it. The cops took that preliminary score sheet I found in Meckel's office to the police station. If they find Barry's fingerprints on it, and they find somebody erased Justin's scores and put in new ones—"

" —then I'd be in trouble," a voice said.

Andrea screamed. So did I. It was Barry Richardson's voice, coming from outside. In the dim light we saw Barry's face above the windowsill. We also saw a gun, pointed straight at Andrea.

"Voices down, please," Barry said, his own voice tight. "Andrea, come here and climb over the windowsill, if you would."

"Barry, what are you doing?" I squeaked.

"If you really want me to shoot you here in Meckel's office, I will. But I'd prefer you to climb out. You've got ten seconds."

His voice was preternaturally calm. Andrea and I looked at one another, each of us hoping the other would know what to do.

Barry broke the silence. "One . . . two . . ."

"Okay, I'm coming!" Andrea yelled.

She headed for the windowsill. I half turned, thinking about making a break for the door. Barry noticed it. "If you step out that door, I'll shoot your wife," he said.

I didn't step out the door. Instead I watched as Andrea climbed up on the sill, then jumped to the ground.

Keeping his gun trained on Andrea, Barry turned to me. "Now you."

"Listen, Barry," I said, "I know you. You're not a bad guy."

"Drop your flashlight now, before you come to the window."

"Get hold of yourself—"

"One . . . two . . ."

Now it was my turn to yell. "Okay!"

I dropped the flashlight, then climbed up onto the sill. I wanted to jump down on top of Barry, but he was standing too far away, and his gun was still trained on Andrea.

"Last time I ever ask you to baby-sit," I said. Then I jumped to the ground.

"What are you gonna do with us?" Andrea asked.

"We're going to take a little walk across the street," he said.

I looked across the street to the Robinsons' house. Immediately I knew what Barry's plan was. He was going to kill us right by their house, to make it look like one of the Robinsons had done it.

"March," said Barry. "And don't make a peep."

I looked up and down High Rock. No trucks, no cop cars, no nothing. Andrea and I both shuffled our feet as we started down the front walk from the school. We were taking as long as we could. Barry was right behind us.

"Just tell me one thing," I said, trying to distract him.

"Shhh!" he hissed, jabbing his gun in my back.

I lowered my voice to a whisper. "Was I right about what happened? Between you and Meckel?"

"Yeah," Barry whispered hoarsely. "Bloody bastard was gonna keep my kid out of the gifted program. I didn't mean to kill him, though. I pick up that stupid trophy and next thing I know, he's lying there dead. Like you Americans say, 'shit happens.' "

"What about Ms. Helquist?" Andrea asked.

"That fool. She calls me up the next day. Asks if Mr. Meckel ever talked to me about the discrepancy in my son's test scores. I say I don't know what she's talking about. But I can tell she doesn't believe me. Sooner or later she's gonna go to the cops. They'll put me in jail, even though Meckel was an accident. It's not fair. So that night I go to her house with my gun. She thinks she's ready for me—she's got her own gun. So I grab it off her and I shoot her."

I said, "How can you—"

"It's their own bloody fault," Barry exploded. "How could they do this to my son? Your public schools in this country are utterly atrocious!"

"But that's no reason to go around killing people."

"Sure it is. Move," he said. "Across the street. Now."

Andrea and I did our slow death march across the street. Never were two people more in need of A Plan.

And then, just like that, one came to me. Maybe it was somewhat desperate, but it was a plan nonetheless. When we made it to the front of the Robinsons' house, I asked, "Up the driveway?"

I was afraid he'd order us to go up the walk to the front door instead. But we got lucky. "Up the driveway," he said.

Trying not to be too obvious about it, I cast my eyes down to the asphalt. About ten or twelve steps in front of me, I found what I was looking for: a dark shape down close to the ground. Mark Robinson's skateboard.

I glanced over my shoulder. Barry was still directly behind me.

Andrea was walking beside me. I nudged her slightly with my hip so that we'd veer a little to the left. That way the skateboard would be directly in my path.

I came to the skateboard. Again trying not to be too obvious, I lifted my legs a little higher so I would make it over the skateboard without tripping.

Then I got ready, my body tensing. And a moment later, I heard the sound I was waiting for: Barry's foot coming into contact with the skateboard.

I turned, lunged, and rammed my head into Barry's body. I was hoping the skateboard had thrown him off balance enough that he wouldn't be able to shoot me right away.

I guess I was right, because when the shot came a moment later, it didn't hit me. Out of the corner of my eye, I saw Andrea go down—I hoped to God it hadn't hit her either. Maybe she was just ducking. Barry and I were both falling hard. The force of my charge pushed him down to the driveway, and I landed on top of him.

His head banged against the driveway. His gun arm flailed behind him and his hand hit the ground. The gun flew from his hand. I could hear it rattling back down the driveway toward the sidewalk.

I started to jump off him so I could go for the gun. But then he grabbed onto me and somehow rolled on top of me. I reached for his neck and tried to strangle him. He got my head in both his hands and practically threw it against the driveway. I think I lost consciousness for a moment.

Next thing I knew, Barry was jumping off me and racing for the gun. Through the fog in my brain, I knew Andrea and I were done for.

Then I saw a shadowy figure down by the sidewalk. It was Andrea. She was holding the gun.

Barry rushed at her. "Stop!" Andrea said. "Stop!"

He was almost on top of her. His arms reached out—

Then I heard the gunshot.

Barry gave a wild banshee scream and fell down. He moaned for a while, and then he was silent.

18

But Barry got lucky—or unlucky, depending on how you look at it. He didn't die. Andrea, who's much better with blood and gore than I am, was able to staunch some of the bleeding from the hole in Barry's chest. The paramedics arrived within ten minutes. Barry spent a couple of weeks in intensive care, then went to jail.

According to Dave, the cops found Barry's fingerprints and alterations on the preliminary score sheet. That, combined with the statement Andrea and I gave, convinced Barry and his lawyer they should negotiate some kind of plea bargain. They're working it out now. I don't know what kind of sentence Barry will get, but I doubt he'll see freedom anytime soon. I hear via the grapevine that Barry's wife and kids are planning to move up north to Stony Creek this fall, to live with Ronnie's parents and try to escape some of the bad memories.

Andrea felt pretty shaky about firing a gun at a real person—it's not something she ever imagined her pacifist self doing. And my kids felt a tad weird going to school with the children of a man their mother had shot. But time helped us regain our balance, and once again, dinner table conversation at the Burns household most days revolves around point guards and Pokémon instead of murder.

Our recovery was helped along by the fact that Chief Walsh dropped all the criminal charges against me for breaking and entering and obstruction of justice. I guess he was afraid he'd look ridiculous throwing me in jail right after my wife and I had single-handedly—or should I say double-handedly—apprehended Public Enemy Number 1. Judy Demarest had splashed Andrea and me all over the front pages of the *Saratogian* and turned us into local heroes. Chief Walsh never thanked us for solving the murders for him, though; he just sort of tightened his jaw and looked away whenever we happened to see him on Broadway. I almost felt sorry for the guy.

But not quite.

Andrea was officially awarded tenure, and the whole family went out to Bruno's Pizza to celebrate. Meanwhile, Elena and Melanie were both rehired for next year. Did they actually cheat on their students' Terra Nova tests? Guess I'll never know for sure.

I got a call from Lou Robinson one morning, and he apologized endlessly for going gonzo on me. He told me that he and his family had started going to a therapist. I wished him the best.

My inmates did their three performances at Mt. McGregor Correctional Facility and got standing ovations every time. Of course, they did have captive audiences. I sent Brooklyn's one-act play to a couple of friends of mine in New York City who run off-Broadway theatres. Hey, you never know.

My favorite thing that happened recently is Laura Braithwaite's new boyfriend—she's going out with a *Schenectady Gazette* reporter who did a feature on her. He seems like a nice guy.

When Andrea heard about it, she said, "So something good came out of this whole business after all."

Life is something else. One moment you'll be sailing along peacefully, and the next moment you'll happen to aim a spelling bee trophy at the wrong part of somebody's head, and your goose is cooked.

The truth is, my family is blessed. And if my kids don't get the best education in the world . . . well, as Charizard would say, even if school is thirteen-fourteenths boring, there's always recess.

WHITING PUBLIC LIBRARY
WHITING, IN 46394